# The Way We Are

## Word Portraits
## of
## Bible Characters

*A work of imagination*
*based on historical characters and facts*

By

George Robert Crow

PublishAmerica
Baltimore

First printing

ISBN: 1-4137-1678-4
PUBLISHED BY PUBLISHAMERICA, LLLP
www.publishamerica.com
Baltimore

Printed in the United States of America

## Author's Introduction

The Bible, the world's all time best seller, is rich in characters. In it we have the rich and the poor, the gentle and the violent, kings and commoners, the good and the bad, the spiritual and the carnal, the religious and the irreligious, the famous and the infamous. The names of some of these characters are better known around the world than the names in any other book. But do those who know these names know what the people who had them were really like?

If the characters of the Bible could step out of the pages and speak to us, how would they explain their experiences, their natures, their motives, their hopes and fears? Of course, we do not know. But we do have something of the record of their lives, some of the important events that challenged them and revealed what they were like. And we have some of the words they spoke. Also we have comments of others in the Bible on some of those events and the people affected by them and these comments give us further insight into their works and ways.

Using my imagination and joining it with the records we have in the Bible, I have put words in the mouths of Bible characters as though they were speaking themselves. My purpose is that the words I have these characters speak will indicate the way they thought and felt, what was at the core of their being, the way they really were.

And I am sure that the way they were is the way we are. This is why, though the characters in this book are all from the Bible, I have called it The Way We Are. Today we are confronted with the same challenges as they were, the same temptations, the same problems, the same promises for the future, the same possibilities of victory or defeat. And we respond to these things as they did. Human nature has not changed, and the characters of the Bible are mirrors in which we can see ourselves.

May God be glorified through this volume and may those who read it be blessed as they come to a deeper understanding of the teachings of the Word of God and of themselves. And may the reading of these character studies inspire a desire in the heart of every reader to read and study the Bible where these truths are found.

# Old Testament Portraits

## Adam

**many years after Eden**
**(Genesis 2:17; 3:6-10,23,24; Romans 5:12)**

Since the day that spiritual death came
to us in Eden's garden, we have lived
a long time, Eve and I, if you call this
living. Compared to what we had before
this is a dying life, a living death–
the splendor then, the peace and the delight,
the weariness now, the accusing heart.
Then the innocent awareness of God,
now the disturbing consciousness of self.

Forbidden fruit entered our mouths, and so
the venom of sin invaded our blood,
and no words can tell that darkness which came
on our spirits, that indelible stain
spreading through our inner man, that dread of
the presence of God, that desire to flee.
We heard the sound of His steps, looked into
the depths, saw nothing but blackness, and sought
asylum there among the silent trees.
And then the voice of our creator God,
the flaming sword, the awesome cherubim!

To leave this body would be welcome now.
For what is there that should detain me here?
Weeds and thorns seem to thrive everywhere,
in all the fields, and in the mind, the heart.
My sweat doesn't seem to keep them at bay.

Now Abel is dead and Cain has gone, and
what the others may do I cannot guess.
And what can I say about Eve? She is

not like she was at the first, not at all.
Perhaps I love her as much as I did,
but can't fail to see the great change in her.
She is still lovely to look at. But some
bloom has gone from her cheek, some sparkle
from her eye. And at times she seems withdrawn
and secretive, at other times can speak
a sharp and cutting word. And I hear her
complain about various aches and pains
(as I also can do). Something there is
at work in us which brings about the most
melancholy fruits. Death mars everything.

I do not blame her now for our great loss.
I took and ate that fruit with open eyes,
with full awareness of the Lord's command.
I know that I have loosed something on earth
that will produce unending trouble here.
And I have earned a name I will not lose
as the first man to sin, so bringing tears
to every eye and groans to every heart,
and cold death hovering near every home.

We shall return to dust, but I am not
afraid. With the slain animal and its
concealing skin He used to clothe our flesh,
God gave us words of hope and then revealed
how to be saved and righteous in His eyes.

But when will the crusher of the serpent's
head come to free us from this misery?
For that most blessed day I groan and wait.
But as I watch and wait, I will fight on
against the sin which has infected us,
and will never give up until my soul
parts from this body of death and goes up
to meet the God who brought it into life.

So now I suffer on, prepared to pay the price
of knowing that for this I gave up Paradise.

## Eve

**(just after losing Eden–Genesis chapter 3)**

Can you imagine how it felt to die?–
that flowing joy we knew now changed to dread,
that sense of desolation coming on,
that feel of something wicked in the heart,
that light in our spirits suddenly lost.
It seemed as though the morning sun had all
at once plunged back behind the world's far rim,
and in the dark our eyes were opened wide,
and we could see what now we wish that we
had never seen or known. To know good is
good. To know evil surely pains the heart
as nothing else on earth will ever do.

I will be "The mother of all living,"
or now say, "The mother of all dying,"
for now all living will be dying too,
and who but I can be the source of this?
Had I not eaten the forbidden fruit,
would Adam then have eaten on his own?
I was the snare the serpent used for him
to draw us both into this misery.

I could pluck out the eye that craved that fruit!
And tear from me the hand that reached for it!
But my traitorous heart–how deal with that?

Now the future must occupy our thoughts.
What is done is done, and can't be undone,
and vain regrets will paralyze the will,
and make it harder now to face the great
unknown and live outside of Paradise.

Pain and desire and sweat–the words God spoke–
foreshadow now troubles enough for us
without time that's past holding us in chains.

I believe this: God has forgiven us,
and with the sentence of death given a way
to live and learn in our brief time on earth.

One thing is sure–submission on my part
to my dear husband is essential now.
For independent action has its risk,
as these dark days have surely taught us both.

Something of a rebel heart I feel, and
so I must remain humbly by his side
and give support in every way I can,
until the offspring of the woman comes
to crush our cunning enemy's vile head.
The Lord has given promise to our hearts.

We have lost much, but faith is with us yet.
With courage now we face what lies beyond.
And with both joy and sorrow we set out to roam
this beckoning strange world and make ourselves a home.

## Cain

**(Genesis 4:1-17–in the land of Nod)**

Since it is common knowledge anyway,
I might just as well admit it–I did
hate my brother, quite detested him.
And I am fully convinced that if you
had been in my place, then most of you would
have hated him. (Or do you also think
yourselves so much better than other men?)
He was too "good," too "righteous"–I mean he
thought he was. And he always made me feel
inferior, made it seem as if I
were the one who was always in the wrong.
So with his death I felt a great relief.

I tried to please God, yes, earnestly tried.
But there was Abel once more with his gift,
which, incredibly, seemed to please God more
than mine. I brought to Him something that I
had labored hard with my hands to produce.
(I did not want to shed the blood of an
animal–what earthly good could that bring?)
My offering was better than his, but
I was rejected, and he given praise.

Naturally, this injustice provoked
me to anger. What else could you expect?
And I was driven to express my grief
and indignation in the most clear way.
But if my killing him was such a crime
how is it that God let me live and come
to this good place to propagate my kind?

I will say straight out that I was filled with

fears when He pronounced judgment in my case.
Facing banishment to this other land,
this land that now I'm glad to call my home,
I trembled. Prospects seemed so dark and far.
But now I see this dread need not have been.
Our nature is adaptable to all
it has to face and always finds a way
to triumph.
With or without God I will
now build a world according to my taste.
And in it Abel's kind of righteousness
will never have a place, but only that
kind of righteousness earned by our hard work.

Man's dominating will and calloused hands
will be the piety our world demands.

## Abel

**whose blood speaks to us from the ground**
**(Genesis 4:2-10; Hebrews 11:4; 12:24)**

Have you ever wondered once why I brought
a lamb to offer to our God instead
of something else, as did my brother Cain?
It was not that he, a cultivator,
and I, a shepherd, brought the things at hand.
Nor was it speculation on our part.

God gave a revelation of His will.
He told our parents what to bring to Him
as an offering for sin. They told us.
So being a great sinner now I thought
such an offering was my only hope.

Cain had his own ideas about things,
and they were certainly not always good.
Our parents had taught us both (often with
tears in their eyes, remembering the past)
that it is far better to believe and
obey God than to pursue our own way.

We heard that righteousness can come to men
only through sacrifice, the sacrifice
of innocent blood. I accepted that.
But I believe Cain never felt his deep
depravity as I always felt mine,
and so he may have thought that anything
he offered would be good and please the Lord,
no matter what He had commanded us.
It seems my brother felt that self-effort
and righteousness we try to gain by our
own works would be acceptable to God.

I was not surprised when God refused him
and his offering, and then accepted mine.
Faith and obedience are what God wants.
And they enable us to bring a more
excellent sacrifice.
Now my blood here
will speak of man's vileness and cruelty
until the end of time, and will reveal
the results of self-will and unbelief.

One day other blood will flow to appease
God's anger, speaking better things than these.

## Enoch

**(just before God took him–Genesis 5:21-24; Jude 14,15)**

Down through the generations the word came:
There is a true and living God to trust
and serve, one who rewards obedience.
I wanted Him more than anything else,
so from my earliest days I sought Him,
and found Him, and began my walk of faith,
a faith that's based on what He has revealed
of who He is and what He wants of us.

Some nights, out under the stars, His presence
was like a vast ocean surging around me,
and some clear mornings in the forest paths
His love breathed on me with the gentle breeze.
Sometimes He was so very real I thought
that I could reach out my hand and touch Him
as He walked by my side. But all too rare
were joyous experiences like these.

More often He seemed hidden behind clouds.
I kept on walking with Him even when
I could hardly see to take one more step.
But whether I could clearly scan my way,
or had to urge myself on in the dark,
I always knew He was there very near,
and I kept my eyes looking straight to Him,
always fastened them on eternal things,
so I could walk a straight and faithful path.

The ungodly were there, watching my steps–
not always easy was this walk with God.
People have made a wasteland of this world.
Then one day came a prophecy from God.

I was not sure whether it was for them,
or for some generation still to come.
God will work all that out in His good time.

"The Lord is coming with thousands upon
thousands of His holy ones, to bring all
men to judgment, and to convict all the
ungodly of all the ungodly acts
they have done in an ungodly way, and
of all the hard words ungodly sinners
have spoken against Him," is what I said.

Now I sense that any day I could step
out into eternity. Even now
do I not hear His swift chariot's wheels?
Do I not feel a strange pull at my heart?
Let this be the day when I see His face.

Gladly here I have walked with Him alone;
much more gladly there when this life is done.

## Methusulah
**(in old age–Genesis 5:25-27)**

I've lived long enough to know what man is.
I am aware of all the passions and
motives which move the fallen hearts of men
to violence and evil everywhere,
and drive them to the ruin of our race,
for in my own heart I have felt their strength.
I am convinced of this: in general
every notion and desire of man's heart
is corrupt continually, and from
his youth he wants to go astray from God.

I sometimes think that God may quite blot out
the human race and start anew if He
can find one fully righteous man on earth.
Perhaps one day He may. I cannot claim
to be such a man, though sometimes I have
tried to hear and obey what God has said.
Being a man is hard, and being a
good man harder still.
I feel that I have
lived too long. For my heart is pained beyond
relief. It will surely break if I see
any more of what I've seen till now–the
savage destructiveness, the lies and mean
deceit that one meets with on every hand,
the arrogance and utter selfishness,
the cold contempt for God and fellow men.
All this must break the very heart of God,
and stir Him up to anger without cure.

Oh, at last to be done with all of this–
this world gone mad, this outward turbulence,

and all this inner struggle and distress,
now so long drawn out and fierce. Through endless
daylight hours I often think "When will night
come that I might rest in sleep." Painfully
long nights bring the thought "When will morning come
to end these groans."

It is enough. There is
nothing more I wish to do, wish to see,
or wish to hear. It is enough. I would
at once depart to my eternal home
and lay me down and rest the long, long rest,
and wait for God to rise to make things right.

For He will surely come with ten thousands
of His holy ones to judge the world and
utterly destroy all ungodliness,
and make another world where all our tears will cease
and man can live with God in perfect blissful peace.

## Noah

**(as an old man, after the flood. Genesis 6:9– 8:22)**

I knew I was one man against the world,
a world in full rebellion against God,
a world of violence, a world gone mad.
But in their eyes I was the one insane–
the ark to them was proof enough of this.

That generation was hard, very hard.
Preaching my heart out I saw no response,
just determined arrogant depravity.
So many cold faces devoid of thought;
so many eyes without a trace of light;
so many voices and all speaking lies;
so many hearts with no desire for God.

When they were not beating and killing one
another, eating and drinking is how
they spent their time, and talking about who
was marrying and who was splitting up.
Warnings of judgment meant nothing to them.
They had no mind for the pursuit of truth,
only a sullen, stubborn ignorance.

Many a night my pillow flowed with tears,
but God was my comfort, my joy and strength.
He called me "righteous," standing by my side.
And later, when we went into the ark,
with His own hand He gently shut the door.

And then the ark became our only world,
its creaking frame rising on the dark swell.
But how can I describe what happened then?
For forty days no sign of sun or star,

but blackened skies and gloom before unknown,
and when the end might be we could not tell.

It seemed that all the heavens had dissolved,
and water was the substance of the earth.
Upward we went, safe in our floating home,
and still on upward till the mountain tips
alone appeared through our airy windows,
and then they also slowly disappeared.

We knew that what remained without was lost,
that all the beasts and men, with all their homes,
had sunk deep down in the chaotic flood,
that water had submerged the entire globe,
leaving nothing as it had been before.

For months we tossed in that strange, liquid world,
much longing to see trees and fields again.
At last the flood was gone, and wind and sun
dried up the muddy ground and made it firm.

Then God called us from the ark, at the time He planned,
and out we came with eager feet to bright new land.

## Nimrod
**(Genesis 10:8-11)**

Give me the open sky and the wild field,
and the dark forest too, and the roar of
the prey, and the yellow eyes blazing in
the darkness, and the deep thrill of the hunt,
and the pride that swells in my heart when I
see those eyes closed forever by my skill.
By day and by night I am a hunter,
for beasts yes, and, so many say, for the
souls of men. Even Jehovah himself,
the god of Noah, acknowledges that
I am a hunter of exceptional
ability–not that I am very
much concerned about what he has to say.

The battlefield holds no terrors for me.
How arousing are the excited cries,
the flame in the eyes, the arrows that sing,
the clash of arms, the red blood glowing in
the hot cheek, and then flowing on the ground!
To see a strong enemy at my feet
gives me more fiery pleasure than the death
of any king of the jungle could do.
What conquering of fear! What wild delight!
I have found no one my equal in war.

But don't think for a moment that my life
is all destruction and gore. Far from it.
I am also an eminent builder–
not of mere houses, but of fabulous
city-states. I am responsible for their
buildings, but also for the spirit of their
societies, and their religious life.

Simply hearing the grand names of all those
magnificent cities gives me a thrill–
Babylon, Calneh, Accad, Nineveh.
I am sure the world will never forget
me, the hunter, and warrior, and builder.

How many generations will there now be
before there is another equal to me?

## Abraham
**at sunset**

God has been my God from that day in Ur
His compelling voice called me from those gods,
and drew me far from home and friends and land
to live in tents and never to return.

I look back at my life, joyful and sad,
sad at the blunders and stumbling and sin,
joyful for all that God has been to me–
God, my shield and my very great reward,
One who always had time to stoop to hear
this poor man who is but ashes and dust.

Do you wonder what drove me from my home
to journey forth, not knowing where I went?
And what made me a pilgrim here on earth,
traveling onward where He points the road,
willing to do whatever He might say?
And do you ever question what brought me
to that lonely high place of sacrifice
where I held the sharp upraised knife above
my son, my promised one, my very heart?
Here then is the great reason for it all:

Faith was that joy which always urged me on,
my unseen hand that grasped eternal truth,
that always kept the city in my sight,
the heavenly one, the city of God.

It was faith that made real those unseen things,
and saw future hopes as sure as the past.
For I thought that the promises God made
He was also well able to fulfill.

Faith was that powerful force in His hands
that always led to light, to life and love,
that changed my outlook, my acts, my aim,
that brought me to humble obedience,
that linked me with the Lord of heaven and earth,
the true and living One, with God my Friend.

And so through me, according to His Word,
blessings will come to nations everywhere,
the blessings of Messiah sure to come.

So I go on in faith, a stranger in this night,
to that much longed for place where faith turns into sight.

## Sarah
**(Genesis 18:11-15)**

There I was in the tent and had to laugh.
The idea seemed so ridiculous.
After all, I was years and years beyond
the age of child-bearing. And for someone
to say I was going to have a son–
well! Wouldn't you have laughed too, hearing that?
I'm only sorry that I told that lie.
I should have confessed then that I had laughed.
Fear often causes us to hide the truth.

But am I to be remembered only
for that? Or for bringing my husband and
Hagar together, and then casting out
both her and her son? Believe me, these things
do not sum up my whole time on this earth.

You have no idea how challenging
things were for me from the beginning of
our married life. One day suddenly he
said, "Get packed. We're leaving." Naturally
I said, "Where are we going?" Imagine
my consternation when he said to me,
"I really don't know. But I do know that
God is telling me to leave our place here
and go now to live in some distant land.
So we must go, my dear, for God's will is
very important to me."
What could I
do? I loved my husband, and never once
thought that he was not the head of our home.
But still, imagine the difficulties
I faced. But I went with him everywhere

he decided he had to go–Haran,
Canaan, Egypt, back to Canaan. And in
Canaan here and there, back and forth. Sometimes
I didn't know from one day to the next
where our tent was going to be set up.
If that's not hard for a woman, what is?

My husband often seemed to be looking
at something no one else could ever see,
though at times I had a good glimpse of it.

Well, I laughed. And I lied. I admit it.
But I also trusted God, the God of
Abraham, and got strength to bear a son.
And I had the good sense to obey both
God and my husband. I wanted God's will,
I fully believe, as much as he did.

And now my Isaac takes up all my days,
and God's great goodness fills my mouth with praise.

## Lot

**(at the end of his life–Genesis 13:10–19:38)**

We need not seek far for the root cause of
my broken life and heart. It was a fault,
a sin dear to us all, unless it is
subdued and conquered by the grace of God.
I mean self-centeredness, born in the heart
of the infant like a pestilent seed,
growing strong and robust in the youth, and
in full bloom with the adult who does not
learn to tread it in the dust.

When I was
asked by my uncle to make that fateful
choice, I looked long at the beautiful plain
of the Jordan, and after an all too
brief struggle with conscience, affection, and
good sense, I let my eyes dictate the choice
to my brain, and so brought ruin to all
that I held dear.

From self-centeredness I
chose this rich place and left that man of God
in the hills alone.
From self-centeredness
I pitched my tent near Sodom, and later
moved right inside and quickly settled down
among godless men.

From self-centeredness
I joined them in their trade and politics,
and sat with chief men in the city's gate
to judge disputes.

Looking back now I must
admit that it would have been hard for men
outside to know whether I had faith in
the one true God, or was a man of Sodom

like all the rest, so closely was my life
and theirs linked and intertwined. Did not my
own daughters marry sons of theirs?
Still I
did believe in God and tried to live a
righteous life, hard as it was in that town.
And my soul was often vexed with the filth
of perverted men and their corrupt lives.
But I wanted to be a believer
and a man of the world at the same time.

And now all is gone–property and wife,
and daughters corrupted by Sodom's way,
and I myself so wrong, so desolate.
Self-centeredness brought all of this great loss.

This is God's lesson, one to educate
our sluggish minds, but learned, by me, too late.

## Lot's Wife
**(Genesis 19:15-26; Luke 17:32)**

I have really loved life in Sodom town.
The friends in high society, our fine
house, all the modern conveniences, and
the good shopping and entertainment spots
have made things here far more agreeable
than they could ever have been in the hills
of Canaan. I must confess that when we
left Haran for those wanderings in a
strange country, I was not pleased, not at all.
But I endured it for my husband's sake.
I was overjoyed when he decided
to move to this delightful fertile plain,
with its river and lake and flourishing
cities.
                    Please, do not misunderstand me.
I am not into this gay life style which
some follow here. I find it disgusting,
as I'm sure every right thinking person
will do. I cannot even imagine
why men–and even some of the women–
do to each other the vile things they do.
But every place has it's bad element.
I didn't find that the people up in the
mountains where Abraham remains are all
exactly saints of the Lord. Far from it.
If we want to get away from sinners,
we will have to leave the world completely–
which we may have to do very shortly,
if God's judgment is really coming here,
as my husband has tried to persuade me.

That is why I am now fleeing with him

and our two daughters for our very lives.
The man who told us to flee also said:
"Do not stop in the plain, and do not look
behind you," but he did not explain this.
I have always hated being told not
to do something without being given
a proper reason for not doing it.
And why should I not look back? All my friends
are there. My home is there. My heart is there.
Am I to leave it all without a last
glimpse, before the awful life that awaits
us in some cave in the hills up above?

And am I not to see if the judgment
the man spoke about really comes on them?
Maybe destruction will not be complete.
Perhaps we will be able to return
to our lovely home. Why would God destroy
all that great good together with the bad?

Should we really feel this intense alarm?
Surely one brief look back can do no harm.

## People of Sodom
### (Genesis chapter 19; Jude 7)

Honestly, we don't know what all the fuss
is about. After all, we are only
doing what comes naturally to us.
If there is a God who created us
(and we haven't seen any proof of this),
He made us as we are, and like every
other created thing we follow our
spontaneous urges. What's wrong with that?
Should we blame whales for swimming in the sea?
Or eagles for soaring high in the air?
If cattle prefer grass, and herons fish,
and lions meat, can we find any fault?

When all of nature, and most of mankind,
pursue the course set out for them in the
way they are made, must we alone deny
our nature and be forced into a kind
of life style alien to our desires?
Why should we conform to standards set by
those who are basically different from
ourselves? Our motto is, Live and let live.
We don't tell others how to conduct their
lives. Why should they try to dictate to us?

Take this fellow Lot. He comes here to make
money and settle down because he did
not like the hills, and the company of
his uncle Abram. We don't blame him for
that. In fact, we don't see how he stood it
as long as he did. We welcomed him here
and permitted him to stay. But now it
seems he wants to set himself up as judge

of all we wish to do.
"Wicked" is the
word he used for our attempt to have some
innocent pleasure. As if there were such
a thing as sin! If following one's own
nature is sin, then all beasts and all men,
and all the gods too, sin as much as we.

It's all nonsense. We will continue to
express what we really are though men rage,
and the heavens seem to frown. Our battle
cry is freedom–freedom to act as we
are without interference from anyone.
And our rights must be recognized by all.

Now this Lot started a rumor about
the judgment of God, and tried his best to
get his two sons-in-law to leave with him.
To them it seemed like a big joke, which is
exactly what it seems to us. Why on earth would
his deity destroy us, even if he could?

But what now is that sound of rushing in the sky,
that ominous yellow light, those plunging flames? Why–

## Isaac
### (after sending Jacob to Padan Aram–Genesis 28:1,2)

A quiet man they call me, and it's true.
For me no loud disputes, no battle cry,
no aggressive demands, no stir and slash.
Strife with my fellow men is not my way.
Rash ambitions's quickened pulse, the hot heart
that must aim at the ladder's topmost rung,
in me have never found a place.
I thought
in any quarrel coming up with men
far better it would be to lose than win,
if by winning peace in God had to be
thrust aside. Peace is that vital to me.

My parents raised me as a gift from God,
long promised, long an object of their prayer.
I was content in their contented love,
and as a mere boy learned to rest in God.
In his great wisdom my dear father taught
faith in God's faithfulness, and steady hope.
He taught me how to give my life for Him,
and how to live too, when God gave it back.

But I confess one thing: my quiet mind
has lately been disturbed by my two sons.
My hopes for Esau were great, but in the
light of recent events his character
looks very questionable. He seems so
irreligious, and so keen on revenge.
If my eyesight were not so dim I would
expect to see destroying fire flashing
from his eyes. I believe that now he has
no care for the things of God, and no faith.

And Jacob is as he has always been–
secretive and sly, grasping in his heart,
so full of self, so lacking in true love.

The end is not yet. Now I pray and hope
to see our God at work in my two boys,
giving more grace, producing love and faith,
bringing through them both glory to His name.

Both now have gone pursuing different ways.
My Rivka is with me still, and is still
my love, my comfort in my final days,
a wife completely loving, good and true.
I praise God for His good and perfect will
revealed step after step my whole life through.

And now my strength is gone, my senses have grown dim.
So I lift my eyes and quietly wait for Him.

## Rebeccah

**(Genesis 24:57-67; 27:1-46)**

I never regretted it, not for a
single day–my leaving family and
friends for Canaan and life at the side of
a man I had never met, never seen.

Was it a love of adventure in me?
Was it the attraction of the unknown?
Was it a lack of proper suitors there?
Or was it only the persuasive words
of Abram's servant? Or was it God who
turned my heart that way to accomplish His
mysterious plan? Or, perhaps, all these?
In any case, I came, that's all I know.
Detecting motives, and thinking of their
results, I confess, is not my strong point.

No better husband could ever have been
found for me than my dear Isaac. No one
is as gentle, kind, and caring as he.
And none ever loved peace and quiet more.

If I, unworthy as I am, dare point
out any fault in him, it would be this–
a lack of judgment in dealing with our
two sons.
                    There, I've said it. If there's one thing
that has divided us at all, it's this.

Esau is a big disappointment, but
Isaac dotes on him. I simply cannot
understand it. Though he is my son too,
I cannot fail to see his lack of faith

in God and his contempt for righteousness.
The pleasures of the world are all he wants.
And it's a grief of mind to see him so.

How different is my Jacob! This son
will fulfill my hopes. Faith means a great deal
to him, and he is willing to do what
must be done for the godly line to go
on and prosper. He is God's chosen one.
Abraham, Isaac, and Jacob it is,
and always will be. This is my great joy.
And now Jacob has gone off to my land,
and Esau, still enraged, will soon depart
and find a place more suited to his style.

Isaac and I, still in love, and alone once more,
await with true faith what the future has in store.

## Jacob

**(in his final days)**

My eyes are dim, and I grope for the wall
when I get up, which is not often now.
It seems to me that throughout my brief life,
groping–and grasping–is what I did most.
Even at my birth my hand was outstretched.
I was always out to grab what I could.

And somehow my vision was always dim.
I mean my vision of heavenly things.
This is not to say I had none at all.
I did have some. I saw God's promises,
darkly, hardly knowing what they could mean,
but desiring their fulfillment in me.
And I groped after eternal things too.

I certainly had a hard time of it.
I confess–my nature was such that things
couldn't be easy, not even easy things.
And I learned that deception has its risk.
There was that ancient principle at work–
reaping what is sown. Deceiving others
meant that I also was to be deceived.
But, tell me, how could I ever once think
that God needed my foolish trickiness
to give me what He wanted me to have?
How could I let myself so long for things
that to grasp them I held out lying hands?

I see that not a trouble came to me
that I did not completely earn, not one.
Perhaps some good also came from it all–
I learned deception is a thing to hate.

And remember, I grasped the angel too.
My faith held Him fast and would not let go
until He blessed me. That blessing is with
me now. In my mind I still see His eyes
when He looked at my heart and asked my name,
and then gave a different one to me.
So very much I have to praise Him for.

Of course, Jacob did not die overnight,
but Israel lived from that morning on.

So now let me speak blessing on my sons,
and tell them what will be in days to come,
and let me close my eyes and so depart
with empty hands, and no longer grasping,
and go to the Mighty One of Jacob,
and see my darling Rachel once again,
the one whom I have loved so very long and well,
and ever live above with God as Israel.

## • Esau

**(Genesis 25:27-34)**

Some criticism I have heard of late
which I don't think I deserve. After all,
who was the one who acted with that hard
selfishness and greed? Certainly not I–
Jacob is the cold-hearted scoundrel's name.
Yet he gets the praise and I get the blame.

And this I cannot hope to comprehend.
To me it seems so utterly unjust.
There I am, hungry as a bear, and he,
instead of giving me some stew out of
brotherly love, makes this unfair demand.

And what could I do? If you had been there
instead of me, weakened from hunger like
me, doubtless you would have done as I did.

In those circumstances what earthly good
was that birthright to me? Isn't getting
what we need now far better than waiting
for uncertain future hopes? We cannot
live forever, and death brings an abrupt
end to everything, including birthrights.
What is more certain and reasonable
than that a bird in the snare is worth ten
in the sky?

Now give me the open fields,
and the sun overhead, and the wind in
the tall trees, and the cedar's sweet scent, and
living things all around to see and touch
and the flowing excitement of the chase–
heaven? To me this is the only one
there is.

And far more desirable this
than the dark tents of some men where each day
self-centered schemes are conceived for the next.
For me each hour is enough in itself.
I live for today, and have my fun now,
and let others brood about days to come.

Why should I regret letting Jacob have
what he craved so much? And if he is now
moping in the tent like a woman, and
making his secret plots, I will leave him
to it. More manly things delight me and
I will go on with my hunting.
And, please,
stop blaming me for my plain, practical
views on life and death. Try to understand.
All I did was what any down-to-earth
man would do when faced with a choice like that.

My motto is easily understood:
Forget the future, seize the present good.

## Rachel
**(Genesis 29:18-30; 35:16-19)**

There was this stranger standing by the well
when I came to give water to the flocks.
He was handsome, but had something of a
sly, secretive look. Still I thought there was
something very attractive about him.
From that first day I think that he loved me.
And I felt drawn to him for that alone.

Later I found he could work very hard,
and he knew how to acquire property.
He knew how to gain my heart too. Seven
years of labor to get me! Was I worth
so much work? He evidently thought so.
When I saw that, how could I not love him?
I am sure that all four of us loved him,
but I most of all. I'm certain of it.

There was something vulnerable in him.
He needed to show love and to be loved,
and so he would listen to suggestions.

It was long a sorrow to me that I
could not give him children. But at long last
God enabled me to give him the best
of his many sons. From the beginning
Joseph was a delight, a handsome boy,
and almost saintly in the way he prayed
and sought for God, and always put Him first.
He had no time at all for the household
gods of my father, which, to be honest,
I really liked–though they were ugly things.

I don't know how Joseph came by all this.
Somehow or other he found his own goals.
Now Jacob, I am sure, believed in God,
but I would not call him spiritual.
He was a strange mix of spirit and flesh.
Certainly he never tried to make his
religious opinions the rule of life
for the rest of us, though, of course, we knew
where he stood on matters of importance.

And I will say this for him–now that we
are in Canaan, it seems to me that he
has been different, more prayerful, more
humble, more determined to obey God.
And I heartily approve of the change.

I think now that I really love his God.
I long to conceive again and present
to my Jacob another precious son.

My trust is in God. Jacob trusts Him too.
We will wait and see what the Lord will do.

## ·Leah

**(as we might hope she turned out. Genesis 30:19-21)**

It was so hard to be second choice, or
worse. I am not surprised at Jacob's
love for my sister, for she is lovely,
and I know I'm not, and can never be.
But was it too much to ask for a bit
of real affection for me, who gave him
son after son?
                                        I felt very grateful
that he did not despise and reject me,
that at least he, well, tolerated me.
But toleration was never enough.
I always craved for a place in his heart,
and found none. Tears at night, and heaviness
by day were often my experience.

At long last, I learned how to deal with this.
After years of sadness and discontent
I found consolation and peace in God.
There I should have looked long ago, you say.
But human nature is not so quickly
or easily trained to seek for the best,
while the flesh demands its satisfaction,
and the heart reaches out for human love.

And who of us does not crave for the love
of others? Do not people sacrifice
their best interests, and even ruin
their lives, to get it? The desire to love
and be loved is the goal we all aim at.
This can drive men–and women–to acts of
desperation, and degradation too.
Without love we all feel an emptiness

which nothing else can ever seem to fill.

And many of us never come to know
about eternal love, the love of God,
or realize that this brings far greater
delight than human love can ever do,
a delight that lasts and grows with the years.

Now I would never trade my faith and hope
in God for anything else in the world,
including a dear husband's affection.
Having tasted God's love, all other love
seems small and unreal by comparison.
And this love is there, seeking for us all.

I believe that my failure to find love
where I wanted most to find it drove me
to look to God alone. In this way our
sad disappointments can be occasions
for Him to show His mercy toward us,
and raise us to much higher, and far better, ground
than, in our own foolish ways, could ever be found.

## Laban
### (musing about Jacob–Genesis 31:22-24)

I think it must have been something in his
eyes, or the expressions I noticed on
his face. Sometimes he seemed to wear a mask.
However that might be, I knew that he
was tricky before he was here too long,
a sharp man who would try hard to deceive
anyone he could if he saw a chance.
I thought I should get the advantage first,
before he made off with everything here.

For starters, I got him to work for me
for practically nothing. Give him that–
he was a hard worker for my two girls,
and did a lot to make my substance grow.
At the same time I got a husband for
Leah, which I had failed to do before.
She was not much of a looker, poor girl.

That task completed, I then set about
getting rich through my brains, and his hard work.
And did too. But then his crooked nature
began one day to get the upper hand.
This had never happened to me before,
and my perplexity was very great.

And then, quite suddenly, he ran away
with my girls, my grandchildren, and my flocks.
And then, get this, God Himself came to me
and told me I must do no harm to him.

At times the ways of God are very strange.
How could He possibly object to my

getting back again what was surely mine.
But so it is, and I must walk with care
and speak to him no more than must be said.
I will not disobey this word from God.

I think now if Jacob accomplishes his plan,
then I will be a sadder, but a wiser man.

## Joseph
**(at 110–Genesis 50:22)**

I have seen human nature as it is,
so I know why my brothers hated me.
Envy and jealousy stir our fallen
hearts to action in irrational ways.
But I should never have been an object
of their jealousy, I, young and naive,
hardly able to go out and come in.

You think I should not have told them my dreams?
Yes, for me it meant the tears, the dark pit,
the broken heart, exile and slavery.
But see what good came of it in the end–
the salvation of those who hated me,
a people preserved in their deepest need.

So I learned what the Most High God is like.
Behind the hard mystery of His ways
with His people, behind the wickedness
of men, behind the bewildering dark,
behind all our desolation and pain,
there always is the Father's loving face,
and bright rays of His healing mercy shine
to produce the most glorious results.
His wisdom works through the circumstances
of seeming disaster and brings us help.

For He can make the sinful acts of men
work together with His great grace to weave
surprising tapestries, with their black threads
among His gold, and bring good from the bad,
and through men's evil glorify His name.

And He can make a fruitful bough from a
dead stick. For what was I that I should be
His choice of savior in my peoples' need?
I see no good at all in me that He
should teach me when to stand, and when to run,
and what I should refuse, and what embrace,
how to lowly serve and then humbly rule.

He it was who took all my hurting heart,
my troubled mind, my remembered grief,
my furnace affliction, my fiery trial
and used it all as sweet steps to Himself.
I found great riches in those gloomy depths.

He was working out His will from the very start.
His my heart's adoration. His alone my heart.

## The Pharaoh of Joseph's Day
**(Genesis 41:1)**

That morning I woke up troubled and tense,
because of the dreams I had in the night.
I felt they had some great significance,
but could not imagine what it might be.

We have many a wise man in our land,
at least those whom the people call wise men.
So I called all those wizards, astrologers,
magicians, and sorcerers who I thought
might be in contact with the unseen world,
who had some reputation for knowledge.
Whatever use can be found for such men
(I for one have slowly become convinced
there cannot be very much), in the whole
matter of my dreams they exhibited
an abysmal lack of ability.
Not one of them could even give a hint
of their meaning that seemed reasonable.

Turning in disgust from these sages,
I heard of an imprisoned Hebrew slave
who once accurately interpreted
some dreams in the prison house. For wisdom,
I asked myself, must I call such a man?
Then the thought came that wisdom might be found
in the most unexpected places, and
real ability and skill locked up in
obscurity. In any case, I thought,
I had absolutely nothing to lose.

When he came at my summons I was struck
and, I confess, somewhat dismayed by his

youth. But in his eyes there was a bright look
of intelligence and strong confidence.
But when I spoke of my dream, suggesting
he might interpret it, I was further
dismayed by his opening words: “It is
not in me.” But he quickly added, “God
will give the answer.” No such statement had
ever been made to me in my life by
any magician or astrologer,
nor any such humility been shown.
I at once perceived that here was a man
of unusual character and mind.

This truth I had much opportunity
to see throughout the many years that came
and went while he was in my service,
or, I should say, in the service of the
whole country. Without him, I can now think,
this nation might not have even survived.

I am deeply grateful, and so is this whole broad
land, for such a profound and holy man of God.

## Amram and Jochebed

**(Exodus 2:1-10; Numbers 26:59; Hebrews 11:23)**

From slave quarters to Pharaoh's palace–this
was God's will for him. What a God we serve!
Believe Him and then watch the wonders flow!
Pharaoh was cruel and tyrannical,
and he was fully bent on keeping our
people Israel in poverty and
bondage. Many of our own friends suffered
under his savage rule. But somehow we
did not fear his wrath. The one who fears the
one true God need not fear anyone else.
For the fear of the LORD delivers from
the snares of enemies.
We both knew that
in some way our infant boy would be saved,
in spite of Pharaoh's order that all males
must be put to death. But the wonder of
God's working, when His purpose was revealed,
filled us with admiration and worship.

Well known was the place where the daughter of
Pharaoh came down to the river to bathe.
What we did not know was what sort
of person she was and what she might do
when she saw a small infant in his ark
there among the reeds on the water's edge.
But by faith we placed him there and by faith
we watched in hope for her to come that way.

And at just the right moment God caused our
dear boy to cry, and that cry won her heart.
So I, Jochebed, continued on as
his nursing mother, bringing up my son

as if he were her son (in line, perhaps,
one day to sit enthroned as Egypt's king),
able to instill in his nascent mind
a love for Israel, and praising God
for His wisdom, mercy and hidden ways,
glorious beyond our expectation.

Trust the Lord and see Him work. Did ever one cry
so change the whole course of a people's history?

## Moses
### (on Mount Nebo. Deuteronomy 34:1-8. Psalm 90)

Alone I stand on this mount near Canaan's
border, yet not alone, for God is here.
And I fix my eyes on the promised land,
the rich fair land I will not enter now.
And I look back at my afflicted life,
its brief time passed under the wrath of God,
and rejoice in His goodness and mercy.

I really do not need to say much more
about myself. It is all written there
in the books God Himself had me write–
the good, the bad, the great successes, and
the sad failure which ended my long quest.
And my outlook on life, briefly put, is
there in the prayer psalm that I composed.

But still a few words might help to make clear
how I ever came to be what I am.
Godly parents–how I thank God for them!
Their faith, their fearlessness, preserved my life
when decrees of death came from Pharaoh's throne.

And my mother–I could never tell all
her wisdom or her loving, caring heart.
She it was who grounded me in the things
of God, and tied my heart to Israel
forever, when the pleasures of Egypt
were before me, and when Pharaoh's daughter
would try to point me to another way.

I was not meek by nature. Nothing good
ever came from my own heart. This is truth,

truth that many will not wish to believe
(people like to put past leaders up on
pedestals, bow down to their memory,
and think that famed ancestors make them great).
I do not think meek men are as ready
to kill as I was, when I slew the man
mistreating my people. It did no good–
at least it did no good at all for them.
And for me it meant forty desert years.

During those hard years I learned more of God,
and of His hidden, mysterious ways,
and far more of myself than I had known.
God was preparing me for a great task,
one no man had ever yet tried to do.
It strikes me now that even forty years
were hardly sufficient for all of this.
And even at the end I could not think
that I was God's man to save Israel.
Indeed, I was not. It was God Himself
who delivered His people. I was but
a feeble, but submissive, instrument
in His almighty hands. Give Him the praise.

Always my name will be linked with the law,
law of God, law of eternal truth,
law that no mere man ever fully kept,
not us, with our sins and iniquities,
certainly not I with my secret sins.

When I saw Israel's sin at the mount,
I hurled to the ground and broke those tablets
of law, but long before that I broke the
law not yet given, and have done so since.

I know well we all need a redeemer,
a priest and an atoning sacrifice,
and a savior from the condemnation
of that holy law which God gave through me.

Lord, you have ever been my dwelling place.
Under your shadow, your sheltering wings,
I lived, even when I was failing you.
O my God, the great, awe-inspiring God,
how I love you, how I would exalt your
greatness, splendor and holy majesty!

O LORD God, how patiently you bore with
a rebellious and disobedient
people! How meekly you bowed down to hear,
to cover our misdeeds, to lead us on!
Oh, how wise, how good, how gentle you are!
Your mercy, your kindness are infinite,
your love reaches to the depths of our sin,
and raises us to the heights of glory.

My work is done. It was not mine to lead
God's people to the promised place of rest.
For that there must come a much greater one than I,
and come he surely will, when God's own time draws nigh.

## •Aaron
### meditating on priesthood

I am the brother of the greatest man
of this generation, and have had a
part in some of the greatest miracles
ever known among men. But this does not
make me great. My sins and failures are known
to you all, and they loom so large in my
estimate of myself that they bring me
down in the dust at the Lord's holy feet.
But I have learned some important lessons
on my pilgrimage which may help you all.

It seems that at the very center of
each religion in the world there is a
priesthood, and that a strong desire for priests
is a part of the makeup of mankind
wherever they may be found on the earth.
No doubt this reflects man's knowledge of his
sinfulness and distance from God, and the
hope that a priest might bring God's blessings near.

I am a priest, the high priest of Israel,
being appointed by the Most High to
represent His people. In this way man's
need of a priest is taught by God Himself.

Among my other duties is this one:
Once each year with the blood of the slain lamb
in my hands I pass through the curtain,
the holy veil, with much trembling and fear,
to the presence of Holy Majesty,
the appearance of the glory of Him
who created the whole vast universe,

to make atonement at His mercy seat.
I say, with fear and trembling! For I know
I am a sinful man. Since the golden
calf and the shattered tablets of God's law
at Mt Sinai, more oppressive still has
been the dark mountain of my guilt and shame.
O Holy One, how do I ever dare
come before you knowing my sinfulness?

Listen, my people, hear me, O my friends.
I have thought much on priesthood and its task.
Learn one thing, a heavenly truth, from me:
a human high priest is but a fallen man.
I dream of a much superior one,
one who is human but more than human,
so he can have compassion on us all,
yet never betray his office by sin;
one who can bring us completely to God,
one who can offer one just sacrifice
for sin forever, one who will never
weakly yield to foolish demands of men,
one with whom there will be no calf of gold,
no envy of Moses, no broken law.

To such a one, the priest of my best dreams,
I bow. Sometimes a thought has come to me–
am I a symbol, a passing shadow
of one who is to come, the higher,
the greater one I'm sure that all men need?

I think this may be what my life has meant.
And so with this I've learned to rest content.

## • Miriam
### (Numbers chapter 12)

Dear brother, I write because I find it
easier to put these things on paper than
to speak about them face to face with you.

The truth is, I'm ashamed, very ashamed.
How I could ever get in such a state
that I spoke a single word against you
and your leadership, I don't really know.
It must have been a long process brought on
by the dreary life we all endure in
this terrible wilderness, combined with
my failure to keep under the fallen
and sinful nature we all suffer from.
(Will these wretched wanderings never end?)

I hope you will not think that I make that
an excuse for my evil behavior.
I have no real excuse for what I did.
It was no business of mine whom you chose
to marry. And being upset about
that certainly gave me no right at all
to criticize the way you do your job.

Forgive me, for I pray with all my heart
that you will overlook my sad offense,
and show once more that humbleness of mind
that has always distinguished you from me
and from most others of the human race.

Dear Moses, dear brother, I have always
loved you. I loved you from your birth, and when
your wee form was committed to the Nile

in that basket, and floated near the bank,
I was there by you keeping loving watch.
You were so beautiful, so sweet a babe.
It almost broke my heart to think that you
were in danger. And when your tiny voice
uttered that cry in the ears of Pharaoh's
daughter, remember, it was I who ran
to her in the hope of helping your life.
And it was I who got our own mother
to be your nurse, and so tied your young heart
to Israel forever.
                                        Oh, how strong,
how powerful you became, how godly!
Oh, cut this tongue from my mouth lest it speak
again one word against so great a man,
so good and righteous and holy a man!

Please accept this apology, I am,
with love and high regard. Your Miriam.

## The Pharaoh of Moses' day
**(after hearing the demands of Moses–Exodus 5:1-9)**

Of all the stupid things I ever heard
this was the most stupid. Let Israel's
god do the worst he can, I will never
let those brutish people go, those weak,
slavish, sniveling people.
                                        Does Moses think
that I have taken leave of my senses,
or that the might of Egypt is no more?

And did you hear the reason Moses gave–
or I should say excuse to keep from work–
to worship and sacrifice to their god!
If they want to worship and serve a god,
don't we have a sufficient number in
Egypt?
                                        And I cannot think any god
of ours is inferior to–now what
did Moses say his god's name was?–Yahweh.

If he comes in with any more demands
we'll be happy to put it to the test.
He will find out that I am a hard man.

The powers of our gods are known to all,
controlling as they do the earth, the sky,
the sun, all the beasts, and the River Nile.
Where does this leave this god of Israel?

This Yahweh speaks big words; we will see his
power. Or, what is far more probable,
we will see his powerlessness. I now
give a challenge to the Lord of Israel.

Let Moses and Aaron now stretch out their rod.
They'll learn that in Egypt I myself am God.

## Israel at Sinai
**(Exodus chapter 32)**

What has happened to Moses? We don't know.
Perhaps some wild animal has torn him.
Perhaps, as he did once before in the
land of Egypt, he has run off somewhere.
It is even possible that his God
has killed him for breaking one of his laws.
Maybe he has been burned up by the fire
on that fearful mountain. How can we tell?

We will not speak a word against any
god, but surely there can be no other
as stern as this Yahweh. It seems to us
right now that he is impossibly strict.
And he's always angry about something
or other. Think of our experiences
in this horrible desert up till now.
He is a jealous God, a consuming fire.
With him how can we ever live and breathe?

Yes, we know, not long back we agreed to
keep all of his regulations and laws.
It seemed a good idea at the time.
And what else could we do? We could hardly
stand there at the foot of that huge mountain
with him on top and say "No, we will not!"
Could we? A refusal might have meant the
end of us, or at least more pain and grief.
We hardly had a choice then, but we do now.

On our way we know we need some god to
go with us, or better still, several gods.
Yahweh, we fear, means danger–that is,

if we try to act according to all
that is in our hearts, which, of course, is what
we want to do. And what can be wrong with
behaving like normal human beings
for a change? Our heart's cry is for a god
(or gods) who will understand and permit
us to do just this.

The calf god we came
to know in Egypt would do very well,
and we will sacrifice the gold we have
to make a form that can be seen and touched
to replace that distant one who conceals
himself behind dark clouds and dreadful smoke,
and thunders with his voice and hurts our ears
with noise far worse than any trumpet blast,
and will not let us even touch the mount
where he remains and sends out his hard rules.
For us no more lightning flash or blazing fire!
No more quaking mountain, or trembling hearts!

Oh for a god who can be pleased, and who will please!
So get up, Aaron, and make us some deities.

## Israel in the Desert
### (at Kadesh Barnea–Numbers 14:1-4)

We're fed up. You would think that a man as
educated as Moses could see what
the real situation is. But common
sense and education are not always
joined in the same man. Does he think we had
it bad in Egypt?

This is worse. Our food's
the same every day, and poor stuff it is.
Our surroundings are intolerable.
Not a flower, hardly a tree can be seen
in this waste howling wilderness, this burning
land, a place of sand and killing heat, of drought
and the shades of death, where no one travels
and no one lives. And can he expect us
to travel on and on enduring this?

And there's all these regulations and rules.
We can't lift a hand to do anything
for fear that we might break some law of his.

It all sounded well enough when we first
heard it, but since then we have come to our
senses and we are not going to let
this man lord it over us anymore.

For now he wants us to go into this
land of Canaan where we will be at the
mercy of giants who outnumber us,
who are far better equipped than we are,
in whose sight we are puny as locusts.
We will fall by their whetted swords and our
wives and little ones will become their prey.

Far better now to return to the land
from which he dragged us when we were at peace.
To be sure, Egypt had its difficulties,
but nothing compared to this. And if we
return of our own free will, perhaps
the Egyptians will welcome us and make
our lot easier than it was before.
We can promise never to leave them again.

If Moses and his brother and those henchmen
of his, Joshua and Caleb, try to
stop us, we will leave their dead bodies here
to rot in this desert they love so much.
Without them we can find our way back home.
If they come with us, who knows what trouble
they may cause? Yes, better to leave them here.

We'll turn back again and by morning light be gone.
Promise of Canaan can no longer lure us on.

## The Sons of Korah
**(Numbers 16:1-33; Psalm 48, etc)**

We are brands plucked from the burning, or
to be more exact, from the deadly pit.
We and our whole families, young and old,
have heard this truth from the time that we could
understand words. It is interwoven
with our childhood memories. Our infant
lips lisp the grim tale of our ancestor
almost as soon as they learn to form words,
and of how it is that we can be alive.

On that rebellious day the very earth
groaned aloud at all the mutinous crew
arrayed against the leaders God Himself
had appointed for our good. It groaned and
split apart, and the pit spread wide for them,
and down they went into Sheol alive,
swallowed up by the ground's wide gaping mouth
and joined the living spirits of the dead,
Korah, with Dathan and Abiram too,
all the wives, the children, and all their men,
fallen deep down inside that dark unknown world.

And we live, memorials to God's grace,
and do not know why our forefather, that
member of wicked Korah's clan, was spared.
Perhaps our compassionate God then saw
in him some tenderness of heart for God,
or some true glimmer of the faith that saves.
We know that He delights in mercy and
is keen not to punish if He can find
a just reason for passing over sin.

So now we all spend our time in praise to
our blessed God, and sometimes clap our hands
with joy. How awesome is the Lord Most High.
He is the great King over all the earth.

Praise Him all you nations, and sing glad songs to Him,
the One who sits enthroned above the cherubim.

## Balak
**(Numbers 22:1-25:16; 31:1-8)**

Encamped at the Jordan facing Jericho,
seemingly Israel was not at all
concerned about us. But I could not know
whether this would last. I did know what they
did both to Og king of Bashan and to
Sihon king of the Amorites, and I
trembled at the sight of them–could we trust
them not to attack?
And later what would
happen if they took Canaan and lived there?
Then would Israel, well established and
stronger still, view us near their borders with
peaceful eyes? Real danger is what I saw,
and felt Israel must be stopped by any
means available to us.
So I had
Balaam brought here. I had to pay him well,
but you expect that in a prophet of
his reputation and previous success.
I was sure his mantras against Israel
would lead to their swift and total defeat.
And what did the fellow do? Instead of
cursing Israel as I told him to do,
he blessed them! Then said his God made him do it!

He was a complicated man, and not
very easy to know or understand.
But in spite of all his pronouncements to
to the contrary, I sensed he loved money and
would do almost anything to get it.
Why, then, did he prophecy as he did?

This was a puzzle to me until I
realized how strong pride worked in the man.
He could hardly bear to think his words
might somehow fall to the ground unfulfilled.
Honors from men meant a great deal to him.
But riches too.
So he thought of a way to
keep his reputation and get his gold
by deceitful scheme, all at the same time–
a thing common enough among men, but
seen, I believe, in excess in that man.
He said to me that if Israel should
fall into sin, they would be punished by
their God and then be weak and vulnerable
on the battlefield.
I followed his advice
and those beautiful Moabite women
did their work of temptation with great skill.
But it all came back to rest on our own
heads. The God of Israel has prevailed.

For Midian is destroyed and all my troops have fled,
and fighting the God he said he served, Balaam's dead.

## Balaam
**(Numbers 22:1 - 25:4)**

For some reason or other people have
always found me something of a puzzle.
Some even think that I have two distinct
personalities (which is, of course, not
only untrue but completely absurd).
Perhaps this is because I am a man
of two worlds, and I try to keep these two
separate in my thinking and actions.

There is, of course, my career as prophet,
of which I am justly proud. Always I
try to get God's message and deliver
it just as I receive it. No changes
in the message are possible to me–
if, that is, I want to maintain my good
reputation as a genuine seer,
which I do. People will lose confidence
in you if you meddle with the message,
and it goes unfulfilled. This is not my
way. I will speak what God gives me and let
the chips fall where they may.

Then there is my
other world, the world of money and the
good things of this earth. I cannot think that
we should be faulted for desiring these.
Do they not also come from God above?
I will admit that when I went to the
king of Moab I had them in my mind,
and I did some things which I am sure some
bigots and religious fanatics will
always attack me for. So be it.

What
was Israel to me? I did not know
that people and really did not care what
might happen to them. Uninvited, they
have come here and caused turmoil everywhere.
I fear they will be a source of very
great trouble to all the nations around
here for many years to come.
Now as to
the reward that Balak promised–that I
did care about. That I could see and touch
and put to good use in my life as a
prophet of God. I resolved to get it,
come what may. So, man to man, secretly,
I gave him some good advice, which he took.
The results you know. But do not blame me.
Israel is the one who sinned against God.

This is my way: to declare to all what will be,
then to get everything that is coming to me.

## Joshua
### after taking Canaan

I was trained under the meekest of men.
But I learned how to fight, just as he fought.
Men sometimes think meekness is a weak thing,
not realizing the great manliness,
the almost superhuman strength of heart,
one needs to meet provocations meekly.
By nature he was something else; he learned
meekness–or else it was a gift of God,
given at the time he needed it most.

For that matter, is anything in us
by birth good? I am no theologian,
but I think not; I too have a nature.
And in my people I have often seen
the hard rebelliousness, the base desire,
the complaining spirit, the fainting will,
the slowness to love, the swiftness to sin,
the slackness to obey.
But I thank my God
that I have also seen them eager and
prepared for exploits and valorous deeds,
equipped by God according to their faith.

About myself I've hardly said a word.
Moses occupied so much of my life,
that he is still there in all my thoughts.
I wish he could have come into the land.
But God had other plans, and it was me
He called to lead, to fight and take this place.

To me one thing alone made leadership
possible–before I took a step

to take this fair land, the Commander of
the LORD's armies drew near and took control.
His leadership it was which won the fight;
my task to follow and obey His word.

God is the mighty warrior, the One who
raises His banner against wicked men,
who lifts His glittering sword to strike at
arrogance and unbelief and all that
vainly struggles against His holy laws,
who marches with His own and girds them with
strength, the Destroyer of all that is wrong.

So I look back with no praise for myself,
but much for Him, the God who fights for us,
the Lord of my life, and of the whole earth.

Trust in our God alone can give our poor life wings.
Faith is the victory that overcomes all things.

## Caleb
**(Joshua 14:6-15–during the battle for Canaan)**

There are still things for an old man to do
besides putting his feet up in the tent
and looking back to former victories.
As sure as God lives, God who gives me strength,
I will fight on and glory in the fight,
and not count up my years as an excuse
to be at ease while still the people war
for the LORD of hosts against His enemy.
I will not sleep the sleep of idleness
while there are still those mountains to be claimed.

If I must die now, I will die in arms
against all that opposes God's sweet truth
and His march of righteousness through the land.

As long as I still have breath I will breathe
out my prayer for Israel's success,
and for my own as I prepare once more
to face the foe and take my piece of ground.

Faith looks not at age, hopes not for delay.
Now, sword in hand, I set out for the fray.

## Rahab
**(Joshua 2:1-21; 6:23; Matthew 1:5)**

It is probably not a usual thing
that a person in my profession has
an opportunity such as I had.
God is great and can use whom He will.
I ran a certain place that was called an
inn, but it could be, and frequently was,
used for purposes I don't wish to name–
not now that everything is changed, and I
am redeemed by Israel's God.
Let me
describe to you how it all came about.
Jericho, and indeed the whole wide land,
was in a state of alarm because of
Israel. For reports had reached our ears
about their great victories over the
Egyptians, over the Midianites,
and over Sihon king of Heshbon, and
Og king of Bashan, east of the Jordan,
indeed, over all who dared to oppose
them anywhere.
And we were no stronger
than those nations, though our city walls were
high, and well fortified and very stout.
But in our hearts we knew it was no use–
Israel's God of miracles was on
the march, and from king to slave everyone
trembled at His approach. I know I did.

Then came the day when those spies suddenly
appeared at my inn, sent by God Himself,
I firmly believe. And I saw my chance.
I hid them there from my own king, and then

I lied to those who made determined search
(do you think that it was a time for truth?).
And so they spared me when the walls collapsed
and the slaughter began, and the whole of
Jericho was demolished and all its
people slain. Such is my story in brief.

One more thing I should say–God rewarded
not my telling lies, but my trust in Him.
I praise Him, the God of truth forever,
who forgives our wrong and remembers our
acts of faith, and the good we try to do.

This whole story discloses God's amazing grace
shown to a fallen woman of a fallen race.

## Achan
**(Joshua 6:1-21; 7:1,16-26)**

What a crash there was when those walls came down!
Thick walls they were, and high, and they fell flat
as could be, flat as our unleavened bread.
The whole land for miles around must have felt
the shock. After that there was a great deal
of confusion in Jericho–people
shouting and wailing and running about
here and there, trying to escape, and quite
a lot trying to hide inside their homes.
We did what we had been told. With drawn swords
we marched in, going straight ahead, killing
everyone in our path.
I doubt if you
can really imagine those grim scenes.
We slashed and cut till our arms were worn out.
Such screaming and crying you never heard.
Blood was everywhere in the houses and
flowing in the streets, and dead and dying
men, women and children were scattered all
over the place. You had to keep your eyes
wide open or you might step on someone.
We even killed all the cattle and sheep.

When the slaughter was coming to an end,
I found myself in a big house where I
immediately put my sword to good
use on everyone in sight. As I glanced
here and there, my eyes fell on what I thought
of as great treasure (I have never been
a wealthy man)–some beautiful clothing,
some silver pieces, and a wedge of gold.

I knew very well what our orders were–
we were not to touch a thing that was there.
It all belonged to God and was to go
into the Lord's treasury. So I tried
to tear my eyes away. But I could not.
It seemed they were in control of my brain,
and kept me staring at those things, when I
should have turned my head away. And the more
I looked, the more desire rose in my heart.
And then desire overcame conscience and
reason and fear, and so I looked this way
and that, and then reached out and took those things,
and went and hid them in my tent, and thought
no man on earth will ever find this out.

Now here I am condemned by God and men,
and very soon the first of many stones
will strike my trembling flesh. Though I have now
confessed my sin, and have some hope that God
has forgiven me, I can't be sure. I
know I deserve to die in doubt and pain.

Are any of you tempted to do as I did?
Then you should be quite sure your sin cannot be hid.

## Deborah
### (Judges 4:4–5:31–looking back)

I really did not want to do man's work,
but know now that when men will not do it
God may call women to work in their place,
rather than have man's work remain undone.
My desire is to be just what God wants,
and available to Him if He calls.
I firmly believe that we should all live
up to our potential, and God may give
to some women work which men may think strange.

I led Israel and went to the war,
and sang, and sometimes I suspect only
the singing was what some men approved.
I can live with that. Are we to please men,
or God who calls us and gives us our task?

But do not think I want to be a man.
I will maintain my womanliness till
the day I die. To behave like a man,
or to try to usurp man's position,
I utterly refuse, now and always.
I believe that if God had wanted me
to act like men He would have made me one.
I encouraged the princes to rise up,
I urged Barak to bravely take the lead.
I arose a mother in Israel,
not a father, and I will remain one.

Now let me return to my poetry.
As a judge, I hear enough disputing.
I will still serve the LORD and Israel,
and sing when I can, and lead when I must,
and praise my God in everything He does.

His will for each of us is the important thing.
Let each one find it and obey our Lord and King.

## Barak

**(after the victory over Sisera–Judges 4:6-16)**

I know, I was far too timid and fearful,
But in His work God has a place for a
poor trembling man whose trust in Him is small.
If very great faith is needed, I am
not your man, though I can wish that I were.
Who knows? from now on perhaps I will be.
Demanding the presence of Deborah,
I did not count enough on the presence
of God, not thinking that God is enough
even when there is no one else at all.

But I learned that a tiny sprout of faith
can be a force in the hands of the LORD,
can put invading enemies to flight.
It is an empty hand outstretched for help,
and even our small faith will see Him act.

Our great victories come by our great God,
and not by our puny efforts and strength.
Remember, it's not faith that's to be praised,
but the One who gives His power to it.

Let us not praise the hand and not the man,
but the One who puts the gift in the hand,
and deigns to use the woman or the man,
the One far above all gifts and all men.

God speaks to us in our weak faith and fears.
and has a work for everyone who hears.

## Jael
**(Judges 4:17-24)**

Is this the man who troubled Israel,
who inspired terror in so many hearts,
this man here resting, sleeping at my feet?
Where is now all that pride and arrogance?
Where is that unholy fire which blazed at
the sight of the holy people of God?
How pale and weary is Sisera's face!
His powerful arm bent, cradling his chest,
he lies there, his head flat against the earth.

Running he came to me, running, fleeing
for his life. "Turn in here, my lord, turn in
to me," I said, "and do not be afraid."
"A little water now," he said, "oh, please,
a cup of water for my burning tongue.
And stand watch in the entrance of the tent."

Milk I gave him, cool milk from the pitcher's
mouth, milk to hush him to sleep. Milk he drank
with thoughts, it could be, of mother and home.

He is a guest here, he has sought refuge
in my tent, but I am fully resolved,
by the strength God gives, this enemy of
Israel will not leave my tent alive.
Will you now think me masculine and fierce?
I am only a woman, a housewife,
strong and aroused for righteousness and truth.

No poisonous beverage sits on my
shelves. No sword is here honed and thirsty for
the blood of man, no spear prepared with skill

to raise and thrust into his pulsing heart,
no arrow to fly swift from the bent bow.
Hammer, and long pegs for the tent to hold
it firm against the earth when strong winds blow,
these I have ready in my eager hands.

Hammer and nail, now do your blessed work–
find through the bone and brain the floor beneath.
Bite through the skull where such wickedness lay,
part spirit from depraved flesh and send it
groaning down to the dark pit's darkest depths!
Courage and faith, now take the victory!
Through a weak, trembling woman, and by this frail hand,
God slays the mighty man who rose against His land.

## Gideon

**(after victory over Midian–Judges 6:11 - 7:25)**

Before I speak about my fleece, I would
explain why I first asked for a sign.
You should not think that I was shrinking back
from doing the will of God, as is the
way of all those who do not trust in Him.

I was willing to do what He would say,
once I was sure He was the one who spoke.
After all, anyone may come to us
and say he brings a message straight from God.
Should we not put that message to the test,
and make trial of such a messenger?

There are many beings, many voices
in the world, and not all of them are good.
But did not my later actions prove my
willingness? Do not forget my yielded
heart, my obedience and daring deeds.

I asked for a sign because God was now
demanding of me an important thing,
and I had no illusions about my
adequacy, no confidence at all
in my abilities. I knew that the
Midianites were much too strong for us
and that on my own nothing could be done.
I had to know beyond all doubt that God
was with me and would give me victory.

Yes, I confess that in my heart there was
some unbelief mixed with my faith, that is,
a doubt that God could use me as He said.

But is this not the way of all mankind?
(Those with absolute faith, who never had
a doubt, may criticize me. Yes, blame me,
if you have never longed for assurance
and certitude and peace, as I did.then).
So I asked for further signs.
                                        And know this:
If I had it to do over again,
I would still ask God to guide me in this way.
I see no wrong in wanting certainty.
For should I bring a risk to Israel
without being sure of God's appointed will?
To set out on so serious a task
in doubt did not seem the way for me to go.

Do not say that I did not believe God,
and so foolishly demanded those signs.
Rather say that I believed that God would
give me signs. I praise Him for doing so.
If you know God's will without signs then praise
Him and do that will.
                                        But do not look down
on those who get signs and then do His will.
Now if I erred in asking God for signs,
why did no rebuke come from God's own mouth?
It is true, without faith one can ask for signs,
in doubt that God will ever speak to us,
or in scornful rejection of God's Word.
But one can also ask in faith. I know.

There is what some men call faith which I call
mere presumption, and reckless bravado.
I will never, never undertake to
do such an almost impossible thing,
until God's presence with me is assured.
If this is a fault, then it is a fault
I wish to see at work in everyone.

God's plan and call for us are vital to fulfill.
So by any proper means, let us find His will.

## Jephthah
**(Judges 11:29-40)**

Oh, my poor girl, what have I done to you!
How could I ever have let such rash and
foolish words fall from my lips as I spoke
then in my haste? Could I not even guess
what might occur when I came back from war?
Could I not see it might be you who would
come first out through the door and break my heart?

Great triumph turned into calamity,
and my excited words became ashes
in my mouth, when my eyes fell on your face.

A vow made to the Lord must be fulfilled.
There can be no retreat, no change of mind,
no altering of even one detail
of the original vow. For that would
make us false to our great God and so earn
His condemnation and His fiery wrath.
It is far better not to vow at all
than to vow and then not perform the vow.

And so you must die, and with you, my heart.
On the battlefield God has given me
a great victory and brought me safe home.
But what are all victories compared to
this great loss? This defeat will send me to
my grave regretting every day I live.
I have become a monster and a fool
in my own eyes, and no doubt in yours too.

Forgive me, my daughter, my precious one,
if you can find a heart to forgive a

foolish man who loves you still, and would be
glad to die in your place, if God approved.

A hasty vow can be an awful thing. It can
mean the death of a man's dear child, and kill the man.

## Samson
### (at life's end, holding the temple's pillars–Judges 16:29-31)

Of men I am the strongest but also
the weakest. I may pull this temple down,
but could be bound by a woman's weak hand.
I could learn how to fight, but not to live.
I could overpower my enemies,
but desire always overpowered me.
I could take a city, but could not keep
a guard on the ramparts of my own heart.
I could stand against a great multitude,
but not against the power of my lust.
I was, sadly, like every other man,
or more fallen and more foolish than all.

I did not learn well that dedication
to God means more than keeping a razor
from my hair, or refusing the wine cup.
A Nazirite from birth, I often lived
for self, not for the One to whom I was vowed.
Though with His help I performed amazing
feats of strength, and confounded all my foes,
did I ever once have the solemn thought
that from me a holy God wanted more?
Wanted a clean life, wanted all my heart?
And what profit is there in a man's great
strength, or his heroic deeds, without that?

So now, deservedly blind, desperate
and sad in the house of these Philistines,
groping, and made a spectacle to them,
here in the presence of their helpless gods,
at full stretch to see my dying revenge
on cruel men, I make my final prayer:

O Lord God, remember again this poor
man, and come and strengthen me just once more.

## Delilah
**(Judges 16:4-31)**

What a snap it turned out to be! Knowing
his reputation for strength I had thought
there could be some minor difficulty,
though I have always known that I can bend
any man around my little finger.

It turned out to be so again, and it
was even easier than I had guessed
it would be. Because the poor idiot
was then actually in love with me.
Or at least that is what he always said.
So deceiving him was a simple thing.

What man likes to suspect that the woman
he thinks he loves is a cunning serpent?
But perhaps he was really not deceived,
but only considered the whole thing a
game, over-confident that he could win,
little knowing that no man has ever
won playing a game with me. Yes, this seems
much more likely.
But whether it was this
or that, the result was the same. Samson
was taken away by the Philistines,
and I have the one thing I really cared
about–the promised silver. And, indeed,
to be perfectly honest, money is
the one thing I can ever care about.
You may think that there is some lack in me,
but to me all this talk of love is just
that–mere talk. I have not seen the unfeigned
thing a single time in my entire life.

When people speak of love they mean they want
something for themselves.
I suppose you will
want to know what I think of the blinding
of Samson, his death, and the destruction
of Dagon's temple with the great loss of
life connected with that event. For you
know that it was my part in this affair
that produced all those dramatic results.

But I'm enjoying the money I earned
and think of little else. I am not proud
of what I did, but I am not troubled
by it, and I feel no worm of remorse.
I am not concerned with politics or
struggles for power, or which so-called great
men rebel, or submit, or live or die.

I received my just reward for a job well done.
Do not look for my thoughts beyond this. There are none.

## Micah in Judges
**Judges 17:1 - 18:31**

The whole matter was quite puzzling to me.
After all, I am a good member of
one of the greatest tribes in Israel,
and a religious and trustworthy man.
You will remember that when I stole
that money from my mother, I confessed,
nor did she have to use any kind of
force for me to own my guilt. You can see
I have a conscience and give in to it.

I wanted home to be a godly place,
and so was overjoyed when Mom got that
good silversmith to make those images.
I oversaw that work and urged him on
to the best work that he could ever do.
And not only this. I made my own son
the priest at our idol shrine. Does this not
show how carefully I brought up my kids
and instructed them in the proper way?

Then there was the day that the Levite came.
I persuaded him to stay and become
our priest. This was not because my son was
not doing a good job. No, but to have
a holy man, one descended from the
priestly tribe in Israel, a man of
experience, as our priest, was, I thought,
a good chance to get more blessing from God
on our home. You can see that God means a
great deal to me.
But what good did it do?
It looks now like I don't mean much to God.

For He doesn't do anything I say.
And in spite of how I earnestly tried
to please and serve Him, He lets these lawless
men from the tribe of Dan rob me of all
that was dear to me. My idols are gone,
my ephod is gone, and my priest is gone.
Nothing at all is left to me. What will
I have to face next if I serve my God?

We live in evil days. No one has a
conscience and no one is teaching right from
wrong. Everyone is out for money and
sells out to the highest bidder. No one
has consideration for other men.
Pathetic indeed are these times of ours.
To see this just look at my own sad case.
There seems to be no standards anymore.
Everywhere we see injustice, violence and lies.
All we can do is what is right in our own eyes.

## The Tribe of Benjamin
**(in Judges chapter 20)**

Now we are almost totally destroyed.
And all because of the meddling of some
other tribes in our affairs. Our hearts are
torn when we see what is left of our tribe,
the frightful fields and all the fallen dead.
We care not what the men of Gibeah
did, it was not right for the whole nation
to decide to attack us as it did.

That Levite did make some very severe
allegations. But was what he said fact,
or fiction? Has any of it been proved?
We know all of Israel believes it,
but does that make it true? People in large
numbers believe in falsehoods all the time.
Perhaps the Levite had some deadly grudge
against Gibeah's men, and sought to bring
them down.
But even if the charge was true,
we think the matter was improperly
handled. The other tribes made their demands,
instead of asking for a meeting to
calmly study what all of us should do.
After all is said and done this was an
internal matter. If some tribes try to
judge others, what becomes of tribal rights?

Now try to see things from our point of view.
The men of Gibeah were our own flesh
and blood, and to us blood relationship
is of extreme importance. We really
could not, just like that, hand them over for

punishment, especially punishment
at the harsh hands of those not of our tribe.
Why, they said they would put the men to death!

The idea is unacceptable.
If we, who have the same ancestry, and
who are in the very same clan, do not
stick together what will happen to us?
We could all fall into feebleness and
poverty. We will never let ourselves
be divided in this dangerous way,
for any reason, imagined or real.

If those men were really guilty as charged
(and we admit that they might well have been),
shouldn't we have been left to deal with it
in our time and way? Should the other tribes
have rushed to judgment as they did? Some men
are much too quick to put hand to sword hilt.
Now let all the tribes learn how to control
their rashness, their bullying arrogance.

Well, now you can understand what was the real core
of the problem, and why we had to go to war.

## Israel Opposing Benjamin
**(Judges chapter 20)**

Today we are hurting, as low as we
have ever been, but we are not confused.
For we are sure that we did the right thing,
in spite of the defeats, and the loss of
life on both sides which caused great searching of
heart. For God Himself gave us His guidance
in what we did, and victory at last.

Is civil war or internecine strife
ever justified? Is not the cost more
grievous than the faults which produce it?
The cost in this sad case was very great–
Israel lost more than forty thousand
fighting men, and the tribe of Benjamin
was almost wholly obliterated.

And all this the result of one night of
sinning in the town of Gibeah in
Benjamin, and their stubborn refusal
to punish the guilty.
But was that our
affair? We thought it was, and think so still.
There was a weighty principle at stake:
The very life of this great nation was
threatened by such wickedness, and to let
such men go free would be to make the land
unclean, and bring down the judgment of God.

We remembered Achan, the troubler of
Israel, who by one sin brought defeat
to the armies of God, and much disgrace.
When that one man sinned, God said "Israel

has sinned." He refused to continue with
us until we put away that evil
from our midst.
He taught us that His people
are all linked together, and that He will
deal with us as a nation, and so our
individual acts bear upon the
welfare of us all. God and evil will
never co-exist, and if we want His
presence with us we must deal with those things
which offend Him and cause Him to depart.

So we knew we could not abandon this
principle because blood was flowing on
the fair fields of our villages and towns.
There are things of far more importance than
our own lives, or the lives of other men.

We say, in spite of all, we took the proper stand.
For our God is not the kind that makes no demand.

## Ruth

Strange and wonderful are the ways of God.
He used a bad famine in Israel
to bring good to me. For because of it
Naomi's family came to our land,
and brought a knowledge I had never had.
Now if that famine had not brought her here
how could I ever have married one of
her sons, or ever have gone to her land,
or ever have met Boaz and become
a member of a great family in
Israel, or, far more importantly,
ever have come to know Israel's God?

For I was of a people who worshiped
idols, who did not know the true God, and,
for the most part, from all that I could see,
had no desire to know Him.
                                        Kemosh was
our god, and a very vile one he was–
almost as bad as horrible Molech,
god of the Ammonites, who demanded
the sacrifice of innocent children
burned in his idol fires.
                                        Looking back I
wonder how I ever could have bowed to
the repulsive image of Kemosh, or
indeed to any such divinity.

How far short all idols come of showing us
what God is really like! They slander Him
instead, and keep people in bondage to
ugly lies. When worshipping that idol
I never dreamed there was such a God as

the great One whom now I have come to know,
though I often wondered at creation,
and looked at the stars of heaven with a
longing, however faint it might have been.

So when, from my mother-in-law, I heard
of Him, I did not hesitate, but sought
Him with my whole heart and soul, and found Him.
That is how it came about that I could
say to her with determination and
full assurance,
"Your God will be my God."
So I was willing to leave everything,
except Him, and the one who had told me
of Him. How well it all worked out, you know.

God troubled His own people, but bowed from His throne,
revealed His great grace and love, and made me His own.

## Naomi
**(the book of Ruth)**

From pleasantness to bitterness and then
back to pleasantness again. This is my
story in brief. In Bethlehem with my
good husband and two sons I was at peace,
and thought that God smiled on us. And I found
life was pleasing and good.
But God in His
wisdom sent troublesome times (He always
knows what the best thing is to do)–a drought
came, the fields dried up, and famine stalked the land.
In this way God sent us to live in a
land close bv, where He had good purposes
to fulfill.
Moab–a place of savage
idols and peculiar ways, where the God
of truth and His righteous laws have no place–
received us and so there we sought our bread
as aliens in an alien land. This had
a taste of bitterness, as you might guess,
but lack of other option bound us there.
Work was found, and spouses for my two sons.

Then into my life more bitterness came.
First my husband and then my precious boys
passed away leaving me sad and alone.
Call me not Naomi, I thought, but call
me Mara, for the Lord has dealt bitterly
with me.
There came the day (oh, the drawn-out
waiting, the many tears) I heard that rains
and harvests once more refreshed Bethlehem.
Without delay I set out to return

to my own people and to my own land,
and with me my Moabite daughters-in-law.
I tried to send them back, knowing myself
the grief of exile far from home and friends.

Orpah returned, but to my great surprise
Ruth would not go, but tightly clung to me
as though I were her one rock of refuge
in a savage sea. And so she clung to
my God as well.
Dear girl! She's with me yet,
and here in Bethlehem her little boy
now crawls on my lap and kisses my cheek,
and so my name is pleasantness again.

To fulfill His plan God uses His staff and rod.
But in the end we see how merciful is God.

## Hannah

**(1 Samuel 1:1 - 2:21. Later in life)**

Who would have thought that the answer to one
prayer could have such a profound effect
on the whole nation. But it did, for that
one answer was my dear son Samuel.
God gave me more than I had ever dreamed.
That's what God is like. Praise Him forever.
He gives joy for tears, smiles for bitterness.

I love all my children–I have six now
(and all this from one who by nature was
barren)–but Samuel is the one whom
God chose for very high and holy work.
You all know who he is and what he's done.
I need say nothing about all of that.
Instead, let me praise the Lord on His throne.

How great is our God, how mighty His power!
How strong His justice, how kingly His acts!
How sternly He deals with the arrogant!
How lovingly He raises the helpless!

The mighty man takes his bow, his arrow
from the quiver. His bow bends, his muscles
bulge. He aims the arrow, his eye is on
the poor and weak, but the Lord breaks the bow.
Shattered it lies in the dirt, the arrow
lies broken on the ground. The mighty man
lies at the feet of the one he despised.
Anguish seizes him, he rolls in the dust.
The enemies of the Lord will perish.
Their name will be blotted out, all their fame
forgotten.

The weak rise, girded with strength,
the needy and helpless ascend the throne,
the beggar rises from the ash heap, he
sits among princes, he inherits the
throne of glory.
Our God weighs the acts of all.
He sends the rich away. Hunger takes them,
they stand by the road with their hands outstretched.
They beg for work, frantic, they plead for bread.
How pale their faces, how gaunt their whole frame!
He feeds the hungry. They rejoice in His
great goodness, they praise Him for His justice.

No one is holy like the Lord our God.
There is no rock besides our Rock, no, none
besides you, O God. No one can do what
you do. You kill and make alive, you make
poor and make rich. You have made the pillars
of the earth. You guard the feet of your saints.
In darkness the wicked will be silent.
Heaven will thunder against them.
The Lord
will judge the ends of the earth. Do not talk
proudly. Lay your hand on your mouth. Forsake
arrogance. Let our God alone be praised.

He has raised my horn on high; I will sing His praise.
My spirit will sing on until the end of days.

## Samuel
**(as an old man–1 Samuel 12:2, 22-25)**

I consider again what great things God
has done for me, and for His Israel.

What a great thing to be an answer to
prayer and to deep longing, and at once
to be devoted to the work of God.
What a great thing to have a mother like mine,
one who loved me too much to hold me fast
when I belonged to God, but gave me up
to live and serve Him in the LORD's own house.

And what a great thing to have such a God,
one who gave me to my mother and then
took me for Himself from her willing hand,
one who stooped to a child and called to him,
standing by my bedside and calling still
until my infant mind could understand.

It was a great thing that He had a place
for a mere boy in His important work,
and gave me words which never fell in vain.
It was a great thing to grow up in that work
and to have Him always so near to me,
teaching me how to judge and how to pray,
delivering me from the sins of men
and giving me eyes to see His great truth.

It was a great thing to see God at work
delivering His people from their foes,
and changing sad defeats to victory.

I had my sorrows. My own dear sons were

disappointments in the Lord's great work.
And so the people turned to thoughts of kings,
and very soon rejected heaven's King.
And Saul–a bigger disappointment than
my sons, a flawed and disobedient
man, who never learned his own heart, or God's.
So I had double sorrow for a time.
But David cheered my heart and brought some peace
about the future of this holy land.
For God will surely bring Him to the throne
and through him save His people Israel.

Now my brief time on earth is nearly done.
God forbid that I should sin against Him,
even in my last days, by ceasing to
intercede for my people in their need.

So I will die just as I have lived–praying still,
and go to rest trusting God's good and perfect will.

## Eli
### (1 Samuel 2:12–4:22–the glory departed)

So this is what I have come to at last–
the sparse gray hair over a scaly scalp,
facial skin beginning to hang in folds,
the chin becoming two, or maybe three,
the swelling paunch and the faltering step,
the inner drive now gone and life fading
fast away, the death angel drawing near,
and regrets beyond any numbering,
almost beyond remembering.
Do I
wish I could live my life over? Not that.
Once is enough, and, I sometimes think, more
than enough. And better it would be not
to live at all than to have to live twice.
Oh yes, as all other men, I wish that
some things could be changed.
As the high priest of
Israel I had many privileges and,
of course, many responsibilities,
and I believe that I was grateful for
the privileges and took all my duties
seriously. I always saw that the
lamps in the Holy Place were burning bright,
that the Showbread was there on its table,
and that the incense was offered to God.

And never did I think to enter the
Most Holy Place without fear and trembling,
and I guarded well, as I would my own
life, the sanctity of the ark of God.
I loved it as much as I did my sons.
And now it has gone away to the war

with them to fight the Philistines, and how
will I ever see it or them again?

My sons–here was my big mistake.
I should say–to be accurate–my sin.
I trusted them too much and took no pains
to see what they were doing. How could I,
a sinner myself, not guess at the deep
depravity concealed in both their hearts?

And once revealed how could I be so weak
in my rebuke? How could I permit them
to proceed in the holy work of God
with their unholy hands? I was not one
to use the rod in discipline, and now
I've seen my spoiled and heartless boys and my
own heart dies. They have brought shame on themselves,
on me, and on the whole of Levi's tribe.

I must state things as they are: I have not done well,
and so now the glory has gone from Israel.

## King Saul
**(at the end, after consulting the witch–1 Samuel 28:3-25)**

All I ever heard was David, David,
David. Everybody was against me,
and no one cared whether I lived or died,
if only they could put him on the throne.
And who is there remaining who can rid
me of that traitorous adversary?

My own son was first to join his side,
and soon all went after that reckless boy,
and left me suffering on all alone.
The only ones who stayed were sycophants
who bring vain words and never any joy.

Samuel too hated and opposed my rule,
inventing reasons why I can't be king,
and at the end would not give me a glance.
Now, dead, he rose up to pronounce my fate,
and looked at me as if I were a fool.
He always was for those who tried to bring
me crashing down, and opened wide the gate
for Jesse's plotting and rebellious son.

What was my fault that all men turned from me?
And what the sin they say that I have done?
Among them all I never harmed a man,
and saw their wives and children with respect.
I have stood tall to fight their enemy,
and even now am doing all I can.
Why should I be the object of neglect?
And why can they not see my unjust woe?

And am I to die? Is it fair to me

that even God should turn to be my foe?
But I will now fight on; I am the stuff
that heroes are made of. My dying breath
will see me still pursuing victory
and never turning back. But that's enough.
Now to the battle and welcoming death.

## Jonathan
### (1 Samuel 18:1-4; 23:16-18)

The first time I saw David in action
I could understand he had qualities
that would make made him a very special man.
He had that boldness of faith, that complete
confidence in God, which overcame his
fear and enabled him to undertake
exploits others would not have dared to try.
Perhaps he really felt no fear at all
in those times of danger which left other
men weak and trembling. His ability
to forget himself and think only of
the honor of God and what needed to
be done, marked him as a leader of men.

I never met a man I admired more,
or loved more. I love him as my own soul.
I know he will be king, not I, and I
am satisfied that this is how things are.
I have no great ambitions for myself,
and am quite content with God's will for me.

My father is of a different mind.
For now the truth is clear that he wants him
dead. He is so full of envy and fear,
so plagued by some spirit of wickedness,
that he appears sometimes out of his mind.
And he is not willing to take second
place to another, especially to
one he considers a rival for the
admiration of the people of God.
And David has proved himself dauntless on
the battlefield, and won the hearts of all.

"Saul has killed his thousands, but David his
tens of thousands"–this is the song that first
stirred up rage and jealousy, which since that
time have led on to such violent ways.

But is there a humbler man than David?
He never bragged of his abilities,
but gave all praise to God. And he has no
desire to seize my father's throne, but wants
only what pleases God, and that in God's
good time. He would not lift a finger to
harm the king, nor ever use his tongue to
disparage him.
But now he suffers in
the desert, hiding there from cave to cave,
knowing the king will come in hot pursuit.

But in His perfect time God will bring release
and grant him a reign of righteousness and peace.

## King David
**in his last days**

Many think of me as a fighting man,
and once the people sang, "Saul has killed his
thousands, but David his tens of thousands."
Can you believe me then if I say that
far more than warring I liked writing psalms?
That being the sweet singer of Israel
was more satisfying than bearing arms?

But God, and therefore I, had enemies,
and so when there was fighting to be done,
I was ready to do it, since the Lord
of hosts Himself had taught my hands to war.

But music was never my second choice,
and poetry was not to me something
to be crowded into leisure moments.
Lifting my heart to heaven, looking for,
and trusting that I found, the chosen word,
the inescapable phrase and form to
convey the high and holy truth that sought
to be expressed through my excited pen,
and feeling the Spirit's inspiring fire,
gripped heart and mind as nothing else could do.

So I became a warrior-poet whose
double pursuit created double tracks.
God too is a warrior, and also writes
His verse, using prophets to record it.
I am in very splendid company.

Looking back now at my venturesome life
and what are counted as its daring acts

(though to me they were simply a matter
of trusting in the true and living God,
and obeying what I knew to be His will),
I praise the Most High God for all His grace.
His were the deeds, and I only a poor
instrument in His all-powerful hands.

So can it be true, as I've been told, that
God called me a man after His own heart?
If so, it was because He Himself worked
in me to produce what He could approve.
I can't trace any of it to myself–
though the devil has tempted me to think
that there was something of my own in it.
What is man that God is mindful of him!

But if a man after God's heart is one
who desires Him more than anything else,
who tries to maintain his integrity,
who loves truth and justice and righteousness,
who, having sinned, hates sin and seeks mercy,
and much trembles to offend God again,
who trusts Him even when all things go wrong,
who dares believe that God will act for him,
who exalts the Lord of all and not himself,
who is full of praise for God's great goodness,
who loves God and His people and His Word,
who looks to a King far greater than all,
then I gladly confess, I am that man.

As king, unworthy as I was, I tried
to follow the pattern set by the King
of the whole universe, and, in spite of
failure and sin, to rule with fairness and truth.
And, in the midst of my troubles, found joy
in God in doing so.

But all in all
I believe my gladdest days were as a
shepherd. There was more time for looking at
the stars, for singing, and for prayer alone.
Afterwards there was so much clash of arms,
far too much blood, too many disasters,
too much agony of spirit and mind.
And sometimes too much of the sensual.

But I know that goodness and mercy
have followed me all the days of my life.
In the midst of many struggles, and much
need of my Shepherd's rod and staff, I have
known quiet waters and green pastures and straight
paths for my feet, and a growing desire
to see the beauty and glory of the Lord
and be forever in His holy home.

There I hope to sing far greater psalms and
make more melodious music, on far
better instruments, than I ever made
in this poor life below, awaking
at last in His likeness, all free to praise
the everlasting mercy of the Lord.

So I will go to that fair land for which I long
with great joy in my heart, and in my mouth a song.

## Bathsheba
**(2 Samuel 11:1 - 12:25)**

That evening while I was having my bath
in what, I confess, was an exposed place
if someone had happened to be on the
roof of the palace nearby, the thought came
that king David himself might well be there
(for I knew he had not gone off to war).

But still I went ahead. Don't misunderstand,
or think that my brave husband did not have
a very large place in my heart. He did,
but being a soldier he often was
away on some far distant battlefield,
leaving me here alone and unfulfilled.

There was (and still is) something terribly
appealing about the king. And it did
come to my mind that if he saw me he
might be attracted to me. And indeed
I found out the truth of this very soon.

When he summoned me to his home, I thought
"Who disobeys a summons from the king?"
although I knew I did not have to go.
So I went, knowing well what might take place,
but never dreaming what my husband's fate
would be as a result. If the thought had
come that it might cost him his life, of course
I would not have agreed to see the king.

But is it not often so, that actions
done in ignorance of consequences
have very tragic ones? In this case the

innocent persons, Uriah and the
little babe, are dead.
But the guilty ones,
the king and I, live on, and are sometimes
(dare I say this?) almost happy. I mean
as happy as it is possible to
be with that dark shadow from the past ever
falling on our steps. And then there is my
grandfather Ahitophel. He is not
much pleased about all of this. He is a
clever man, and gives advice to the king,
but how long will he do so? and how well?

The Lord loves Solomon, our dear son, and,
I believe, will raise him to a high place
in the kingdom of Israel. Higher
than anyone of David's other sons.
Or is this only a mother's fond hope,
without foundation in reality?
But has not experience taught me that
God's kindness and mercy are very great?
One thing is sure: I will try to banish
ignorance from his mind and make him love
wisdom and knowledge. And then we shall see.

Looking to God I have learned to expect the best.
I will do what I can and leave with Him the rest.

## Nathan
**(2 Samuel 12:1-15)**

I am remembered as the man who dared
point the finger at the king and declare
the truth. Believe me, before I did that
I had pointed the finger at myself
more than once. No one who does not know his
own heart should ever do as I have done.

I was told later that it is a rare
thing for a servant of God to confront
a great ruler. I don't know about that,
but I am convinced that it is something
that ought always to be done if the event
calls for it.
Justice and righteousness
are exceedingly important to God;
they should be so to every one of us.
All too often men (and women) go their
own way, bringing much dishonor to God
and ruining their lives, and no one speaks
up either to challenge or to rebuke,
or to offer a way of escape from
the devil's trap. Certainly it takes some
courage–as I know from experience–
but this fortitude God will surely give.

As for David the king, of course my heart
was in my mouth when I went to meet him,
even though I knew he was a good man,
and was unlikely to persecute me
for my attempt to turn him back to God.
A good man–but how dreadful was his sin!–
and those ensnared in wickedness can turn

violent when exposure is at hand.
So going to him, I was not without
a vigorous stir of apprehension.

But when God says to a prophet, "Go," he
goes. A true prophet fears God more than men,
and must do many tasks that men in more
ordinary positions hesitate
to undertake. That is our hard burden.
But it is also our honor, one for
which we are willing to suffer and die.

When our leaders sin, and do not repent,
their lives and their souls are facing great loss,
and they are bringing trouble on all the
people whom they rule, and reproach to God.
And if a man must die attempting to
make matters right, well, there is no better
way to die–and no better way to live.

So I will live–or die–always doing what He
says to do, as long as He gives His grace to me.

## Asaph
**(1 Chronicles 25:1,2; Psalm 73)**

I am a Levite, so God Himself is
my inheritance. How could I ever
forget this? But I did, and began to
envy unrighteous men when I saw their
prosperity. Yes, and the easy time
they have of it, both in life and in death,
while every day I knew God's heavy hand
in discipline. For them it was always
health and wealth and ease, and for me pains and
burdens and tears.
I thought it all in vain
to keep myself pure and serve God in my
integrity, and doubted God's wisdom
in dealing with men. I, a man who had
been appointed to sing songs of praise and
joy in the tabernacle of the Lord,
began to quarrel with God, and so fell
into self-pity, depression and gloom.
In His presence I became like a beast,
as utterly senseless and ignorant.

Envy is sin, and no small sin at that.
It is self-centered, greedy, and cruel,
and leads to the destruction of all good.
Envy corrupts and embitters the heart,
robs men of worthy aims and drives them on
to the most lawless and violent deeds.

It was envy that rose against righteous
Abel and spilled his blood on the hard ground.
And if its arms were powerful enough,
it would send its venomous dart flying

at God Himself and take all that is His.
And so it brings its slaves under His wrath,
and in grave danger of His eternal
condemnation.
                                        And envy had almost
seized control of my own poor heart and life.
My footsteps had slipped and were going fast.
But then one momentous hour in God's
sanctuary, light streamed into my mind,
and I saw again the final end of
evil men, and my own appointed place
as a servant of God. I remembered
my inheritance in heaven and that
God was my eternal portion, and on
earth the strong Rock of my heart and my life.

And I chose Him again to be all that
I want here and now, and after this brief
life is done and I go to be with Him.

Our flesh and our heart fail in everything we do.
Save us from ourselves, O God. Make us strong and true.

## Absalom
**(pursuing David–2 Samuel 18:9)**

Yes, I will admit that I liked my hair,
cutting it only once a year, and then
gazing at all the five pounds weight of it.
But do not think for one moment that I'm
a vain man or an empty-headed fool.
Believe it or not, I've a passion for
justice, and will act strongly for what I
think is right.
Take, for instance, the case of
my brother Amnon. What he did deserved
death, so I killed him. And my dear sister
Tamar needed a restful place to stay,
after the cruel and ungodly deed
perpetrated on her, so I brought her
into my own home. I always tried to
do the best thing that opened up to me.

You will blame me, I know, for my revolt
against my father the king. But this may
be because you don't understand all the
circumstances which made that suitable.
He had completely lost his sense of what
was fair and just.
When he permitted my
return to Jerusalem, he would have
nothing to do with me, would hardly look
me in the face. Did he not understand
that I killed Amnon because I knew that
he would do nothing about the crime of
that scoundrel? He was always too weak to
judge and put away evil men. To know
this is true all one needs to do is to
think of Joab.

Not only this. I clearly
saw that he was no longer capable
of ruling the land as it needed to
be ruled. My way of gaining the throne by
turning the hearts of the people to me,
might seem to some of you as a method
not fully ethical for one of my
very high standards.
But what other way
was open to me? In this case at least
we can surely think that the good end was
justified by somewhat less than good means.

Now I must pursue my poor father and
finish off this whole sad business. For long
enough I faced scorn and rebuff. Now I
will strike with the hot sword of offended
justice, and then cause right to reign once more.

I love these wild dark woods, these overarching trees,
this purposeful ride, my hair streaming in the breeze.

## Joab
**(1 Kings 1:7; 2:28)**

I know that in some ways David was an
outstanding man, brave on the battlefield,
a great leader of men, loyal to friends,
generous toward enemies–perhaps
too generous toward his enemies.
Yes, to be honest, I must say that in
this regard he seemed to me to show some
weakness. I have observed this also in
other men, that conscience often makes them
hesitate when resolute action is
called for. When dealing with ruthless men one
must be ruthless, not wait for God to be.

And did not David more than once admit
that we sons of Zeruiah were too hard
for him? Certainly he showed himself weak
against me when I had done something he
condemned. I learned to smile at his rebukes,
being sure that he would not act at all.
And was not David really weak in the
matter of Saul? I would not have withheld
my eager sword from Saul's throat if I had
been given a good chance to plunge it there.

And was he not weak in the matter of
Amnon, Tamar, and Absalom? He was.
And toward the end of his reign I felt
he was no longer fully capable
of ruling in a satisfying way.
I will confess that I admire, almost
above everything else, simple strength and
determination to gain and hold power.

Give me a man who will stop at nothing.
Almost Absalom was such a man, but
somehow I could not join his rebel group.

But Solomon I could not tolerate.
For one thing, he was not next in line for
the throne. Adonijah was and still is,
and would make an excellent king in place
of David. He's a right determined man.
And besides all this, I could not but fear
that in some ways Solomon may be as
weak as his father often proved to be.

Also, I know that he does not like me,
that I would lose my place if he were king.
Now the bitterness of being wrong has
made my own position precarious,
and, dreadful as it is to say it, weak.
But perhaps not quite as weak as his who,
an old man, still sits on the throne. I doubt
that he will take action against me now.

However that may be, I will be strong in what
strength remains to me and will leave to God my lot.

## Adonijah
**(1 Kings 1:5-10)**

It is not right or fair that Solomon
should be the chosen king instead of me.
By reason of age, since Absalom's death,
I am next in line. And I feel that I,
in every way, am more qualified than
my younger brother to take the reins of
power over Israel, regardless
of what my father may think.
I fear that
he has become somewhat senile in his
old age. I know that Solomon is his
pet, and that he has made some promises
which he never should have made. But when it
comes to ability I am not at
all behind any leader in the land.
And in the near future I intend to
demonstrate this in the clearest manner
possible.
The great general Joab
agrees with me and stands willing to use
his not inconsiderable power in
my behalf to oppose the injustice
being committed against me in the
name of God. And Abiathar the priest
casts in his lot with me, and shows that he,
a servant of the Most High, knows full well
the justice of my cause. And I am sure
the rest of the king's sons will bow to me,
and accept my regime.
Victory comes
to the bold, my soul, so now boldly act!
Give concrete form to all your heart's desire!

And clothe your secret dreams with real events!
Succeed where your brother Absalom failed
in his attempt to overthrow the king,
and wrest the throne at once from a usurper's hand,
and reign in power and glory over this great land!

## King Solomon

**(1 Kings 3:3-12; 11:1-43. At life's end lamenting)**

Now before the pitcher breaks at the well,
before the snapping of the silver cord,
before my soul goes to God who gave it,
I would confess my failure and my sin.
God gave me a great gift, but I failed Him.
Given wisdom I played the utter fool,
let my low desires draw me from my God,
and made images my intellect abhorred.

My wisdom was not such that it could keep
me from folly and base wickedness.
Wisdom tried to teach my heart but could not
control it, could not make it true and good,
did not have the power to overcome
my terrible innate depravity.

Our nature is a mad determined thing,
an evil power struggling for our will.
Good advice never deterred it at all.
Rebellious to every command of mine,
bent on satisfying its own desires,
it had no time for my sagacity.
Inspired sayings may occupy the mind,
but our nature follows its own aims and
draws us into the dark whirlpool of the world.

Mine was a restless mind and curious,
never satisfied with mere surfaces,
desiring to know what is underneath,
aspiring to discover what is good.
And I went deep to the bottom of things,
but found only still deeper emptiness.

I set out to explore every pleasure,
every work that men undertake to do,
every thought that ever entered man's mind.
And I have found what wisdom cannot do.

Unaided by revelation from above,
it can never find the reason for life,
never see the purpose in anything,
can never bring contentment to the mind,
never begin to cleanse man's filthy heart.
Left on its own it never can find God.
And without God life is empty and vain.

Among my many regrets and sorrows,
one thing cheers me as life draws to its end–
I loved God as a bride loves her bridegroom,
and longed for Him even in my worst days,
when I submitted to my wives' demands.
My faith, even then, did not wholly fail.
So He who has set eternity in
our hearts, at last, I think, in love will welcome me,
and then instruct my mind throughout eternity.

## King Rehoboam
**(looking back as an older, wiser man)**

I suppose it was the arrogance of
youth that made me behave like I did then,
that strange conviction that only the young
can really know what is going on,
that with age comes, not wisdom, but a mind
that will weakly draw back from daring acts,
preferring the status quo, desiring
ease and security, and reluctant
to confront with strength newly emerging
circumstances.
                    However that may be,
I foolishly listened to the advice
of my foolish young friends and rejected
the good counsel of wiser, older men
which, if listened to, would have secured the
kingdom of the twelve tribes for me. But as
it is, I have just two, and much regret.

It is part of this business of growing
old, not just to learn by experience,
but to sadly realize that youthful
acts rashly committed have their results
which cannot be changed.
                    So here we are at
one another's throats, Jeroboam
and I, with little hope for either one
of obtaining enduring victory.
I almost think that this bifurcation
of the kingdom came about because of
the judgment of God, bringing punishment
on a land that had turned its back on Him.

I am not a very religious man,
but I am appalled by what Jeroboam
has done in Israel with his golden
calves, false priests and idolatrous altars.
You will doubtless say, "Look to your own land.
There you find altars to false gods enough,
and many detestable practices."
Yes, I intend to look into this some day.

I should say something about my father
Solomon. No doubt he was a very
wise man, but I didn't get to know him
all that well. The affairs of state, and his
studies and writings, not to speak of his
seven hundred wives and those three hundred
concubines, occupied most of his time
and attention.
But it seems to me that
even with all his wisdom he did some
very foolish things which had dire results.
Is this the way of all flesh?
I fear that
no man is ever wise enough to become free
of faults in his nature and personality.

## King Jeroboam
### (1 Kings 12:25-33)

If you ask me (though I don't think you will),
I think I was a brilliant strategist.
Having wrested ten tribes from Rehoboam
(a very foolish man), I set about
to unify these tribes by giving them
a religion. For, I thought quite rightly,
what can be more unifying than that?
If men can worship at the same altar,
they are more likely to stick together
when it comes to far more important things,
like fully supporting their king, that is,
me, against the rival one in the south.
So I devised a religion for them–
not the ancient worship of Sinai's Lord,
but something more dear to the hearts of men.

Long ago they revealed their true desire,
when, with Moses gone away to the Mount
and to his God, they made their golden calf.
I made them two, and set them up in spots
north and south so that people in both halves
of the country would not be far from one.

And, as everybody knows, festivals
delight the common folk, and so I gave them
a festival, and sacrifices too.
For people also want sacrifices,
as long as they are not asked to make them.

And people love to have priests to do their
praying for them, and all the altar's work.
So I gave them priests as vile as themselves.

Now, not hearing the law's condemnation,
and all its constant talk of holiness,
they can worship here to their hearts' content.

Then, no doubt, they will remain true to me,
their religion's head, and not go again
to Jerusalem, with all the danger
to me that could possibly entail.

If this was not clever I do not know
what is. Giving the people a good mix
of easy religion and politics
is the way to keep the average joe
content and unrebellious here below.
And up above is there anyone there?
If so I'm still waiting for Him to show
it. But, really, I can't say I much care.

## Prophets, Young and Old
**(1 Kings chapter 13)**

### The Young Unknown Prophet

I cannot guess why God chose me for that
important task. There were other prophets
available to Him, including the
one I just left–as strange an old man as
I have ever met with in my brief life.
He lied to me and because I believed
his lie and went with him, he prophesied
about my death, and seemed to indicate
that I may not even reach home at all.

But now why should I take his word for this?
Since the first thing he told me was a lie,
do I have any grounds for believing
the second? A liar is a liar
and can never be trusted when he speaks.

Of course, I can't help but feel just a bit
uneasy, for I did actually
disobey the word of the Lord to me.
But, after all, the man was a prophet,
and when he spoke to me in the Lord's name
I felt it was safe to believe his word
and go with him for a quick bite to eat.
He seemed so friendly, and so concerned for
me. And at the time what reason was there
to doubt his truthfulness? The thought of food
was very appealing, my mouth felt hot and dry,
and I was facing a long trek on foot.
I thought the Lord must have relented and
was showing me a little reward for

a difficult task faithfully performed.

Surely God will overlook my mistake
just this once and protect me on the way.
Did I not stand boldly before the king?
Did I not say exactly what God told
me to say, and rebuff the king's attempt
to get me to go back with him? It is
hard for me to believe that just one act
of disobedience (and that in a
minor matter and in very stressful
circumstances) can now have the results
that old man declared. No, it can't be true.

I have learned my lesson, and from now on,
all my life through, exact obedience
to the Lord's word will be my central aim.

But what moves there in the dark trees? Is there not
something coming now? That sound in my ears–what–

**The Old Prophet**

Who could have dreamed that it would end like this?
A life so promising given to the
lion's mouth!
                    Here I have been a prophet,
willing always to speak out for my Lord;
and would have done so again this time, but
there came this young prophet, this neophyte,
and I learn that it was given him to
cry out against Jeroboam's altar.
And I remained forgotten in my house,
and then heard of it only through my sons!

This shows a proper regard for my work?
This is the fitting treatment of prophets?
Am I so useless, so expendable?

Don't think that I am bitter. I was just
determined to show who is the faithful
prophet around here. Had he stood the test,
he would have been honored by me as well.
But he fell into disobedience
and I am the one who had to cry out
against him. But now he has paid the price
for rashly ignoring the Lord's command.

But he was a prophet. I respect him,
for what he spoke against Jeroboam,
as surely as I live, will be fulfilled,
just, I might add, as my own words have been.

You say that I am a liar? Telling
one lie does not make a man a liar.
And you have no idea how much truth
I have told during my long life as a
prophet. Understand this: What I said to
that young man was just to test and prove him.

Being a prophet is a mysterious thing.
We must all be careful of just what this can bring.

## King Asa
**(on his death bed–2 Chronicles 16:11-13)**

I have seen that man is strange–I am strange
to myself, and, perhaps, seem somewhat strange
to you who have, and have read, the condensed
story of my life. I was one among
twenty-two brothers and sixteen sisters
and in the king's palace there were thirteen
other wives of my father besides my
mother. Sometimes there was some confusion–
you may have difficulty in even
imagining a household like that one.

I emerged as the Lord's choice to be king
in my father's place. All this you may know.
But you may not know that all my life my
own grandmother Maacah, who was the queen
mother, opposed me in every good thing
I tried to do. In her heart she always
loved idols and actually made one,
a very repulsive one, and I loved
the true God, Maker of heaven and earth.
This meant bitter conflict through all the days
of reformation I undertook in
my nation Israel.

God gave to me
that great desire for Him, and faith to see
the work through to the end. I removed the
idols from the land, those detestable
slanders on the most holy name of God,
and repaired the altar in His house.
God enabled me to do much good in
Israel and to turn many people back to Him.

And in battle He gave me great faith that
He would fight for us, and courage to face
the enemy. Looking back now I am
amazed at those confident words I spoke:
"Lord, there is no one like you to help the
powerless against the mighty. Help us,
O Lord our God, for we rely on you,
and in your name we march to face the foe."

But after all those God-given victories,
shameful fear of the king of Israel
began to capture and afflict my heart.
And, believe it if you can, I sent gold
and silver from the treasury of the
Lord to the king of Syria, and leaned
on him, not God, to save me from that man.
And when Hanani the seer dared to point
out my fault, I imprisoned him, and then
persecuted some of my citizens.
And later on in my illness, I sought
doctors, not God, to heal my diseased feet.

I've learned from Solomon's case, and mine: A good start
is not a good end. We must always guard our heart.

## King Ahab
**(in the great drought in Israel–1 Kings 18:2–10)**

In my apple there is only one worm,
and forever he seems to be right there
pointing the finger with talk of judgment
to come. I mean Elijah, my fierce foe.

What business is it of his if I have
a certain woman as my wife? Or if
I buy a needed piece of land? Or if
I follow my fathers in making my
choice of gods and religion and altars?

Are these no longer personal matters?
Am I not the king? Must I always hear
strong condemnation from that wild-eyed oaf?

On the whole I believe I've borne it well.
But now he has gone entirely too far.
Somehow he has persuaded his Yahweh
to keep the sky from sending down its rain.
So he is killing our cattle with thirst,
and making us all face a cruel death
by starvation.
                    And yet he still has the
gall to call himself a servant of God.
If you ask me, he is acting more like
a servant of the devil.
                              Enough is
enough. I can endure no more of this.
If I do not have his corpse at my feet
before year's end, then I am more a fool
than a king and do not deserve to reign.
Not a nation, not a kingdom on earth

will hide him now from my determined search.
I will rid the earth of this pestilence,
and forever blot out his disgraced name.

In coming days no man will ever hear
Elijah's name, or think he was a seer.

## Elijah
**(at Sinai–1 Kings 19:8–18)**

O my God, as always, I am alone.
Alone I have served, alone fought the fight.
Alone let me hear your voice in this mount,
mountain of Moses, holy mount of law,
mountain of the one true and living God.

I've come to hear your voice, my God, my life.
I am weary, not of your service, but
in it, so sad, so shaken, so sinful,
I could die now here on the mountainside.

How could I ever once have had the thought
that I was better than my ancestors?
I am, alas, a man like everyone.

Away from the din of a world insane,
after the wind's explosive violence,
after this earthquake, and this blazing fire,
after the zeal and rage of my own heart,
let me hear your still quiet voice again.

I have been a man of few words, O Lord,
wanting every word I spoke to be yours,
hating the vain and empty chattering
of the foolish ones who do not know you.
But now let me speak from my troubled heart.
In fear of death I turned my back and ran
from the menace of Jezebel.
I'm so ashamed I can't lift up my head.
Restore me to the place where I can speak.

All I ever wanted was to serve you.

My soul has heard the secret trumpet sound,
so life without serving you is but death.
To stand waiting before your holy throne,
and then to stand straight and tall before men–
this has been the one delight of my life.

O my God, I would live, and die, serving.
So let me stand again in the ancient
vales and hills of Israel, speaking your Word
again before I end my days. For now my heart
is moved at your dear voice. Yes, now let me depart.

## Baal's Priests
**(1 Kings 18:19-40)**

We should have had no trouble proving that
Baal is the true God, and not Jehovah
whom Elijah foolishly follows, and
whom he wants the whole of Israel to
worship–as mad a scheme as the brain
of man ever conceived, and one that is
in opposition to both our great queen
and king, and to all the powerful idols
in the land.

Now you have observed, we're sure,
that in this dispute, we are in the vast
majority. Priests, leaders, and people
all agree with us. And can anyone,
able to reason at all, think that a
minority of one is in the right,
and all of us wrong?

But now the king has
forced us to play this game, and we admit
that Elijah has put us on the spot–
what would the people have thought if we had
refused? Not that we fear the outcome, but
he will surely gain from this what he has
long desired: a stage for his ideas and
some needed publicity for himself.
But we agreed to this test he proposed
because we are sure that for the good of
the people his sort of false, divisive
religion, this insane insistence that
there is only one way to God, should be
seen for what it is, and he and all his
followers, if any, be put to death,
and that this is a way to achieve this.

More importantly, we welcomed this as
a fine opportunity to show once
and for all that our great Baal is the Lord
of lords. Day by day He shows His power
by giving us many offspring, and much
cattle, and flocks of sheep and goats, and each
spring grants to us fertile fields and rich crops.
And we're still sure he will work through us now.

But how are we to take this long delay?
What has gone wrong? These many hours have passed,
the sun is terribly hot, and the knife
wounds in our flesh burn from the sweat that
our leaping up and down has now produced.
Still our God does not respond, in spite of
Elijah's sarcasm and mocking words,
and our throats are raw from repeated cries.

O Baal, you are our only hope. You must not fail!
O Baal, hear us now! O Baal, hear us! O Baal, Baal…

## Elisha
**(at the end)**

I didn't mind being in the background,
or washing the hands or feet of so strange,
so great a man, while he remained on earth.
But when it was time for the arrival
of the chariot, and his departure,
I wanted to do all Elijah had done,
and, if possible, even more than that.

I saw he was twice the man that I am,
so I knew I needed at least double
the power and spirit that he had shown.
I could see it was a daring request,
and he also said it was difficult.

But why would I want to do more than he?
To make a name for myself as being
greater than Elijah? Think what you will.
I think, because it needed to be done.
The people of God still suffered and wept,
a tyrant still sat on Israel's throne,
and behind him idols still ruled the land.

I sometimes feel I should have been more bold
and asked for ten times the spirit he had.
What is our brief life if we cannot serve,
and serve with all the power we can get?
But a double portion of his spirit
filled all my days with travel and hard toil.

If I had been given more than double,
I doubt if I could have been more stretched out
for God than I have been, or labored more.

We may not understand all that we ask
when our hearts are aroused and we are fully bent
on godly exploits. But now I am quite content.

## Gehazi

**(2 Kings 5:20-27)**

In case you don't know, I am the servant
of Elisha the prophet, a wise man
in many ways, but in worldly matters
not so wise. Or so it appears to me.

As evidence for this I set before
you the fact that he lives as a poor man
when he might be rich. He goes about on
foot doing good to others and never
takes a thing for the miracles he does,
and his prophesying brings him no gain.
Now I ask you, is this the way astute
people behave? Doesn't he understand
that faith in God should mean prosperity,
or even wealth?

This man reminds me of
that other prophet, Elijah. They say
there were times when the ravens had to bring
him food. Here ravens have not been employed
in this way yet, but now I fear if our
noble seer continues on as before
he will soon sink to living in that way.

Here's more evidence of his strange conduct:
That Syrian general, that Naaman,
has just been here. Through the gracious words of
my master, the man went to the Jordan
and returned here healed from his leprosy.
Now listen to this–he opened his bags
and showed us a huge sum of Silver and
Gold together with some fine apparel,
and offered it all to my dear guru.

And what did said guru do? Believe this,
if you can. He refused it all, I mean
the whole of that Gold and Silver and all
of those beautiful Syrian-made clothes!
His words were, "I will not accept a thing."
I simply cannot understand this kind
of mad behavior. Now what harm could there
possibly be in accepting a gift
offered in gratitude for a good deed?
And the loss, think of the loss!
I know what
I will do. My master refused a gift
he could justly have taken. I will go
and persuade that general to give me
some of it even if I receive it
unjustly. Yes, if I must lie to get
it, then I will lie. Surely the good Lord
will overlook a small lie to gain such
great good. And I will be perfectly safe.
No one will ever find out what I've done.

Right. Get on with it then and do not hesitate.
A stroke of luck like this is rare. Don't be too late.

## Great Woman of Shunem
**(2 Kings 4:8-37)**

I know a man of God when I see one.
And Elisha is one without a doubt.
Humble, pure, prayerful, wise, full of God's
Spirit, faithful to God's call, speaking God's
great words in God's way, making no demands,
not even asking for what he might lack.

And never would he have had to ask me.
God put the desire to help him in my
heart, so I did whatever I could do.
And, of course, he did far, far more for me.
A bed, a chair, a table, and a lamp
brought a great gift, because he asked his God.

Soon my husband and I were able to
have this delightful boy to bless our home.
A wonderful bargain, I thought. My aim
in helping him was not so that I could
get something in return, but simply to
fulfill the desire I had to help him.
But kindness expressed produces kindness.

Then came that day when my poor boy cried out,
"My head, my head!"–and later passed away
on my lap. Now my husband is not young,
and, I'm afraid, he's not a caring man,
and he lacks understanding of God's ways.
I went myself to see the man of God.
He gave his staff to Gehazi and sent
him ahead.
I stayed with Elisha. I
have eyes, and could discern in Gehazi

a lack of faith and care, and a lack of,
well, an honest heart. He could do no good,
even with that rod placed on my dear boy.

Then Elisha came, and God came with him,
and entered the room where my dead son lay.
And soon my boy was in my arms again,
alive and well, a cure for all my pain.

It's not Elisha, but Elisha's God I praise.
Mysterious and marvelous are all His ways.

## Naaman
**(2 Kings 5:1-14)**

What good were all those accolades to me?
And the appreciation of the king?
What benefit my proven bravery,
or my strength, or my possessions and gold?
For one day I woke up with the dreadful
apprehension that I had leprosy.
I went to the best doctors that I knew,
and they all confirmed it. There was no cure
for one in my condition, and no hope.
So for a long time hopeless I remained.
Only one with that dire disease can know
what suffering I was going through.

But someone looked at my case, and thought to
do me good. A servant girl, captive from
the land of Israel, said to my wife,
"There is a great man in Samaria,
a prophet of God. And I am sure that
he can heal my lord of his leprosy."

Though skeptical, I was willing to hear
what she had to say. (What had I to lose?)
When she told me fully what that man had
done, I was inspired to give it a try.
So off I went carrying rich rewards
for one who could cure me of leprosy.

When I arrived at his place–and a small
and dismal place it was too–he did not
even come out to see me but sent word
through his servant to tell me what to do,
as if I were a nobody and had

come with no good purpose. He displayed no
interest in my gold. And his message
was quite incomprehensible to me:
"Go wash in the Jordan river." Indeed,
has the Jordan such almighty power?
Is it greater than rivers in our land?
was what I thought and would have gone away
full of bitterness and wrath had not my
good servant given me some sweet advice.

Almost my anger and my fierce pride (things
frequently joined together in the heart)
robbed me of healing and drove me home sad.
"Why not go and try?" he said. So I did.
How ridiculous I felt when I dipped
in that narrow stream and then dipped again.
Seven times I dipped, then quickly looked at
my skin. It had changed to that of a child!

None of our many gods could cure my leprosy.
Israel's God is real; there is no God but He.

## King Jehoshaphat
**(2 Chronicles 17:1 – 21:6; 21:18 – 22:10)**

I think I have shown by the way I live
and reign over this kingdom of Judah
that I have a high regard for the Lord
of the universe, Jehovah of hosts.
I have tried to obey His laws and I
have despised all idols and false gods.
And I do not, I repeat, I do not
approve of the way king Ahab bows down
to Baal and follows a mistaken path
in the way he now rules in Israel.
And Jezebel is not exactly one
of my favorite people.
However,
I consider cooperation and
peaceful dealings between neighboring lands
a very good thing, and am willing to
ignore the faults of Ahab and his wife
in order to pursue this. Certainly
friendship and mutual helpfulness is
better by far than antagonism
and unending preparations for war.

And remember that the people of that
northern kingdom are our brothers. We are
all children of Abraham. We have all
been given this land of Canaan as our
eternal inheritance. We have all
been called by one God and blessed by one God.
Whether we like it or not, we and they
are united both by history and
by our hopes for the future. Should we not
stand shoulder to shoulder against outside
enemies?

And can there be a better
way to seal an alliance of this kind
than by arranged marriages? So I see
Ahab's daughter and my son united
in sacred wedlock and cementing this
much to be desired close relationship
between our two peoples.

Am I to be
criticized for this? Should not all of God's
children be one and live in harmony?
Can't we overlook the faults in others
to gain this great good? We need not adopt
their ways in order to cooperate
in joint ventures. And who knows? Perhaps our
influence will turn them back to our God.

But now comes a prophet known to be stern and bold.
So I wait here to learn what the future may hold.

## Jehu
### (riding into the palace grounds–2 Kings 9:30-33)

The Lord has given me a job to do,
and I am determined to do it, and
to do it swiftly and without showing
favor to anyone, high or low, man
or woman. The word "compromise" is not
in my vocabulary, and for years
I have despised all that Ahab stood for
and that polluted heathen wife of his.

Now to be chosen as the instrument
of the Lord's fiery vengeance against them
fills my heart with great zeal and joy and pride.
I know I am a man of destiny
to root out wickedness in Israel,
bring to a quick end an evil regime,
and eradicate the worship of Baal
from the fair hills and valleys of this land.

Would to God that Ahab still lived on earth
that my sword could be stained with his heart's blood!
At least his offspring now will know my power.
Not one, I swear, will long draw breath on earth.
Just now my hot arrow has struck between
his grandson Joram's shoulders to the heart,
and his corpse, given to the dogs, lies there
in the field of Naboth the Jezreelite,
which Jezebel stole by lies and treachery
to satisfy the whim of her vile mate.

Now here's the palace gate, and here the life
of that cursed Jezebel will be ground
beneath my horses' hooves.

And what is that?
Through the window her painted face appears!
Can false hope in detestable false gods
be at work in that false heart? She will know
that her false face stirs me, not to pity,
but to true wrath and true violence.

Who is on my side? Who? Now falls the crown
of that apostate house. Now "THROW HER DOWN!"

## Jezebel
**(2 Kings 9:30-37)**

So here comes the general out for blood,
slaughtering each man he meets on his mad
rampage, urging on his chariot wheels,
as only he does, to our palace door.

I can't guess what has stirred him up, but I
feel somewhat threatened. I wonder what his
attitude toward women is. Is he
vulnerable? Is he a gentleman?
Is he attracted to a well made-up
face? If so, I think I am well able
to handle Jehu the fierce fighting man.

The use of a little powder and paint,
a few coy glances, and a smile or two
can bring to heel the most determined male.

I have had much practice in dealing with
men, and powerful men at that. Think of
my husband Ahab. Strong and brave in war,
but so easily conquered by my skills.
As his wife I did everything I pleased,
and made him like it. Yes, he really did.
It is the wife's rightful place to see that
her husband always conforms to her will.
This I have thought for years and think so still.
At my table dined Asherah's prophets,
four hundred strong, and fifty more than that
of the prophets of Baal. He never said
a word, but bent his knees to that great god,
and shelled out gold for all that they could need.

Think of Naboth and how firmly he stood
against the king's request to buy his land.
But he did not stand so long against me.
And, to tell the truth, no man ever could.

Think of that mad Elijah and his hope
to defeat me and my powerful god.
In the end we know who it was who turned
and ran, like the cowardly dog he was,
and resolved to hang up his prophet's gear.
We saw his face no more in these locales.

But now here's this slight problem confronting
me in the person of this rabid man.
His horses' hooves trample the palace yard.
I'll look from my window and face him now.
Surely my queenly presence will make him
pause. But what is this I hear? "Throw her down!"
What? Throw me doooooooooooooooooooown????!

## Athaliah
**(2 Kings 8:16 - 11:20)**

I am justifiably proud to be
a member of a powerful family.
My father Ahab and my grandfather
Omri were two of the very greatest kings
Israel ever had, wise, strong and brave,
and above all, faithful to Baal, the
God of gods.
Ahaziah my brother
reigned in Israel in my father's place,
and my husband Jehoram ruled down here
in Judah's land, and, after him, my own
dear son Ahaziah. Surely all this
is reason enough for pride.
But I have
not mentioned the greatest reason of all–
my mother was Jezebel, queen and all
queenly in all she undertook to do.
She is the great model I emulate,
the one who put my feet on the right path,
the path that led to the pinnacle of
power and glory. I can never praise
her enough for her determination
to have a woman's voice heard in the land.

All too long women and their rights had been
suppressed and their wishes ignored or scorned.
Then came my dear mother and changed all that.
She set about to liberate women
from the hard, heavy and painful yoke men
had placed on them, and introduce a new
way of living, a new relationship
between them and their male counterparts. To

be equal was her goal, and she more than
achieved it.
                    Nothing and no one could long
stand against her! You remember Naboth,
that stubborn foolish man, and that so-called
prophet Elijah, wild and murderous.
And did she send him running off, or what?
Men like to think they are the ones who are brave,
but was one ever brave as Jezebel?
And what a beauty she was! And she knew
how to use her beauty to bring about
good ends. And she imparted her vision
to me.
                    Now all of them are gone, and I
alone remain. The assassin Jehu
has done his savage work in Israel,
but touch me here he cannot. For now my
Baal has elevated me to the throne.
And with Jezebel's vision and strength I will wear
the crown, and do here what my mother did up there.

## King Uzziah
**(2 Chronicles 26:16-23)**

Yes, I should have known, and, in fact, did know,
that all pride is detestable to God,
that it will always earn His punishment.

Was it not pride in Pharaoh's heart that brought
ten appalling plagues, with the death of all
their firstborn and great grief in every home,
and plunged his armies under the dark sea?
And then was it not pride in Miriam
which brought to her that dreadful leprosy?
Was it not Nadab and Abihu's pride
which moved their dark, defiant hearts to take
false fire and offer incense to the LORD,
and brought the fire of God down in response?
Was it not pride in Korah's rebel band
that made the very ground divide in two,
and sent them down with terror to their doom?
Was it not pride that expelled Lucifer
himself like a lightning flash from the heights
of heaven?
And is it not pride that takes men
down to dark Sheol's lowest, darkest depths?
Pride will appear before destruction's hour,
and a haughty spirit before a fall.

All this I heard, and knew it to be true.
But truth in the mind does not always mean
that truth governs the heart. In spite of truth
known and believed men may foolishly go
on and fall prey to what they know is wrong.
So it was pride that brought God's wrath on me.

For years I served our God with love and faith,
delighting in His blessing on my life.
Did I grow cold to Him? Did I forget
the ground of blessing is obedience?
What haughtiness may possess the hearts of
those with some authority, who forget,
for even a brief time, the living God,
and their own weakness and tendency to sin!

One somber day I thought that I, the king,
could be and do exactly as I pleased.
So recklessly that day I went inside
the temple of the LORD and straight on in
its Holy Place, reserved for priests alone,
and thought that I, like them, could offer there
the fragrant incense to the Most High God.

Anger produced by arrogance burst from
my heart against the priests who came to stop
my vain and foolish act of wickedness.

And then leprosy did to me what it can do.
For pride, the mighty destroyer, had struck me too.

## King Hezekiah
**(on his bed of sickness–Isaiah 38:1-27)**

I have finished weaving the tapestry
of my life. It is rolled up on the loom,
and the Lord Himself will soon cut it off.
And I must leave this land that I have loved,
this crossroad of nations, center of the world
and its one haven by its savage seas,
this dear spot flowing with honey and milk,
place of the shining tents of Abraham,
this ground of glory made by God's own hand,
this realm of grace, whose hills and streams and fields
I would embrace and hold fast to my heart,

this single land where heaven touches earth,
this splendid site, well known to angels' feet,
of celestial vision and revealing dream,
of victorious battle and quiet rest,
of exploits of faith and valiant deeds,
of righteous works and godly miracles,
where eternal promises are received,
this blessed land where God's own voice is heard,

this holy platform for prophets and seers,
this trumpet calling to the whole wide world,
and earth's one altar for the one true God,
by His own hand anointed high above
all other lands for His temple and home,
for the ark, the glory, the sacrifice,
this fragrant aroma of Paradise,
this transcendent sacred land of Israel.

And in the prime of life must I go through
the doors of death and leave all this behind?

Must my poor fragile house be now pulled down
like a tent, and not set up again?
I moan like a mourning dove. Looking up
my eyes grow dim, and my desperate prayer
I speak against the wall. Remember me,
O Lord, I have walked in your truth, your faith.

And now the word has come–fifteen more years!
The anguish of my soul has brought me good.
Pondering all the wonders of this place,
thinking of those vast and mysterious
skies above, and of our contemptible
pettiness and sin, in the God-given
words of my great ancestor, to God I
would say, to God my life, my joy and strength,
“What is man that you are mindful of him,
or the son of man that you care for him?”

But you do! In love you, my Lord, have kept
me from the pit of destruction, and cast
all my many sins far behind your back.

Living I will praise you, and your great name confess,
and all of my brief life will walk in humbleness.

## Sennacherib

**(just before the battle for Jerusalem–2 Kings 18:13–19:37)**

I am the king of kings. No one has, and
no one can, stand against me. One city
after another, one country after
another has been subdued under me.

For I do not depend on my own might.
Assyria has the greatest of all
gods. Just to think of their names fills me with
strength, courage and confidence–Asshur, Bel,
Anu, Ea, Nergal, and my personal
favorite Nisroch, before whom all the
gods of the nations tremble and bow down.
These names will live on to the end of time.
Against them no god has been able to
defend his own people from my attacks.

Where are the gods of Hamath and Arpad?
And where are the gods of Sepharvaim
and Hena and Ivvah? Could all of them
together save Samaria from me?
When will the people of Jerusalem
learn that there are no powerful gods in
all the world but the gods of Assyria,
whom I worship, serve and heartily praise.

Sidon, Arvad, Byblos, Ashkelon and
Lachish, and numberless towns in Moab
and Edom are crushed. And forty-six strong
walled cities in Judah have submitted
to my yoke. And will Jerusalem stand?

They trust in their weak Jehovah, a god

who has not saved the rest of this land
from my armies. And already the king,
Hezekiah, for fear of the splendor
of my lordship, has sent tribute to me.

I think we can persuade them to give in.
but if, perchance, they decide to resist,
let Jerusalem fight, and fight the best they can.
I don't believe that we will lose a single man.

## King Manasseh
**(2 Chronicles 33:1–20. At the end)**

Did any man ever do what I did,
and with it all show such contempt for God?
I do not glory in my evil deeds,
but if I name them it may help you see
something of our God's astonishing grace.

I built shrines on the high places for gods
whom God calls no gods, and I worshipped them,
and these gods the most evil, degraded
gods I knew about. I bowed down to the
sun and moon and the starry host above,
making created things my god rather
than God Himself who created all things.
I consulted witches and mediums,
and practiced black magic and sorcery.
In Ben Hinnom's valley I built altars
to fierce, demanding gods, and to those gods
I sacrificed my own sons in the fire.
And I made innocent blood flow like rain
water in the streets of Jerusalem.

Above all, I insulted the Most High
by placing a carved image in His house,
so that His temple was made a temple
to all that was base and hateful and false.
I did more to provoke God to anger
than all the nations He had driven out
before His people Israel. I was
the worst man I ever knew, worse than that
Ahab, king of Israel, who was the
most evil of Israel's evil kings.
Hating all God loved and loving all He

despised, I merited a thousand times
utter damnation and eternal death.

But then our God, whom I had grieved so much,
in just judgment (and tender mercy) sent
the fierce barbaric king of Babylon.
By hooks and iron shackles I was led
to that far place of dreadful punishment.
But God may use the savagery of men
to wake us up and bring us to His love.

No way can be cruel that leads to Him.
And in Babylon for the first time since
I was a small boy at my father's knee
I called out again to my fathers' God,
and sought His favor and begged Him for grace.
And found it! I, the vilest of all men,
contemptible, controlled by lust and pride,
insulter of the Majesty on high,
found mercy with that all-merciful One!
Now listen, then, to me, and learn great truth:

No one who will repent and humble himself and fall
at God's feet is beyond mercy's reach, no one at all.

## King Josiah
### (2 Chronicles chapters 34 and 35)

When he ascended David's throne, the last
to be left alive in the royal line
when Satan used Athaliah to try
to make the Lord's promise to Israel
null and void–the promise that David's house
would never lack a man who could be king,
Joash was only seven years of age.
I was eight, and often I think of him.
Now for these thirty-one years I have served
the Lord God of Israel with all my strength.

True revival has been my hope and prayer.
I've used every means at my command
to bring the people back to God, for they
had strayed far from Him in my father's reign,
and bowed again to gods of wood and stone.
God gave me great zeal to remove idols
from the land and encourage once again
the worship of the one true God in the
temple restored and made holy and clean.
I praise Him with my whole heart for what He
enabled me to do.
But the words of
Jeremiah have sometimes made me doubt
whether much of what I saw was at all
real and deep. He receives God's messages
for us in these latter years of my reign,
and it is quite clear that God is not pleased
with the condition of His people and
threatens again and again severe trials
and troubles to come on Jerusalem.
Here are some of his words, words that have come

from the Lord above, from the living God:

"My people have committed two evils:
They have forsaken me, the fountain of
living waters, and have dug cisterns for
themselves that can hold no water," God says.

Again the prophet said, "We lie down in
our shame, and our reproach covers us.
For we have sinned against the LORD our God,
we and our fathers, from our youth even
to this day, and have not obeyed the voice
of the LORD our God."
All my work for naught?
is the question that can trouble me in
dark moments when I look at the people
and their fickle ways. But I encourage
myself by thinking that although the mass
of men go their own way and only pay
lip service to the things of God even
in what seem to be times of reviving,
the few are brought to Him and seek His face.
Revival lasts for a day, man's evil
nature rules the man to the end of days,
save in those few whose hearts are truly changed.

And now Egypt's king would march through our land.
Is this the beginning of the troubles
Jeremiah warned us about? But I
will stop Pharaoh in his tracks and send him
back in shame to his idolatrous realm.
He has dared to say he has a message
from God for me. Nonsense! How could this be?
Here in Israel is where the prophets are.
And here is where the voice of God is heard.

So I go to fight our foe. O God, you know how
I've spent my life for you. Will you not help me now?

## Huldah
**(2 Kings 22)**

I know–most of you never heard of me.
But my name is in the Bible, and you
will find it if you are willing to search.
I am one of many unknown women
who were glad to serve God behind the scenes
of history. Their work, though hidden, was
not without its importance, because it
was God's work, and there can be no work of
God without significance, though men may
not recognize it.
Some there are, I know,
who will not lift a hand to help in the
work of God unless men are there to see.
So what they do is not for God at all.
The Most High has, I believe, given me
a different mind. I want, when I can,
to do my work for Him in secret ways.

I am known as a prophetess, but this
I did not seek. God's compelling voice called
me and I could not refuse to speak His
word. I did not run with messages to the
king and his officials. They sought me out.
And God revealed what I should say to them.
It was a good word, and I was content–

and am content now, as then, to be without fame
and serve not myself, but the glory of God's Name.

## Ezra

I am a teacher of the Word of God,
called to this service by the Lord Himself.
In its study my whole life has been spent,
and in expounding it to other men.

I turn my mind again to lessons learned.
I know of all the difficulties and
dangers and snares created by our foes,
faced first by Zerubbabel and then by
Nehemiah and all the rest of us.
If we are serving God, I know that the
enemy of our souls will always try
to bring us down and rob us of our strength
to continue on in fruitful work.
He
will attempt to destroy our faith,
will try to drag our good name in the mud,
will do his best to thrust us into sin,
will then tell us that God will not forgive,
will try to demolish past ministry,
will do what he can to shatter our health,
will go all out to discourage our minds,
will attempt to pierce the guard at our hearts,
will not leave a single path unexplored,
will aim at the exposed chink in our wall,
will always tempt us at our weakest point,
will go on tempting, and never give up.

And what makes matters harder still is this:
a wretched traitor lives here in our breast
who recklessly and wickedly betrays
to the enemy all of our best and
highest interests and seems as resolved

as he to pull us down to the dark depths.
We're like a leaning fence or tottering wall
that one slight shove sends crashing to the ground.

And we have one resource and only one:
The strength God gives to war against our foe,
and against our self which must be denied
and not permitted once to interrupt
our holy walk with the true and living God.

Keep close to Him. The joy of the Lord is
your strength. Confess your faults, and pray and work,
and still fight on, and you will see that God is kind.
So let the Word of God live in your heart and mind.

## Nehemiah

As always in any true work of God,
so now we have had to face hard problems,
and continual opposition from
the enemies of God. I have learned to
expect them. When they are absent I tend
to suspect that we are not doing the
right thing, or if the right thing, then not in
the right way.
                              If we are not making a
good impact in this evil world then will
God's enemies try to resist us still?
But if we are doing a great work for
God they will do their best to make us stop,
and harass us in every way they can.

Life was untroubled when I served the king
of Persia and brought the wine cup for his
royal lips. But here in this divine work
a nest of furious adversaries
has been stirred up. They all hate the Jews and
God, and are content only as long as
both are suffering.
                              Sanballat, Tobiah,
the Ashdodites, Arabs, and Ammonites
were all wholly resolved that we should fail.
But God made us more resolute than they.
So with trowel in one hand and sword in
the other we kept at the job until
the walls of Jerusalem rose again
strong, and to their former height.
                              Besides this
resistance from without, from within too
difficulties constantly raised their heads.

We had among us some unfaithful men,
and selfish ones who put their own concerns
above the work of God, and cared not what
might happen to that as long as they got
what they desired.

In my little book I
have revealed the matters which made our task
harder than it otherwise would have been:
ridicule, threats of violence and plots
of one kind or another, temptations
to discouragement because of unjust
acts, the spreading of falsehoods about us,
attempts to bring dishonor on my name,
other attempts to create fear and dread,
false prophets who tried to intimidate,
and a traitor who sided with our foes.

But the greatest danger of all was this:
sin in our camp which aroused God's wrath.

It was then I greatly feared we had lost our chance,
and begged God for mercy and His continuance.

## Four in Esther

### Mordecai

Haman–a descendant of murderers
of my people, and quite as murderous
as they–am I now to bow down to him?
I know there are many who flatter those
in places of wealth or authority.
Such people always fill me with disgust.
This I will never do, even if my
refusal costs me my life.
                                        Yes, he is
in a high position in the court of
the king, but I will bend not one righteous
principle for any man, no matter
how exalted he may be, no, not for
any advantage it could ever bring,
or to save myself from the lurking noose
of the hangman.
                        For what is wrong is wrong,
and will always and forever be wrong.
I worship God and trust in Him alone,
and will not cravenly bend my neck to
an evil man to save it. If the scaffold
awaits, I will face it courageously,
without compromise. I know that, soon or
late, God will deal with those who spurn His law,
who persecute the people in His care.

So Haman schemes to do away with me
and with all the Jews in this entire realm.
But can I not trust God to save us now?
Is He powerless in the face of threats?
Can He not make the plots of wicked men

ensnare them, bring good to us, and glory
to His name? I believe He can and will.
The God of Joseph, of Hezekiah
still lives now with His exiled people here.

Perhaps for such a time as this Esther
has been made queen, and will fulfill the hopes
I had that she will do great good for all
Israel. But even if she does not,
God, from some other source, will bring us help.

Never is God limited to this or
that person to accomplish His good will.
He is the LORD of hosts, and myriads
of angels in the sky, and men on earth,
bend to His sovereign rule to complete all
His gracious purposes toward His own.

Though His way of saving us is not yet made clear,
I will trust Him alone and not give in to fear.

**Esther**

I hardly understand it to this day.
I was a Jewish girl, a foreigner,
in this large city of Persia's great king,
the foremost monarch in the whole wide world.
My parents were dead and, though I was raised
by my older cousin, a true father
to me, prospects did not seem very bright.
I had no wish for fame or a high place,
but still, one wishes to make one's life count,
find some happiness, and serve God and man.
One thing, so I was told, I had–beauty.
But from what I frequently saw, beauty
can be more of a curse than a blessing.
Many a beautiful girl has fallen
into vain ways and has become a prey

to bad men who are attracted by a
lovely face.
My cousin was a wise man.
He foresaw possibilities I could
never have dreamed of, possibilities
of helping our own people in this land.
So when the queen grew proud and was deposed,
and search was made for one to take her place,
my cousin Mordecai looked long at me
and thought that I might win King Xerxes' heart.
A palace life held no appeal for me,
but no one could resist the king's demand.
What the king wanted the king always got.
And I found out what he wanted was me.

My cousin gave me comfort and advice,
and told me I might now do good to all
Israel. The rest you already know.

I was willing to do what I could do,
even if it were to cost me my life.
I seemed to myself a most unlikely
instrument for the help of my race,
but the Most High does not think as we do.

We can learn something here about God's gracious ways,
and how He saves His people in perilous days.

**Haman**

I never saw a Jew I liked, and I
have seen plenty of them–far more than I
ever wished to see, I can tell you that.
Here in Susa my life would be a joy,
except for one disagreeable thing.
I mean that arrogant Jew, Mordecai,
who thinks he is too good to kneel to me
and show me the honor that is my due.

Am I not the favorite of the king,
promoted by him to the highest place?

That man Mordecai is a thorn in my heart.
Believe me, he will pay for his conceit.
I am proud to be an Amalekite,
and to know our people always hated his,
and fought and killed them when they had the chance.

Now that I have the king's ear a final
solution of the Jewish problem is
at hand. For I have easily convinced
our gracious monarch that his kingdom will
not prosper as it should until they are
gone. And by "gone" I do not mean exiled
again to some other place. I mead dead.
And mighty Xerxes has agreed with me.

Their time is short. Soon not a single Jew
will remain in any province of this
realm. And Mordecai himself will feel my
rope about his neck, high on the gallows
I am having built. At last justice will
prevail between us, and I will have peace.

And I will not feel even one twinge of
conscience when the last Jew falls by my sword.
They are all as worthy of death as he.
For don't they all show the same arrogance,
claiming, as they do, to be a very
special group and heaven's own chosen ones?

If there was even the least grain of truth
in this, why did heaven see to it that
they were forced into exile from their land,
with hardly a rag of clothes on their backs?
If this is to be the chosen ones of
heaven then my desire is to be the

chosen of somewhere else! It surely is
a marvel that the king has let them stay
here and corrupt this fair domain with their
presence, their false dreams and pernicious ways.

So now may our great God prosper my brilliant plan
and rid the empire of this degenerate clan.

**King Xerxes**

Vashti, Esther, Haman, and Mordecai–
I've had to deal with some unusual
characters lately. Pride and love
and hate and righteousness have been on show,
and with all their many consequences.

All this has brought interest to my life,
and it is much better than fighting wars,
especially if you do not win them.
Kings must be occupied with something, or
else die of boredom, which is not pleasant.

Vashti with her independent ways had
become intolerable. When women
will not obey their own husband's wishes,
it is high time to put them in their place.
She was beautiful, but I don't miss her.

Esther is also beautiful, and so
much nicer than Vashti in every way.
But I was much surprised at her steely
purpose when it came to helping her own
people. Her cousin's presence behind her
might account for some of this, but not all.

I must admit that Haman had me fooled.
Rulers in general, I suppose, are
not careful enough in their choice of those

who work for them. It's a tedious business.
I gave him far too much latitude in
decisions regarding the state's affairs.
Why, it now seems he could have made me
guilty of genocide. Wretched fellow!
At last it appeared that he was filled with
hate, and could not control his evil lust.

Divine justice worked quite well in his case.
To be hanged on gallows one has prepared
for another is the very sort of
irony that pleases me. I must find
ways to work things like this more frequently.

Mordecai is a most remarkable
human being. Once he saved me from death,
and later saved me from great foolishness,
the second being better than the first.
I have never met a man so fully
reliable and upright in my life,
at least not my life as king. The palace
seems to breed flatterers and sycophants.
How refreshing to know a man who talks
straight and tells you exactly what he thinks.

Well, just a few notes about life in a king's court.
One deals with people of just about every sort.

## Job
**toward the end of his life**

If only I had not been so lacking
in knowledge I would not have said those hard
things about God, things which I did not know.
I would have laid my hand over my mouth
long before I did. Ignorance was an
acute problem, though I had others too.
But those others would not have been such hard,
such crushing problems if I had known more.

Suffering when one knows why is one thing,
suffering not knowing is something else.
Suffering when one knows God very well
must be different than suffering when
one knows only a little about Him.

I have repented now and wish to make
no excuse. But perhaps this can be said:
We may be quite early in God's program
to teach mankind His ways and will and truth.
I had no writing in my hand, no book
informing me what God was doing then,
no way to know the mystery of His acts,
the words spoken there behind the dark veil.

Being at the mercy of ignorance,
I found that ignorance has no mercy.
So in the raging of the unseen war
when Satan and God each had his own plan,
and neither of them told me what his was,
I suffered much in my uninformed state.

In my absorbing pain and bafflement

I said those many things I now regret.
But one thing I did–I kept trusting Him,
trusting that in the end God would prove true.
He brought me to the edge of black despair.
My agonized spirit, my intellect
went plunging into gloom by His strange ways
with me.
                But I trusted Him. Trusted when
I could see no secure ground for my faith,
except a dim sight of His character,
His revelation of Himself to my heart.
Will you ever know the comfort it was
when He called me His servant at the end?

Looking back now I can, and do, praise Him
for my suffering, yes, for all of it.
I found priceless treasure in those dark depths.
There I obtained more knowledge of myself,
and through intense suffering saw the Most High bring
more knowledge of Himself. This was worth everything.

## Eliphaz
**(Job 4:1, etc)**

I will speak for myself and my two friends.
We all shared the same views, had the same aim.
We were convinced that Job was in the wrong,
a man of pride who would not bend his neck
and a guilty man who denied his guilt,
and so deserved all that had come on him,
surprising as that was to contemplate.
We thought that we could bring him to his knees
to confess his sin and find peace with God.

You all must know what our position was:
God never punishes the innocent;
but God has sent great punishment on Job;
therefore Job is a very wicked man.

We thought that we were wise. Our principles
of judging matters, long and fondly held,
did not permit new light to penetrate
our rigid minds. Of course, we could not know
what had taken place in the unseen realm
where God sits on His throne, viewing the world
and working out His plans for every man,
where the contest between Himself and the
wicked enemy of our souls goes on.
Nor could we know that Job was the best man
of our times, far better than ourselves who
did not comprehend the truth, and could but
increase his unbearable grief and pain.

We must confess that we were arrogant.
We spoke of things too great for our poor minds,
things beyond the reach of any man. We tried

to make God fit into the mold our thoughts
had made for Him, and would not let Him be
God.

At last we learned that His thoughts and ways
are not like ours, but higher than the heights
of heaven, deeper than unfathomed depths.
So now we no longer desire to be
philosophers, but simple believers
and lovers of God, and lay our hands on
our mouths, and do not speak, except to praise
the everlasting King and Lord of life,
who speaks from the storm and instructs our hearts.
Speaking of things too high for us is how our lives were spent.
God in mercy revealed Himself and taught us to repent.

## The Song of Songs

### The Loved One
### (Read Song of Songs 5:2-8)

O heart, now raise your words to touch the theme
of themes, to sing the song of songs, the song
of love to my Lord, the Lord of love, brave
to love beyond our best and highest dream
of love, with love everlasting, as strong
as death and jealous as the relentless grave,

*

love that's a blazing fire, a mighty flame,
unquenchable by overwhelming flood,
by any river of adversity.
I will sing this old song to your dear Name,
to your dear heart, loving to tears and blood,
wanting my hesitant love, keen to see

*

it strong as yours. You stand there at the door
to win with winning love my wasted heart
that's poured its love on vain unworthy things.
And all the love I have for you seems more
love for myself as loved by you, a part
of the fallenness my poor nature brings

*

to all I am and do. In me no spot?
(These are your words of love.) All spot I feel
I am, with nothing that is good and true.
Come now, my Lord, and make me what I'm not –
a lover worthy of love. Come and heal
my lovelessness, my disregard for you.

*

At length I touch the lock, but at the gate
your sad departing footsteps sound.
Return, my love! See how the door is opened wide!
But silence fills the night. So I will wait,
and I will search for Him. He will not spurn
my prayer, my hunger to walk by His side.

*

I am His and He is mine. I know well
my Lover will suddenly come to me.
Seeking His face can never be in vain.
So there on Bether like a young gazelle,
until the day breaks and the shadows flee,
turn, my Beloved, on the hills again.

**The Lover
of the Song of songs**

The day is breaking and the shadows flee.
Arise now, my dear one, and come away,
and let me see your lovely face again,
and tell how very dear you are to me.
Beautiful you are as the dawn of day,
radiant as the sun shining through rain,

*

fair as the moon, pure as the morning light.
My life, my joy, how delightful you are!
There is no flaw in you, my peerless one.
Nothing can dim your beauty in my sight,
nothing ever diminish, nothing mar
the work of grace in you that God has done,

*

nothing at all can ever take your place,
nothing you do or say can make us part.
Oh, how captivating you are, my love!
One glance from your eyes, one look at your face
has utterly stolen away my heart.
I am yours forever, my spotless dove.

*

Beautiful as Tirzah, awesome as an
army advancing with banners, regal
as Jerusalem, you marched through my mind
taking captives. Before your love began
I loved you, was willing to turn from all
I had to win you, leaving it behind.

*

In the cleft of the rock, behind your veil
dove's eyes look out at me, moving me to tears.
My fair one, my lovely one, waiting there
do not fear my love for you will somehow fail.
It will remain through all the passing years.
There is no trial, no wound I cannot bear.

*

Undying fire for you burns in my soul.
What sorrow my deep love for you has brought!
What gladness! What compelling joy! What pain!
Nor will these end before you reach the goal,
until your love is like the love which first sought
you, and pursues you now again and again.

*

O prince's daughter, my sister, my bride,
how beautiful are your feet on the hills!
Like the dance of Mahanaim, your feet–how
they dance and leap coming here to my side!
And how sweet is your voice! How my heart fills
as it speaks from your heart! Let me hear it now.

*

See, the winter is past, the rain has gone,
flowers appear on the earth. The fig tree
puts forth new figs, and in the land the voice
of the turtledove is heard. My pure one,
my bride, no more tears, no despondency–
now is the time to sing and to rejoice.

*Author's note: It is my belief that the Song of songs, whatever other meanings it may have, speaks of Christ's love for His people, His Church, forgiven, justified, and sanctified forever.*

## Isaiah
**just before his death**

I had a hard, demanding job to do–
I might even say, two jobs to do–
pronouncing judgments on ungodly men,
and speaking of the coming Holy One
to some who wished that He would never come.

Always I tried to make my words and style
suit the subject of which I spoke and wrote
(but as to that, it was God who gave me
the language to use and the very words.
But this most men are quite slow to believe),
so that I would not be much astounded
if in distant days some might even think
I was two Isaiahs writing–or more.

But, come, I am no more two Isaiahs
than God is two Gods. He varies his style
of language to suit the matter at hand,
and so do I. I am one Isaiah,
even though it seems possible that soon
I will be sawn in two and so depart
from this sad earth.
Though I said some hard things,
and recorded a world shaken by God's wrath,
the thing I loved to do was to predict
the great Messiah's needed suffering
and all the glories which would follow that.
Such words God gave me! Such visions of Him!
It was as though the future were before
my eyes and those things which are still to come
were as events which happened in the past,
or time present with me there looking on.

I saw Him in grief and despised by men;
and I saw Him pierced for our many sins,
our God's sacrifice for our lawless deeds.
Then I saw Him coming to earth again.
And I saw His pure and glorious reign,
and the new heaven and earth yet to be.

With unclean lips I once thought to begin.
But God gave me clean and privileged lips
to declare these pure things to Israel
and to set forth this holy truth of God.

All praise be to the Majesty on high
who helps the one who trembles at His Word,
who lives in the high and holy place,
and with the lowly in spirit and heart.

Soon I will see the King in His beauty, the Star
of Jacob, the eternal land that stretches afar.

## Cyrus
**(Isaiah 41:2,25; 46:11; 48:15; 44:28-45:7)**

That man Daniel, much honored as a great
man in Babylon, and, as I have come
to know, a very remarkable man,
one day not long after my arrival
in that city after its fall, brought a
scroll to me, quite old in appearance and
much read, and written in the Hebrew tongue.
In it, he said, were many prophecies
recorded a hundred and fifty years
beforehand by a man named Isaiah.

And Daniel drew my attention to a
specific part of the scroll, and then he
pointed with his aged finger at a line,
and below it to still another line.
And twice he pronounced a name, and it was
my name, Koresh, sounding in Hebrew much
as it does in my native tongue.
                                        At first
I could not believe that what he said was
there was actually there. I'm sure you
can imagine my wonder at hearing
my name from a scroll written long before
my birth, in a land far away, and by
a man of another race who couid know
little of my fathers or my fatherland.
But I had it thoroughly checked by the
best scholars in the whole of Babylon.
My name was there.
                                        And not merely my name.
The scroll spoke of me (not always by name)
several times, and revealed what I would do,

before a thought ever came to my brain,
indeed, long before either I or my
father came into existence.
You will
agree that here was an amazing thing,
And this was in a sacred writing much
venerated by all the Jews I saw
as being inspired by the Most High God
Himself. I think I can believe it too.

Of one thing I am sure. I'll do my best to see
that all those great prophecies are fulfilled through me.

## Jeremiah

**as an old man, regarding his tears**

To be a prophet was not my desire.
At last I agreed–God persuaded me.
But it was against what was in my mind.
And the cost was many a mournful day.

You can mark me down as melancholy.
I'm not ashamed of it. For God puts his
people's tears in His bottle. He stores them
up as nectar. They are a holy drink,
they quench His thirst–His thirst to see human
beings who care for the important things.
Oh, that my eyes were a fountain of tears,
to satisfy more fully His great thirst.

For I've learned to weep for something larger
and more meaningful than my own small griefs.
Those called by His name demand all my tears,
those forsaking the holy living streams
and vainly digging their waterless wells,
those turning from blessing to just judgment,
those fallen on dark idolatrous fields.

How can I cry over my petty cares,
my troubles, passing, insignificant?
I will find my satisfaction only
in satisfying Him. I will tear down,
destroy and overthrow, build up and plant.
And I will go on weeping till the day
when there will be no more weeping, ever.

There were times when I also had some joy.
The knowledge that God could cause me to stand

against a whole people whose hearts were brass,
and speak His word through me, cheered my poor heart,
and brought me comfort in my many pains.

And it was to me that our God revealed
His truth concerning a new covenant.
A new heart, a new spirit–these are the
crying need. And these Israel will have,
when once this present judgment runs its course,
and God once more turns in mercy and love
and blesses His people more than before.

It will not be in my time. Cruel foes
are at the door and captivity looms.
Seventy years this people will be gone,
and the land will be desolate.
But I
will still go on trusting and serving God,
and being joyful in Him whenever I can,
and weeping with Him too while He fulfills His plan.

## Ezekiel
### (before his death)

The thought has come to me that of all the
seers I may be the hardest to understand.
I myself did not understand many
things that I wrote, so difficult they were,
and given in such strange symbolic ways.
And there were times when I could not be sure
whether I was in the body or out
of it, whether awake or in a dream,
whether what I saw was reality,
or visions pointing to reality.

I am sure that to this day not one man
comprehends all the things that I wrote down.
Perhaps no one will until that future day
when prophecies become realities.

But there were things I wrote so very clear
that those rebellious ones in Israel
who never wanted to obey the truth,
were much dismayed to hear me speak of them.
But prophets speak for God and so must speak
even if all the world is reprobate
concerning God and truth and righteousness.

And prophets must, of course, obey the Lord.
At times this was a great trial to me.
I had to do some things that seemed bizarre.
I did them, believing that God knew best
what to ask of His servants, and aflame
to please Him even if I looked a fool
to men, which I think I may well have done.
But what is important–that I appeared

like a fool, or that men received the truth?
If strange behavior helps to open up
reluctant minds to listen to God's words,
I will not be concerned if I seem strange.

You may not comprehend what I say now,
but like the other things that I have said
it is the truth: The whole theme of my book
is the glory of God, the outworking
of that glory which I saw at the first.
Some day this glory will fill the whole earth.

For above and through all the wickedness of man
God goes on fulfilling His great eternal plan.

## Gog
**(Ezekiel 38:1-23)**

I suppose you are interested in
my name because that man in Israel
long ago wrote mistakenly of me.
And this disinformation was kept in
their scriptures along with some other lies.

And so even to this day, these many
centuries later, I am viewed by some
with fear and loathing. But I am not the
sort of man they think I am, not at all.
For I am neither a beast, nor the Beast,
but simply a man ambitious for my
Russian motherland and glad to see her
once more rising up to heights of power
and dignity among the great nations
of the world. And should I be blamed for that?

For long enough she lay prostrate and weak,
hardly able to feed her people well,
and looked upon with contempt by the more
affluent and aggressive lands of earth.

Now she has risen from the ruins caused
by all her disastrous policies and
her experiments with democracy.
And with the strong leadership she enjoys
she is once again in a position
to shake up a few nations around here.

My plans are not secret. Intelligence
has discerned them for some time. So I don't
mind being a bit specific with you.

As a start, I mean to control the whole
of western Asia, and wield strong influence
over the rest of this great continent.
And when all those vast territories are
in my hands, we will see who goes with cap
in hand groveling to whom, as lately
those ruthless finance lords have made us do.

There will be sudden movements of armies,
huge and well equipped, and nations will be
invaded and crushed by the Russian bear
and all her many allies in the world.
Magog, Meshech, Tubal, Persia, Cush, Put,
Gomer and Beth-Togarmah in the north
will be united with a common aim,
and will be a force to be reckoned with.

You may believe Ezekiel if you choose,
but if you do, you will find out too late
that his dramatic sketch of my defeat
came not from God but from his mixed-up brain.
Gog is the man for the future of man,
and no one at all can thwart his great plan.

## Prominent Men in Daniel

### Daniel

You may think of me in the lions' den,
but God did much more in my life than that.
A gloomy den or halls of royalty–
He made all such acceptable to me,
and kept my feet on straight and level ground.
This was a miracle just as great as
keeping shut the hot mouths of savage beasts.

He gave me a heart craving purity–
a thing of much importance in my eyes.
During my long life not once did I give
in to fleshly lust and sensual sin.
I would rather die than sin against Him.
I often thought of Joseph all alone
in Egypt, and learned how to stand alone,
and shun all evil, all forbidden things.

And when intimidation showed its face
He always gave me special grace and strength,
and so protected me from compromise
with ungodly men and corrupt desires.
I would not bend one holy principle
to gain advantage or security.
This also had its great significance.

I should mention the wisdom that God gave
so that I could understand many things–
though one has always greatly puzzled me.
No, I am not referring to the beasts,
symbols of nations determined and fierce,
although they too can much puzzle the mind.

My perplexity has another source–
He called me a man greatly beloved. Why?
I never thought myself a favorite
of heaven, never dreamed I deserved love.
All that was good in me was His own work.
Anything I had was a gift from Him.
My sins were all mine, my successes were
all His; my part to bow low at His feet.

One thing alone I always brought to Him–
my sincere and willing and trusting heart
(of course, this too was His work in me).
I wanted the best of His best for me,
and sought for it with full earnestness,
and this also for His own people's sake.

My visions troubled me, made me quite ill.
But I learned to leave these matters to God.

So soon I will rest, and leave to another day,
and to many others, interpretation's way.

## Shadrach, Meshach and Abednego

We really don't know how it came about
that when confronted with that crucial choice
we had such untroubled courage and faith.
Of course, Daniel was an example to
us, but that hardly explains everything.
Even when examples are good, meeting
with danger nature tends to take its own
course and may soon forget the model seen.
We had some faith before, developed by
our study of the Word of God and prayer,
but not faith we could think exceptional.
We feel it must have come by God's good grace

given on the spot. For as danger grew
our faith also grew.
                    Nebuchadnezzar
the great king could be kind to those he liked,
but he was a fiercely determined man.
People simply did not say "no" to him.
But for us it was either that or else
dishonoring and angering our God.
In His Word we saw instances enough
of those who brought on themselves. His hot wrath
by bowing down to idols of false gods.

Then somehow the faith came that we would not
perish in the flames now awaiting us,
and so we could say with firm confidence:
"And our God will deliver us, O king.
But even if He does not, yet we will
never worship the image you have made."

We cannot deny the sudden surge of
apprehension when we fell through the air,
with flailing arms, all helpless to avoid
the fierce heat that rose up to meet us there.

And then, quite remarkably, it was cool
as though we walked about on some autumn
day with its chill air, and warm sun above.
And all the flames could do was to consume
the bonds on hands and feet and set us free.
And One walked with us in the fire and spoke
words of encouragement to our tried hearts.

It was not an experience we will
forget tomorrow. Nebuchadnezzar
too will remember it for a long time.
You can give him this–when faced with the truth
he would bend his neck and acknowledge it.
He did once before and he did it now.

He learned that God could rescue from his hand,
and instantly was vocal in His praise.

This is the God whom all the world should come to know–
the God of Shadrach, Meshach and Abednego.

**King Nebuchadnezzar**

I really thought myself the greatest man
on earth. And not without some reason too.
Who else had invaded so many lands,
conquered so many different people,
defeated so many powerful gods?
And who had ever constructed such a
magnificent city as Babylon?
In man's towering image of the world,
I was (and am) the head of gold, and all
kings following will be of lesser stuff.

Giving me the plain meaning of my dream
the youth Daniel made a deep impression
on my mind, and I began to see that
his God was no commonplace god as those
known to me. But my proud heart was not changed.
To symbolize my prowess and my might
I had that monstrous idol erected on
the plain, and demanded its worship from
every nation and people in my realm.
And then the process of enlightenment
took a forward step. There were three men
who refused to submit to my commands,
and resolutely looked me in the eye,
facing the fiery furnace without fear.
Such boldness I had never seen before,
and, believe me, my fury knew no bounds.
Into the blazing fire they went–and stood
there with a fourth, all untouched, unharmed by
leaping flames. Evidently, some great God

beyond my experience was at work,
and I could only wonder and admire.

And Daniel. In my long life I have known
many men, men of great ability,
men of power, in touch with the unseen.
But never one the equal of this man.
All the wizards and astrologers in
the land were as nothing compared with him.
He could peer over the high rim of time
and look into the eternal expanse.
His God seemed to be a personal friend
who told him how things are, and things to come,
and helped him day by day and kept him pure.
I had strange dreams, which were not strange to him,
and he interpreted each one with ease,
and humbly claimed no credit for himself,
giving all to God on high. The last dream
was the most disquieting of them all
and ushered in a time of great distress.
For seven years my reason went away,
and like a mindless beast I roamed the fields,
hardly aware of what I was or did,
until I learned to say from humbled heart
that God is the Sovereign of the world.

He knows how to deal with the arrogant,
and can raise up or abase any man
and teach him that God is God and man is
man, and a great gulf is between the two.
Humbling, of course, was then my greatest need,
and I thank God that this is what I got.
Now I praise the King, the King of eternity,
the One who brought me down to give new light to me.

**King Belshazzar**

Now I have always regarded my great

ancestor, and founder of this mighty
kingdom, as more than a little crazy
at the end of his life. I do not refer
to his eating grass like an ox, as sad,
and as indicative of an unsound
mind, as that was. No, my meaning is this:
He brings all those hopeless Jews here, and then
adopts some of their religion! Even
worships their god!
But if their religion
is so good and their god so powerful,
how is it that he could not save them from
crushing defeat and exile to this land?

I have always believed, and still do now,
that defeat of a people means defeat
of that people's god. A god that cannot
protect devotees from attack is not
a god deserving of our reverence.

I remember once there was talk about
some strange fellows called Shadrach, Meshach and
Abednego who, some say, were rescued
from blazing fire by the miraculous
intervention of their god. As for me,
I cannot believe it for a moment.

It sounds exactly like an old wives' tale,
originally invented by some
fertile mind bent on providing the Jews
with a phony reason why they should still
go on believing in their god who has
routinely failed to help them in their need.

I've just thought of a perfect way to show
how strong my convictions are in all this:
I will now have those golden goblets brought,
the ones Nebuchadnezzar took from that

temple of their god in Jerusalem.
And from them I will drink my wine, and praise
my gods, the mighty gods of Babylon,
and so put that god to an open shame.
And let that feeble one do what he can.
When dealing with him there is no need for tact.
If he is a god at all, now let him act!

**Darius**

We had expected more difficulty.
After all, Babylon had been a great
empire for many years, in fact the most
powerful on earth. Its armies were large
and well trained, with a reputation for
savagery, its conquests legendary.
Called a bitter and hasty nation,
terrible and dreadful, it marched through land
after land, violently seizing captives
as numerous as the sand of the sea,
scoffing at all kings, scorning every prince,
laughing at forts and fortifications.
Its horses were swifter than leopards, more
fierce than evening wolves. Like eagles they flew
to the prey.
Its walls were exceedingly
high, strong and magnificent. Behind them
both rulers and people boasted in their
idols and trusted in their gods and thought,
no doubt, that they were all forever safe.

In one night, with hardly any trouble
or resistance at all, we entered and
took the city, coming, not through the gates,
or over those high walls, but under them,
on a stream bed from which the water had
been diverted. Nothing and no one was

able to oppose us, no troops, no ruler,
no hero, no idol, no god.
And so
it came about that I could meet Daniel,
far and away the best and greatest man
I ever met, one whose walk with the true God,
the great Creator of the universe,
was incredibly close, honest, and real.

You know, of course, how that fearless man faced
the lions in their den, with no tremor,
no anxious word, and how God rescued him
from their mouths. I myself was witness to
that miracle, and I have not been the
same man since. Now I know of a kingdom
far above the arrogant kingdoms like
Babylon which, in a moment, totter and fall.
God's kingdom is eternal and rules over all.

## Hosea

Israel behaves like a prostitute,
seeking the many gods of the countries
all around–no, not like a prostitute,
but an adulterous wife who leaves her
own husband and runs after other men,
not for money, but to satisfy lust.

God is the husband, eternally true;
Israel is the vile unfaithful wife.

A hard thing He asked of me, our great God.
He wanted me to be a symbol of
all this, an object lesson to all men.
I had to marry an unfaithful wife.
And go to her again and bring her back
when she had fallen so low that my heart
felt a mixture of loathing with my love.

Does God feel less than man when those He loves
and unites with Himself by covenant,
break their vows, reject His words, spurn His law,
prove unfaithful, and refuse all appeals?
Has He who made man's heart, and taught it love,
Himself no heart to love, no heart to break?

And cannot that same heart loathe the sin which
drew you from His embrace and made you vile,
and loathe with infinite loathing and love
with eternal love, both at the same time?

Oh, Israel, now learn the heart of God.
He wants you back, all defiled as you are,
all degenerate to your very core.

He weeps for you, He holds out loving arms,
He calls with breaking voice, and His one word
is "Come."
                    Oh, return to the Lord our God.
He will forgive, He will receive you to
His breast. Take with you words and say to Him,
"Forgive our sins. Receive us graciously.
Sick to death we are of unfaithfulness.
Now we cast false gods to the bats and moles,
and come to you, our God, and come to you."
Then you will truly be a people apart;
for then will come healing of the mind and heart.

## Hosea's Wife

I'm not sure you can understand, unless
you have been victimized by your own lust
as I have been. When I say "victimized"
I am not suggesting that I am free
of guilt, only that I am a guilty
victim. I cannot stand against the pull
of my desires. I fall, and fall again,
and hate my falling, and still fall again.

Often I am sick because of what I do
to Hosea, and, on top of that, sick with
longing for other men.
I am a bad
woman who sometimes wishes to be good,
but find out that my badness will prevail.
It seems to me that I am made of sin.
Against my better judgment, and against
all my husband's affectionate appeals,
and against the troubling voice of conscience,
I turn back again to wickedness and
folly, and so disgrace myself and break
my poor husband's heart. And all this for what?
A momentary satisfaction of
a low desire that will not let me rest,
a hunger to add new burns to old scars.

You who are pure may think, "It can't be that
hard to say "no." But how can you know the
power of old sins to recreate themselves.
How can you guess the inflaming memories,
the brooding strength of idols in the heart,
the grim fascination with the ugly
and depraved. And how can you know how the

pressure builds, and the urge nags again and
again and fiercely demands the obedience
of its slave–me–so that sometimes it seems
impossible to utter the word "no."

Believe me, no resolution can stand
against it long. I believe this is true
of all powerful desires which enslave
people, especially true of the kind
that afflicts me.
And who is stronger than
my lust? Who can deliver slaves to new
life from such disgusting bondage as mine?
And who cares enough? Hosea tells me
that his God does, that I should turn to Him.

When I really believe this I will cry
out to him until my throat's raw and can
cry no more, until my heart is made new.
One time, desperate, I prayed for either
victory or death, but received neither.

I'm trying to decide if his words make good sense.
Should I try it? I want no more disappointments.

## Amos

I never thought of myself as "prophet,"
though God used me to prophesy His truth.
Why do people think that those who do so
are some kind of extraordinary
beings, far above the usual man?
I was, am, nothing at all to boast of–
a mere shepherd and tender of fig trees.

And I think something along this line may
be said of nearly all the prophets
God has used. They were but ordinary men,
given an extraordinary work,
and so endowed by God with special gifts.

But they were not without the fears and faults
of other men. They shared the same nature,
the same weaknesses, longings and desires.
Whether learning to live, making choices,
coping with problems, occupied at home,
or going about the business of life,
as others, they could make many errors.

But when they spoke for God it was not so.
Then they were infallible in their words,
for they were the words of the one true God.
All of their extraordinariness
was in the Most High God, not in themselves.

Now I go out for starry skies to seek
their Creator for more strength for my task.
Their distant beauty almost breaks the heart.
They point me Godward more than anything
else ever does, except, of course, God's Word,

and His Spirit speaking to my inner man.
I find it hard to live without a frequent sight
of all those eloquent stars in the sky at night.

## Jonah

Fame did not interest me in the least,
yet I have become quite a famous man–
more for what I refused to do than for
what I did. I should say tried to refuse.
My efforts to escape from God were well
planned, it seemed to me, but not successful.
Instead I found the truth of the psalmist
in my case to be very true indeed:

"Where shall I go from your Spirit or where
shall I flee from your face? If I take the
wings of the morning and dwell in the most
distant part of the sea, even there your
hand shall lead me, and your right hand seize me."

Not on foot, nor by ship, nor even in
that huge sea creature, could I evade Him,
not for an hour. What had been to me
only a magnificent song, I came
to know was absolute reality.

And another verse became meaningful
to me–"Out of the depths I cry to you."
And God heard my cry. How else could I have
survived that monster's dark interior?
And when it grew sick of me and spewed me
out on dry land, that land was not se far
distant one, or some hidden island's beach.
It required no ship for me to proceed
to Nineveh.
So at last I gave up,
concluding that disobedience was
far greater trouble that obedience.

"If God wants me in Nineveh, then to
Nineveh I go," I thought, and set out
for that forbidding place of wickedness.

On the way, I was again disturbed by
the fear that the people there might repent.
If you ask me why this should be so, the
answer is simple. In general I
am not very fond of Gentile sinners,
and especially have an aversion
to those who have long been enemies of
my people. I simply do not want God
to bless them. Let Him destroy them instead,
was the thought running through my mind as I
went on my journey to that evil place.
And, this is why, at first, I ran away.

Well, at long last I learned to do what must be done,
for there's no hiding from the Omnipresent One.

## Habakkuk

My poor mind was in utter disarray,
for I could not understand a thing God
proposed to do. And I very much longed
to understand. The Lord is a great King
over the earth, and I submit to Him.
But His reign, hidden and mysterious
as it is, baffled all my highest thoughts.

I know that my (and His) people Israel
have fallen away from Him and disgraced
His holy name and brought grief to His heart.
Everywhere injustice and scorn of law
prevail, and my prayers about all this
seemed to go unanswered. I was amazed
that God did not judge the many evil
ways among us.
At last God answered, but
what He said filled me with more dismay.
He would punish His people, He said,
but with a nation more wicked than they.
This brought another complaint to my lips.
How could God even think of doing this?
Surely His eyes are too pure to look on
evil, or to use a depraved people
to destroy His own.
Then I thought I should
wait for God to speak again and give me
what explanation He would choose to give.
And His word was this: A man does not live
by explanations, by understanding
the mysteries God keeps hidden from us.
But the righteous man will live by his faith.

God will never reveal to us so much
that faith becomes unnecessary. He
will tell us only enough for faith to
act and trust Him even without any
more revelation or understanding.

It is not our work to find out what He
has not revealed, but to believe Him in
what He has revealed. We must let God be
God, and know that never will He do wrong.
Man in unbelief says God is unjust.
Faith says God is just, even when it sees
injustice and suffering on every hand.

So the thoughts of my heart now know a change:
Though the fig tree never gives fruit again,
and though all the vines are without their grapes,
though no olive is seen on the olive tree,
and no sheep, no cattle appear in the pens,
from me God will hear no more complaints. My voice
will be lifted in praise, and I will rejoice.

## God is the Judge
**(Zephaniah and Nahum)**

God is a stronghold in every day of
trouble. And trouble there will be, for His
whole nature burns against all wickedness.
God can do no wrong, not then, not now, not
ever. Evil He will never condone.
The earth will crack, the heavens will dissolve,
peoples will be destroyed, nations will fall,
this globe will totter and stagger like a
drunken man, will sink under God's anger.
For His justice is awake and on the march.
It will take hold of its glittering sword.
It is armed to put down all wickedness.

God is good. He loves this world of His too
well to permit the ungodly to go
on indefinitely polluting it.
He takes severe action. Cancerous growths
must be excised, the body must be saved.

Look how He has sent disasters to the
earth. See how many of its inhabitants
have been crushed like the moth,
and learn with certainty one important truth:
God's nature burns against all that is wrong.
So seek righteousness, seek humility.

God is the Judge. He well knows, and not we,
what, whom and when to punish and destroy.
He is the Creator. He is the King.
Does He have eyes of flesh? Does He see as
man sees? Is not His view of things far higher,
better, more just than ours could ever be?

Against Him do not raise your lofty thoughts.
Do not babble to Him of good and bad.
Do not explain to Him kindness and love.
Do not give Him rules for executing
justice. You are a sinful man. You are
a worm that deserves crushing under His
heel. Do not presume to enlighten Him
regarding His ways with the universe.

Do not think you can teach Him the best way to reign,
you who are but dust and go to the dust again.

## Haggai

"The time to build the Lord's house has not come."
You who say this, will the time ever come,
you who are keen to build if it is for
yourselves? What mansions you will erect if
you are the ones to live in them! You will
choose the best carpenters, the finest wood,
daily will be seen at the building site,
and watch with joy as stone rises on stone,
and can hardly wait to move yourselves in,
when you have furnished it with the best things
available.
And all the while God's house
remains in ruins, daily suffering
the ravages of neglect, a home only for insects
and rodents, instead of for Him. And you
builders for yourselves do not take it to
heart, and thus you show your contempt for God,
for to disregard the house of God and
the work of God is to scorn God Himself.

And you who do this are the children of
Abraham, and you profess to believe
in the God He worshiped and served so well.
And God has brought you back to this blest land
and promised you blessings as He did before,
blessings above all other people in
the world. And thus you would repay God's grace.

And now you reap the unhappy harvest
of the conduct you have sown. And will reap
still more of such until you think on your
ways and give your hearts to Him.

The great day
is coming! God will shake the heavens and
the earth. Down will come houses small and great,
and thrones will totter and crash, and horses
and chariots fall. Then where will be those
palatial homes erected for yourselves?
The very earth shall reel to and fro like
a drunken man. It will collapse like a
shed in a storm. And will it matter then
whether your house was a mansion or a hut?

But God's kingdom is an everlasting
kingdom, one which no one will ever shake.
So come now, show true faith and gratitude.
Sacrifice your rich interests for His.
And worship the true and living God in a way
He accepts–by what we do, not by what we say.

## Malachi

I could never stand for very long the
words and actions of the people I served.
I often felt as God reveals He felt–
contradicted, insulted, or ignored.
To this day some of the things they said seem
quite impossible for them to have said.
But they said them, there is no doubt of that.
Sometimes they drove me to tears and almost
to despair.
For a thousand years they have
been taught by God, led by great men, blessed when
they obeyed, warned by faithful seers, sometimes
punished for their sins, but reasoned with and
pled with again and again. And what has
been the grand result? Do you want to hear–
you who probably think you're better than they?
Then listen to their words:
"How have you loved us?"
That was not said by those whom God had scorned,
by those hard Egyptians who perished in
the sea. It was not said by Amorites
being annihilated and driven
from their land, or by unclean Edomites
given up to their gross darkness and to
their detestable, murderous false gods.

Believe this if you can: That was said by
the people of God, called to be His own,
borne on eagle's wings and brought to this land,
given God's Word, loved with eternal love,
and blessed far beyond any measurement.

Hear again. When God said (with reason plain

to all with open eyes), "You have despised
my name," the arrogant words came back: "How
have we despised your name?" Do you think this
was said by blasphemers? By ignorant
sinners rolling in the mire or by those
who never once let themselves be found in
the sacred temple courts of our great God?

Then think again. It was God's priests, the priests
who presented defiled food to Him, who
deliberately offered defective
sacrifices, the blind, the crippled and
diseased, on the holy altar of the
great King of the whole universe, and thus
dared to show consummate contempt for Him.
Have you a desire to know any more?

God has more to say to you, if you care to look.
You will find it written down in my little book.

# New Testament Portraits

## The Angel Gabriel
**(Luke 1:11-38)**

In long service as an angel of God
I've been sent to many sites on many
missions to the place the inhabitants
call earth–a very sad, rebellious and
unholy spot that has a great need of
angelic visitations. But these last
two journeys there have been the very best.

First I was sent to a man of God named
Zechariah. "Yahweh remembers" is
the meaning of his fine name, and after
many years and many earnest prayers for
a child sent to the Throne by him and his
good wife, and after the hope of having
one had all but died in their gentle hearts,
I was sent to him with the happy news
that Yahweh had indeed remembered them,
and that his faithful prayer had been heard.

And what a child he will turn out to be!
No one greater in the thousands of years
of man's history has opened eyes there.
And what a great work will be his to do–
preparing the coming Messiah's way!

If angels were given to envy (and
I'm very glad to say that we are not)
not one of us could help envying John.

But that first visit, happy as it was,
can scarcely compare with that made to the
insignificant town of Nazareth,

now become significant forever.
When I saw Mary alone I drew near.
To me she seemed hardly more than a child,
and was much alarmed at the words I spoke.
Such sweet timidity drew from my heart
compassion and tender reassurance.

I was delighted to say "Do not fear,"
and then to bring my message which would cause
eternal changes in the universe.
Heaven's immortal King had made His choice
of that humble person through whom His Son
would be born on earth to redeem His own,
and lead them safely on to stand, pure and
spotless, before the holy throne of God.

Mary means "rebellious" or "obstinate,"
but no shadow of such a thing was seen
in her, but rather instant submission
to the heavenly words of the Most High.
I can see how good God's choice of her is.

I am sure she will be the mother that our Lord
will want in early years of growth in God's sure Word.

## Zechariah and Elizabeth
**(Luke 1:5-80)**

### Zechariah

That day it was my turn as priest of God
to offer incense at the temple in
the presence of the Holy One. This was
always an act I looked forward to with
great eagerness. The mystery of that
which lay there behind the concealing veil,
and the heightened sense of the nearness of
the Most High God never once failed to fire
all my imagination and my love.
And as the incense sweetly rose so did
my prayers for myself and my dear wife and
for all the holy nation Israel.

I was not then thinking of the many
prayers for a son I had often sent
above (prayers, I am ashamed to say,
in my old age, I doubted God had heard
or would hear, prayers I was prone to forget).

Quite unexpectedly the angel came
and stood by the altar of incense there.
Do I need to say that I trembled and
shook with fear? But he was sent with precious
promises, and each of his words was good.
But at first I gave in to unbelief.

How could he really mean what he now says?
was my immediate thought. And I sought
for further assurance to fight my doubt.
And got that too in a surprising way.

God will give us signs when it's signs we need,
but they may not be very pleasant ones.

When once again I was able to speak,
my tongue had some very excellent themes–
the greatness and goodness of the Lord God,
and the redemption of His Israel.

His mercy has brought us the best years of our life.
And old now means good. Here's a word from my dear wife:

**Elizabeth**

According to our Holy Book nothing
is impossible to God. And in our
own experience we have found this to
be true. I had been barren all my life,
and, when I heard the news, was long past the
age of bearing children. But what is all
that to God? He has done great things for us.

And so my little son now runs about
the house and lightly dances in my heart.
And he will be great–this the angel said–
and do great things for all of Israel,
making a people ready for the Lord.
So should there now be limits to my joy?

And Mary! Wonderful as this story
is of my husband and me, hers is an
even greater wonder. Never having
known any man, and then to bear a son–
a virgin bringing forth Immanuel!

Oh, what great times we had together there
in the Judean hills! Three solid months
filled with joy and praise, which have not yet died,
but grow and grow as our dear children grow.

How blessed are those in the center of God's will!
Their blessedness goes on, ever increasing still.

## Mary the mother of Jesus

A joy that knew no bounds, and then a sword
in my heart. And after that, joy again.
This is what it meant to me to be the
mother of Jesus. Always it was a
blessed thing, beyond anything I dreamed.
But I must confess that sometimes it was
also a puzzling thing.
As a boy He
was always perfectly obedient,
perfectly loving, and perfectly pure.
But he would say such strange things, things which we
could not understand at the time, and not
until much later. But when I fully
understood who He was and why He came,
then, of course, everything became quite clear.

One thing that has never been clear is this:
Why our great heavenly Father chose me.
For I was just a poor girl and had no
special qualifications I could see.
And I had (and have) a sinful nature
like all people (please never once dream of
idolizing me, or exalting me
to some high position that is not mine).
I knew temptations and my weaknesses.

Oh, from beginning to end it was all
the mercy and grace of God toward me.

Now, looking back, I can see that I had
one thing–I trusted in God, truly loved
Him, and was willing to do what He said.
But I'm sure that many others were not

at all behind me in any of this.
And even my trust and love and heart to
obey were a free gift of God above,
who is the one and only source of grace.
So grace will be my song until I die,
the undeserved kindness of God to me.

And now Jesus, crucified, has risen
from the dead, the Son of God and Saviour
of sinners like me. I am blessed indeed
to be the mother of His humanness,
but let Him, and not me, be the object
of your praise, your living hope, and your faith.
I am happy to have Him who was born
to me be my Lord forevermore. This is bliss.
And there can be no greater blessedness than this.

## Joseph of Nazareth
**(Matthew 1:18-25)**

You all know the story–it is one of
the best known of all stories, and I need
not repeat all the details to you now.
But a few remarks about how I felt
at the time might be interesting to you.

I come from a good, solid family.
I mean an honest, hard-working family,
that respected others and had faith in
God. And it was a family that could
trace its lines clear back to David the king.
But we did not boast about this, or feel
we were somehow great ones because of it.

We were not rich–quite the opposite.
Mary's parents too were poor. But neither
one of us cared for luxuries and show.
It was enough that I had steady work.
I was sure that if God continued to
grant me health and strength, I would be able
to provide well for a wife and children.
Carpentry work is always needed in
the community.
So we decided
to proceed and get formally engaged.
This bound us together as though we were
man and wife, and I could hardly wait for
the day when she would come to live with me
in our own home. But that other day came,
the day when she was found to be with child.

Try to imagine yourself in my place.
It was as if on a clear summer's day
without even a whisper of thunder
in the air I suddenly had been hurled
to the ground by an impossible stroke
of lightning. Believing it seemed out of
the question. When we became engaged she
was a virgin and pure. Everyone knew
this was true. And now the unthinkable
had happened.
When the evidence could no
longer be denied, in my bewildered
state I had to think what could be done to
save her, if she could be saved at all.
According to the law the penalty
for adultery is death, and death by
stoning. I did not know whether such an
end awaited her. But in any case,
I wanted to save her from the disgrace
of exposure, so I knew I could not
tell the matter to the authorities.
Instead I thought to put her away as
quietly as possible, and try to
get on with my life.
And now an angel
of God has appeared and brought the good news.
Good news? Better news than this the world never
had before! The long-awaited Messiah
is to be born! And my Mary is not
guilty of what I feared, but His chosen
mother! And I am the one to become
His legal father while He's in our home!

I can't even guess what joys this will bring.
My thoughts are in a tumult once again–
this great One entrusted to us to train!
What wisdom it will take to raise the King!

## The Shepherds
**(Luke 2:8-20)**

We are beginning to learn something of
God's ways, and hope this does not make us proud.
We had a privilege no one else had.
For the angels came, not to the rulers
of the land, or to priests or Pharisees,
or to clever and educated scribes.

We were the chosen ones–we who were, and
are, absolute nobodies. Perhaps it
is nobodies that God most loves to bless.
We have heard it is with the contrite and
lowly in heart that He chooses to live,
and those who tremble at His Word. But still,
does not this whole matter seem very strange?
He is the great King over all the earth.
Why does He care for nobodies like us?

We cannot begin to describe that night,
the unexpected glory, the sudden
fear, the company of all those angels,
voices in the sky, and the word of peace.

Our lives were changed, but not our daily work.
We continue on caring for our sheep,
leading them out to pasture and clear streams,
and watching over them when they are sick,
and guarding them from the attack of wolves,
and willing, we suppose, to risk our lives
for them, if it should ever come to that.

Seeing that great sight did not make us great,
but it made us happy and satisfied
with our lot on the earth. Our job is good.
It gives us time to see the beauty God
gives us all around, and at night we have
the stars, and quiet godly solitude,
with opportunities to think and pray.
Our King David was once a shepherd, and
so is the LORD, according to His Word.

We will go on in this and not aspire
to so-called higher things. But we will speak
of what we saw and heard, and love all men
and pray for all our neighbors and our friends,
and keep our trust in God all our life through,
doing from the heart what He would have us do.

## The Magi
**(Matthew 2:1-12. As old men looking back)**

Let us try to explain how matters were.
We were astronomers–astrologers,
we might say, though we did not follow all
the superstitions that people often
associate with such men. We sought truth,
and wished to know and worship the true God
(a thing not true of most astrologers).

That night it was no ordinary star
we saw, and we knew it heralded no
ordinary event. We had learned that
some day a King of the Jews would arise
to deliver them. We had been told that
centuries ago Israelites spoke
concerning it in our part of the world
(when that entire nation was exiled here).
And in our day we heard of such from Jews
who live among us, and we read their Book.
So we learned of a star that would come out
of Jacob, a scepter from Israel.

But the star that night was unexpected,
to say the least. It moved, not as planets
do in their regular orbits, or as
stars in the fixed wheeling constellations,
but as if guided by some sagacious
Power on a course not previously
known to man. Low in the sky it went straight
to the west, without being influenced
by any other celestial bodies,
that we could tell.

In Jerusalem it
turned due south (a thing no ordinary
star could ever do), and led us to that
house in Bethlehem. And arriving there,
it stopped so low in the sky that we could
see it standing there directly above
the house where the new King of the Jews lay,
not at all like the normal stars so far
away, which were above the house, but so
distant that it was not possible for
any of them to point to just one house.

But there was no mistaking this new star,
or where it stood, or what it signified.
There was no need to search from house to house.
We had found Him, and we gave Him our gifts,
and bowed in adoration at His feet.
After a time we took our departure
back to our land, the same, but not the same
ever again, praising the Lord God all the way
for all the many signs and marvels in our day.

## King Herod
### (Matthew 2:1-18)

You can well understand, I am sure, that
the matter set alarm bells ringing in
my mind. Having some strangers from afar
suddenly appear at the palace gate
asking for a king other than myself
was not an every day experience.

And then to hear them speak about a star
they saw in the east–the star of the king
of the Jews–to me was a further shock.
They even spoke about worshiping him.
Plainly a rival had been born near here,
and no ordinary rival at that.

Their words brought to mind the old Jewish hope
of some messiah or other who would
come on the scene and put everything right–
or what Jewish leaders consider right,
which is a completely different thing.
Need I say that their views about all this
I consider nonsense? Messiahs are
not my thing, and I will kill anyone
anywhere who will try to take my place,
even if that person is my own son,
or the messiah of the Jewish race,
who, they say, will be sent by God himself.

Really, all this talk of God drives me mad.
Tell me, what did God, if there is a God,
ever do for me? I shake my fist in
the face of whatever God there may be.

And so I did what I needed to do.
Now if this meant the death of several
children in the area of Bethlehem,
it could not be helped. I had to make quite
sure that any rival to me was stopped.

In any case, was the death of the whole
lot of them much of a loss? That is a
poor place, the people uneducated,
and, on the whole, a miserable lot.
It could matter little whether most of
them lived or died. Their lives were empty things.
Now I will be quite safe for years to come.

And surely this is far more meaningful
than even many infants' life or death.
We know that kings have a significance
that common ones of earth can never have.
And I am not in the least distressed that
a few baby Jews had to face the sword
in order for me to retain my throne.

For we all live in a cutthroat world, and the one
who cuts first will remain when all is said and done.

## Simeon
**(Luke 2:25-35)**

God reveals things to me. I do not know
why He's chosen me for this, but He has.
So I had been aware for some time that
I would not die until Messiah comes.

Now I think my death is near, for this day
I saw Him in the temple, being led
straight there by the Holy Spirit of God.
And I saw Him, not, as one might suppose,
in the power of His high position,
or in the splendor worthy of His name.

He was in His mother's arms, an infant,
new, tiny, without strength, hardly able,
it seemed, to keep His eyes open as her
rite of purification was fulfilled.
But at once I knew, ah, in that infant
heart and brain the one hope of Israel's
salvation lay incarnate. I worshiped
Him.
I then spoke to Mary words from God's
own heart through mine to hers: "Because of this
child, and what He will be and do, there will
come a rising and falling of many
among our people. He will be a sign,
but against Him there will be many words;
the thoughts of many hearts will be revealed.
Your soul will feel a piercing sword, but know
He is the glory of God's people Israel,
and a light to enlighten the Gentiles as well."

## Anna
**(Luke 2:36-38)**

I am an old woman, and have been a
widow more years than most of you have lived.
have been waiting, oh so long, for the
redemption of Jerusalem, and have
prayed God for this more days than I can count.
I never leave the temple now, and I
have no wish to do so. Can there be a
better place to live than this? Here I have
all I want. I desire no luxuries,
and crave no entertainment. All my needs
are simple and easily met. And my
interest in outside events not great
enough to entice me into the streets.

It is divine events which interest me.
And if I cannot understand them here
in God's own house, would I be likely to
if I journeyed abroad? And one thing at
least I have now understood. God wants our
humble prayers, our hearts and our worship far
more than our understanding, though that too
has its importance.
So day and night I
pray. I pray with fasting, and pray without.
To me prayer is more important than food,
but to keep alive some food is required,
so I sometimes eat, but pray as I eat.
Not an hour goes by that my thoughts are
drawn from Him.
Today a wonderful thing
took place here in my holy home. A child
newborn and in his mother's arms was brought

here. I felt an irresistible urge
to go up to him, and then, when I did,
there was this strange stir of adoration
deep in my heart which I had never felt
toward any human being.

I did not
then know his name, but immediately
I knew that he was far more than met the
eye, and in my thoughts at once he became
related to all of my deepest prayers,
and with the salvation of Israel.

Again I thought how marvelous are God's ways
and my mind was filled with light, my mouth with praise.

## John The Baptist
**(at the end, in prison–Matthew 11:2-11)**

What He said of me filled me with surprise.
When they told me Jesus said it I turned
away in confusion. I knew myself
too well to think as they all said He thought–
"Not one ever greater than John Baptist."

Even now how can I ever think it?
Must I believe that Abraham, Moses,
Samuel, Elijah, and other such men
were not greater than I? But if He says
I am so great it must be so, for He
is the true One, and always speaks the truth.

And as I turn this over in my mind,
and try to see the sense beyond the words,
I ponder what true greatness really means.
Such greatness is not a man's own doing,
not something inherent and natural,
or something earned he can take credit for,
but the work of the great God in a man,
a matter more of character than deeds.

Such greatness is never to be measured
in terms of military victories,
or of political ascendancy,
or of man's religious activity,
or of those things highly esteemed by men,
or of achieved place or fortune or name,
or of the robes and palaces of kings,
or of the halls of the world's honored ones,
or of raging ambition to be great.
It is not found in self-exaltation,

but in self-denial and lowly mind;
in giving service, not demanding it.

If I am so great listen to me now,
and hear the qualities true greatness has:
A steady faith in who and what God is,
a humble submission to all His will,
a desire to be His devoted slave,
a firm rejection of all that God hates,
a godly character and holy life,
a willingness to be nothing at all
so that Christ alone can be everything,
and an undying love for His great name,
His great Book and His great work on the earth.

Without these, what people may call greatness
is not real greatness, but mere prominence.
Being, as we all are, sinners by birth,
if God did not do His great work in us,
greatness would be as far beyond our reach
as holiness and righteousness and truth.

I was filled with God's Spirit from my very birth,
His gentleness alone has made me great on earth.

## The Apostle Peter
**(when his death drew near)**

Call me headstrong, call me a man of words,
talking on, whether making sense or not.
Call me a rough impulsive fisherman.
Call me weak, prone even to deny Him.
But call me also a man who knew change
when that rushing sound fell swift from heaven,
and the Spirit came on each of us with
the fiery tongues.
Then I could die for Him,
and speak to His murderers without fear.
The work of God in man is wonderful.
And altogether His own work, not man's.

But do not think that I did not love Him
even when I shrank from that servant girl
and would not admit that I knew my Lord.
I loved Him from the day He came and said,
"Follow me." I loved Him when I failed Him,
when His words brought confusion to my mind,
when He rebuked me for my foolish words,
when I sinned so grievously against Him,
and when He gave me that long loving look
on His way to judgment and cruel death.
(I still always wince at a rooster's cry.)

And now I love Him even more than then,
with more understanding, more constancy.
And I will love Him till I lay life down,
and on this earth can no more speak for Him.

My mind and heart are always filled with Him,
Not an hour that He is not in my thoughts,

and what He is and what He did, and does.
And I preach Jesus, risen from the grave,
chosen to be the Church's one true Head,
the one Mediator between man and God,
the one and only hope of human kind,
my suffering Savior and coming Lord,

Now I know that my departure is at hand.
Forgiven, blessed beyond measure, at peace,
joyful, I go to His kingdom above,
there to love and praise Him forevermore.

For Jesus was the one who loved me from the first,
who seemed to love me most when I was at my worst.

## The Apostle John on Patmos
**(The Book of the Revelation)**

What I really liked to do was lean on Jesus,
look in His face and listen to His words.
To be in His presence was my great joy.
As the prophet has said, nothing in his
physical aspect was remarkable
for its attractiveness. Yet for all that,
when He was with us the air seemed charged with
wonderful mysteries. There was not an
event that was not clothed with divine fire,
that did not bring eternity to life.

And His very substance seemed made of love.
It always radiated from His eyes,
touched my spirit and energized my life.

In my account of what He did and said
I always used the most simple of words–
of course, the words were not mine but His,
but they completely suited my way of
writing, and thinking and speaking, and His–
simple words clothing the most profound truth,
words given as black and white with no grey,
and always pointing to the great unseen,
to everlasting life and light and love,
to the great eternal Triune God.

Strange as it seems we thought that He was dead,
gone from us forever. Repeated words
about His resurrection from the dead
fell on unhearing, unbelieving ears,
until we saw the empty tomb and knew
our Savior God was with us once again.

Now here on lonely Patmos I have seen
what eyes have never dreamed to see–the Lord
Himself in glorious apparel come
to show us future things and to inform
our slow and simple minds of how to live
when evil is let loose without restraint,
and wickedness howls loud in every street,
and God's great enemy and ours is fierce
to destroy all that is of God on earth.

But our Christ Himself, coming from the sky,
will put an end to all the devil's works.
He will be king over a world made new,
and then prevail forever, all victories won.
Come, Lord Jesus–this my prayer, my final one.

## The Apostle James
**(in jail–Acts 12:1,2)**

I am the James who is the brother of
John. Together with him, and Peter too,
what undreamed of privileges I had!
I mean exceptional privileges,
besides those which all His disciples had
of going about with Him, seeing his
many miracles and hearing His words.
Remember, I was just a fisherman,
and never once thought to be more than that.

Then suddenly the Changer of lives changed
mine. What He saw in me, I do not know.
There were fishermen all around, and most
of them could fish, and do everything else,
as well as I. And, though I had faith in
God, I was certainly no paragon
of virtue. And more than once I had let
my temper get the best of me and had
said and done things that brought me much regret.

But one day sitting there in the boat with our
father, with no thought that such a thing was
possible, He called John and me. I don't
think we spoke a single word, even to
dad. We just left the boat and followed Him,
not thinking about where we were going,
but feeling happy and secure with Him.
Even more strange to me, before long I
was one of His inner circle, with the
other two (again, there's no use asking
me why). And those privileges mentioned
above began.

When the little girl, the
daughter of Jairus was raised from the dead,
I was there.
When Jesus was transfigured
on the mount, and His face shone like the sun,
I was there.
And when in the Garden of
Gethsemane, His face sweat drops of blood,
and he struggled agonizingly to
drink the cup the Father above had given,
I was there.
Now here in jail I have the
the privilege of suffering for Him,
and soon may have an even greater one,
the privilege of being the very first
of the original disciples to
lay down this earthly life for Him. And you
should not think I fear to die. I do not.
Death for me is only an opener
of a door through which I much desire to go.

I have tried to write all this down as best I can–
all this astounding grace toward a fisherman.

## The Wise Builder
**(Matthew 7:24-27)**

Why would anyone want to build his home
on sand? You would think that if a man had
even the least degree of common sense
he would know that a bad foundation means
danger to the whole house.
                                        And yet we see
on every hand builders of lives, even
religious lives, constructing them on most
precarious ground. Outwardly they seem
safe and secure. But then the tempest comes,
the winds beat, the floods rise, and they collapse.

These people take considerable care
with the walls, to exclude what they want to
exclude, and with the roof, to keep out what
comes down from above, and with all the rooms,
to keep separate this activity
from that, and with ornate embellishment.

But their foundations others cannot see,
so they pay little attention to them,
living, as they do, for other men's eyes.

Do they not well earn the name of foolish
builders? They would take great pains to see that
a house of wood or brick rested on a
secure base. They would dig down in the soil
to discover if some concealed pit or
loose dirt waited to swallow up their work,
and would carefully place the well-cut stones,
in every way, acting quite sensibly.

How is it then that in a thing of far
greater importance, the building of a
life, they are guilty of such gross folly?

They will not even look at the source book
which informs us just how this should be done,
will not inspect the plan God gave to men
for this exceedingly important work,
and will not consider that to ignore
the one proper basis of religious
life is to invite certain destruction.

We have learned that in this matter of how
to build our lives for the Lord our minds are
inadequate, our judgment defective.
By your grace we perceived this, our gracious Lord.
We looked to you, O Christ, we believed your Word.

## The Leper
**(Matthew 8:1-3)**

"Unclean! Unclean!" is what I have to cry,
if anyone comes near, out here beyond
the city wall. I am cut off from life
among family and friends, and have viewed
myself with disgust as my face and form
became more disfigured, and with fear as
slowly I lost sensation in my limbs.

Isolated, desolate and afraid,
with torn clothing and uncut, uncombed hair,
with my lower face covered with this cloth,
by day I rove about the walls that shut
me out, and by night seek rest beneath the
bright blind eyes of the stars and the closed ears
of the cold universe, with heart grieved far
beyond any telling.
Time after time
desperate inspections of my flesh find
no cause for cheer, and the faint hope I once
had, is almost dead.
So here, judged by God,
and excluded from the presence of both
God and fellow men, and blaming myself
for all my fruitless prayers, I have waited,
and waiting, longed for sweet release in death.
Only lepers like me can ever know
what I go through, how intolerable
such a life can be.
I really don't
know why, but I do not doubt His power.
This is not my problem at all. I have
heard of His miracles, and seen what could

have been some, I think, some distance away.
I'm sure there is little that He can't do.
They say no incurable disease is
incurable to Him.

But in my mind
I have some doubt about His willingness.
Not because I think of Him as heartless
and lacking compassion, but because I
am less than a nobody, and a quite
disgusting sight.

Why would a man like Him
condescend to look at me, let alone
exercise His power in my behalf?
But then I have nothing to lose. He may
be more willing than I think. If I ask
and he refuses to hear me, my state
will not be more hopeless than it is now.

Here He comes. I may not get another
chance. I'll rouse myself then, and boldly go
and speak to Him–"If you are willing you
can make me clean." Yes, if he his willing–

Oh my heart, His hand touches me. What can it mean?
And His voice of love is saying, "I will. Be clean."

## The Centurion
**(of Matthew 8:5-13)**

As a soldier in the army of Rome
I know the meaning of authority,
for I have followed orders many times,
and also given orders to my men.
Among my hundred there is not a man
who will not do what I tell him to do.

I have heard many orators, teachers,
and such like, but none who could be compared
to Jesus. He doesn't give opinions,
or quote the so-called authorities. He
speaks with power and tells things as they are.

And when it comes to dealing with disease,
a word from Him can cure the very worst.
When He commands, evil spirits in men
immediately depart and leave their
helpless victims behind cured and in their
right mind.
                    I know that Roman soldiers can
be rough and insensitive, and perhaps
not many of them feel as much concern
for their own servants as I do for mine.
I'm afraid that many treat them like dirt.
However that may be, when that dreadful
paralysis came to my man with that
intense suffering of body and mind
(whether from a demon or some other
cause, I can't say), I wanted help for him,
and I wanted it fast.
                    And so I thought
of the Man from Nazareth, and waited

for Him to return to Capernaum
where I was. Knowing my unworthiness,
I did not ask Him to come to my house.
And I knew there was no need to trouble
Him to come, that when He speaks, it is done,
and that my servant's illness would obey
His command.
And so it turned out to be.
To this very day he has perfect health.

All the Lord's words and actions have an enduring
effect. He is a Man who was born to be King.

## The Paralyzed Man
**(Mark 2:1-12)**

Friendship is a very wonderful thing,
ordained, I'm sure, by God for our great good.
Without it how much poorer a place would
this poor world be! How sad the state of those
who never have a single friend to share
their thoughts, their hopes, their sorrows and their joys,
to pray for them, to help them in their need,
to care at all whether they live or die.

I have sometimes thought that if they had not
had that beautiful friendship both David
and Jonathan might have been much lesser
men than they became. Friendship can help make
us more nearly what God wants us to be,
or destroy us, depending on the nature
of our friends.
So now I will praise my friends.
It is hard to be either desperate
or helpless. I was both. Desperate to
get to Jesus and helpless to do so.
And I wasn't sure that if I got to
him I would be healed. I thought I might be,
but other thoughts came as well, such as these:
"And how would the Lord ever notice me?
Around Him there is always such a crowd.
And even if He saw me would He care?"
In any case, to me the question was
academic–I could not get to Him.

Enter my friends, who had more faith than I.
"We will get you there," they said, "and He will
heal you. There's no doubt of that. So here we

go. Hold on to your bed." And off they went
with me, one at each corner of my cot,
and I marveling along the way at
friendship and all the kindness of my friends.

I thought that after this all would be well.
But the crowds! We couldn't get even to
the door, let alone inside, so my heart
fell, faced with this impossibility.

"Take me home. I can't bear to be so near,
and yet so far," I whispered. "Oh, not so,
dear friend," they said. "Hold the bed tight now. Up we go
to the roof." And so they did. All the rest you know.

## The Demoniac of Gadara
**(Mark 5:1-15)**

The tombs were my only home–a fitting
one it was too. For I was dead to God,
dead to the ordinary life of men,
dead to sanity. A horde of evil
spirits had invaded me, completely
taking me over, leaving me only
a small corner of my body and less
of my mind. I felt guilt about letting
them in, but forgot how it came about.

I really did not know who I was,
or where I was, or what I did. Always
I felt terrible pain and dread, but I
didn't know why.
                              I kept hearing voices
in my head. They drove me mad and almost
brought about my death. At times I would wake
with wounds in my flesh and not remember
how they came, or who was responsible.
Sometimes I was chained, other times not, and
I saw broken chains lying on the ground.
But I had no idea who broke them
or why. I didn't think I had that kind
of strength.
                              I say "think," but actually
what I then did can hardly be called thought.
I felt, but my mind then was not at work.
Once flashes of memory about a
former life came–a home, parents, and friends.
But then they swiftly went. It was as if
my entire brain were severed from my self,
and only an occasional spark of

knowledge or memory darted across
that aching chasm, and then left me more
in ignorance, more forlorn than before.
I can't even begin to explain this.

I think I must have wailed and howled a lot.
If it was not I who was it? Noises
like that rang in my ears, and no one else
seemed to be around at the time. To say
I was sad is not to say anything.
There are no words to describe my utter
desolation, my hellish sorrow that
never knew alleviation or end.

And then Someone came, Someone the legion
of demons in me, not I, recognized.
I suddenly ran to Him and knelt down
in His presence–or did they use my legs?
He has very great authority. They
cried out some words, but I did not know what
they meant. They used my voice, but not my mind.

Suddenly my brain was mine again, and I came
to my senses. Then I learned Jesus is His name.

## The Apostle Matthew

I could not believe my ears. There I was
in the tax collector's booth, working for
the Roman State (hated by all for this),
and preparing for another day's work,
thinking of things that I had seen and heard,
peerless new things in our Capernaum,
when quite unexpectedly this serene
commanding presence, this voice of love, called
me to another life, and, just like that,
without a word, I rose and followed Him.

And I hardly knew Him, or what He wished.
I only knew that one look at His face
giving out that call to me was enough.
For quite suddenly I had no past life,
but only a glad future filled with Him.
It was incomprehensible to me
that He would want to choose me for His own,
inviting me to follow in His steps.
I could only wonder where He would go,
and what uncommon purpose led Him there.

Being quite ignorant of all of that,
I thought the paths of glory opened wide
before me and bright dreams of the kingdom
of God arose in my excited brain.

And for a time all seemed to point that way.
Then displeasure and even hate was seen
on the faces of men in authority.
And He began to speak of rejection,
affliction, and death. We were not ready
yet for this and so shrank back from His words,
believing not for pain.

Little did we
understand that the paths of glory for
Him led through the conquered grave, to new life
beyond the grave, His resurrected life.
And now our whole life is bound up with His.
Whether we live or die to us it's all the same–
We want no glory but glory for His dear Name.

## Jairus
**(Luke 8:41-56)**

I have learned something of the great power
of faith. Or I should say the great power
of the Lord Jesus Christ when even small
faith is placed in Him. He is the one who
performs the mighty works, not our poor faith.
But somehow, in a way I do not now
fully comprehend, faith frees Him to act.

No doubt most of you can well understand
my deep concern when my precious girl fell
sick and was at the point of death. You too
have had dear ones helpless on a bed with
little hope of recovery. But I
had one advantage that you may not have.
I knew of Jesus and His power and
His merciful desire to help us all.
Then too I had the thought to go to Him,
and faith that He could work a miracle.

I went to Him and saw his willingness
to come with me, but then there occurred that
distraction and agonizing delay.
Why then of all times must this woman come
and take His time while my poor daughter dies?
This was the selfish thought that struck my mind.

My heart cried out, please, my master, let
nothing keep you here, for now my heart breaks.
But then I thought, her heart is breaking too,
and she has seized this opportunity,
perhaps the only one she's ever had,
and is just as anxious and desperate
as I; and surely this will not take long.

But now men came from my home, their faces
sad, their words sadder still: "Why bother the
teacher any more? Your daughter is dead."

But then our great Master spoke the word to relieve
all of our doubts: "Don't be afraid, only believe."

## The Apostle Thomas
**(John 11:16; 14:5; 20:24-29)**

Somehow the idea has gotten in
people's minds that I am a man of doubt,
and not a man of faith, and some call me
(so I hear) "Doubting Thomas." I am not
much concerned about my reputation,
but for the sake of truth I will say that
before you accept this view you should know
of a trait which has ruled me from my youth–
I like real certainty about things which
are important to me. When I receive
such certainty, I am a man of firm
purpose and resolute conduct, and,
by God's grace, of strong and active faith,
willing to face death for my convictions.
I say, "by God's grace," for no one has faith
like this, or any real faith, without that.

Now as to the report some disciples
made that Jesus had risen from the dead–
on a matter of such significance
could you really expect me to take their
word for it, without further evidence?
Would you have done so, if you had been in
my place? I knew that they were good men, and
truthful, but did not think they were beyond
the possibility of a mistake.
Can men not wish for something so strongly
that they imagine it has taken place?
When the truth of what they had reported
was established I joined them all in glad
acknowledgment.

And it was established!
With my own eyes I saw Him, my hand
touched the healed wound scars in His hands and side,
and my ears heard His voice speaking to me.
I knew at once that He is Lord and God.

Now here in India that moment is
as fresh and real as ever in my mind.
Because of that one overwhelming night,
these many years I have lived and labored
among a people numerous and strange,
who bow down to a multitude of gods.

Do I hear you say, "If you would not take
the word of the disciples about this,
why should we take yours?" I do not ask this.
My word is only one small part of the
total evidence. Examine it all.
And know this fact: Peter and John and Paul,
(and I), and a very great many more,
were willing to leave everything they had
and gladly suffer and die for this one
firm belief: The Lord Jesus rose up from
among the dead and showed He was alive.

But seek Him for yourself. He lives to hear
the voice in prayer of those who want the truth.
He will reveal to you who He is and from whence
He came to earth and why. He is the evidence.

## The Original Disciples of Jesus
**(Luke 14:26-35)**

From the beginning our Lord made it clear,
and we had no illusions about the
cost of discipleship. We also knew
this: Refusing to be His disciple
means to be lost in rebellion and sin.
How can anyone have a valid hope
of eternal life without bending his
neck and his heart to learn from Jesus Christ
the incarnate God, going on learning,
and beginning to practice what he learns?
Even the very thought that a man can
believe and be saved and yet not submit
to this is opposed to everything we,
His disciples, heard from the Lord Himself.
Why, without learning from Him one cannot
even know what salvation really is.

Be assured of this: He calls us all to
discipleship, and salvation is not
to be found in continuing revolt
and in rejection of Christ's revealed will.
No, it is not in claiming to take the
narrow way when one's heart is still in
the broad way; not in profession of the
lips when the life, the mind, and the will are
still not surrendered; not in believing
some facts about Him while pursuing one's
own aims and ambitions; not in a thin
veneer of religion over a strong
determination to keep one's own course;
not in embracing rituals with no
earnest pursuit of holiness and truth;

not in feeling good about oneself, but
in renouncing self and feeling good
about Christ; not in putting self on the
throne, but putting it on the cross,
not in self-esteem, but esteeming Him.

Yet many deceive themselves in all this,
and make a boast of faith without good works,
and salvation without following Him,
without submitting to Him as their Lord.
And they seem to think that they are safe and
secure now, and that discipleship is
another thing–which they may (or may not)
undertake some time down the road, if and
when they please. Is this not to emulate
the foolish man who builds his house on a
foundation of sand and invites ruin?

Why do we emphasize discipleship?
This is our great commission. "Go," He said,
"and make disciples of all the nations."
Do we need to state another reason?
But is the gospel alone not enough?
The answer is clear: We preach the gospel
to make disciples, just as Jesus did.

Discipleship, the gospel, salvation–
these are all very closely intertwined,
and the first is evidence of the last.
Do not mistake what we are saying now.
We all know it is God's grace which saves us,
positively, altogether God's grace.
And that grace is received through faith alone
apart from any works of righteousness.
And no kind of perfection do we claim.
For we are well aware that we are such
sinners that without the mercy of God
we could never survive a single day.

But we are sure that Christ's gospel, when it
is truly preached and received by a real
and living faith, results in discipleship.
God's grace through faith–if it is saving faith–
brings to live in us the Spirit of God
who enables us to obey and follow
Jesus our Lord. It brings into our hearts
an undying love for Jesus Christ and
for His Word and ways, and a mind to hear
and obey what He says. As He Himself
said, His sheep will hear His voice.

And our love and obedience will be
tested in these ways: By what we are willing
to learn from Him, to give to Him, to bear
and suffer for Him, and to do for Him.

And the cost of discipleship? Would you
know that? The cost is everything we have.
We must abandon our control of it,
give up all claims we think we have to it.
And He will not undertake to teach us
His truth if we are not willing for this.
Did He not plainly say, "Whoever does
not renounce all that he has cannot be
my disciple"? Do you believe His word?
Can you think this was for us, not for you,
and that His sheep no longer follow Him,
Him who had no place to lay His dear head?

Can you think you may greedily hold on
to all you have and make it your great aim
to get more for self or for your own ends,
and then find yourself in heaven at last?
We are sure that the devil laughs at such
presumption, and jeers at your ignorance.

The cost of discipleship is quite real,
but it is no sacrifice. And there is
no drawing back for those who truly love
the Lord Jesus Christ, in whose heart the grace
of God is at work, who put the proper
value on the things that He promises.

Giving our little all for His great all–this trade
He offers us. Was better offer ever made?

## The Sadducees
**(Matthew 22:23-29; Acts 23:8. After Christ's death)**

Sometimes, we fear, we are linked in people's
thinking with the Pharisees. This may be
because we have joined together with them
in opposition to a certain strange
individual from the village of
Nazareth who would have destroyed everything
we hold dear. But in some matters of great
importance we don't agree with them at all
(not to mention the fact that we cannot
endure their boasting about giving tithes
of mint and dill and cummin, and other
such foolishness, but we won't pursue that).

Let us give some illustrations of this.
As strange as it may sound, the Pharisees
actually believe in the future
resurrection of all the dead bodies
of those who have passed away! In doing
so they display how lacking they are in
intellectual ability, and
how unenlightened are their attempts to
interpret the Scriptures.
                                        And speaking of
the Scriptures, again they show their utter
incompetence to expound them, and the
pathetic narrowness of their minds, by
insisting, contrary to all reason,
that every word there has come from God and
is altogether worthy of belief.

And so, of course, they maintain that in this
world of ours there are spirits of all sorts,

both good and bad, and angels and whatnot!
And this, even though no one has ever
seen one, or any good evidence that
they exist. The fact is, they are extreme
fundamentalists, and we are quite the
opposite. Then why join with them in the
struggle against that bogus messiah?
Because he was a threat to both of our
parties and a danger to the whole of
Israel. So we determined that we
must rid the earth of him even if we
had to sit down with the devil himself.

Even theological enemies,
when facing such a critical problem,
may agree on some good course of action,
without compromising any of their
basic convictions. So we could unite
even with Pharisees in this good fight.
And we won–that is the important thing.
He is defeated, crucified and gone.
And though there are a few blind fanatics who would
preach him still, we are sure that he is gone for good.

## The Scribes
**(Matthew 23:2, 13-36)**

If there is anyone in Israel
who truly knows the Word of God it is
we. We know things which can come only by
a lifetime of study–careful, constant
study–and long and rich experience
in teaching others the Holy Scriptures.
We've had much practice in discerning truth
and error, and can sniff out heresy
without difficulty.
                    We do not think
that just because someone goes about as
a teacher and gains popularity
with the masses that he must be teaching
the truth. We weigh each word such a man speaks,
and compare it all with the words in God's
Holy Book, and with the traditions and
golden teachings of holy men of God
which have come down to us for centuries.

We live in a day when there is much talk
of messiahs, and recently two men
of the most common, uninstructed sort
(one, we know for sure, some variety
of desert nomad, the other a mere
carpenter) have risen up and gained some
prominence by their fanatical talk.
They have said that their message comes from God,
and have ignored the Pharisees and scribes.
John the baptizer, is no more, having been
arrested by Herod and judged by God.
He lost his head in prison in disgrace–
an end that seemed to us to suit him well.

The other, that Jesus, is still out there
somewhere, making of himself some great one,
and opposing us and the truth we teach.
Many of us are now fully convinced
that his course also should soon end in death.
Hearing for ourselves some of his rash words,
we see he is guilty of blasphemy,
and so among the lowest of the low.
He calls himself the very Son of God,
thus equating himself with the Most High.
The penalty for such a sin is clear.
Such a wretch should not be allowed to live.
Justice cries out against him. So do we,
and will continue to do so until
we see his body given to the grave.

We are the upholders of the law. We
are for strict justice and will always be.

## The Pharisee and the Tax Collector
**(Luke 18:9-14)**

### The Pharisee

What other kind of righteousness is there
besides that which our own efforts can gain?
I'm sure that no one is likely to give
righteousness for nothing to those who will
not work hard to acquire it for themselves.

All of our greatest and best authorities,
all the famous scholars who have composed
godly commentaries on Scripture text,
are in complete agreement with my views,
so I am sure the ground I'm on is safe.

And our God's holy law is also plain:
"And this shall be your righteousness," it says,
"if you do all these things commanded you."

So, being a lover of righteousness,
and a sincere follower of the law,
I set out to obey every single
jot and tittle.
                    No, I am not perfect–
not one of us can think that of ourselves.
But for sure I am not like sinners and
tax collectors–like that one over there.
I give tithes of everything I possess.
I fast religiously twice in a week.
I am never unjust to any man.
I am not an adulterer or thief.
And if I should not thank God for all this,
what on earth should I ever thank Him for?

So regardless of what some people say,
imbibing now the teaching of that one
from Nazareth whom some call a guru,
I am set for the defense of the truth
of God's great law concerning righteousness.

And if he wants to teach that tax collectors
and such like are justified by beating
on their chest and begging for God's mercy,
he will find a worthy opponent here
in me. He can be very sure of that.
If such men are not put down when they raise
their false heads, what will Israel come to?

For I am quite certain that this is always true–
our righteousness can come only by what we do.

**The Tax Collector**

I could hardly get myself to come to
the temple today. I feel like such a
hypocrite, treading this sacred spot and
knowing what a sinner I am. I would
be like that godly Pharisee over
there, praying so confidently, but I
know how impossible this is for me.
For I can't even lift my head in this
holy place. Well, God who can see my heart
need not see my face. And when He sees my
poor heart He will read there sorrow for sin,
and, I hope and pray, repentance true and deep.

I don't know why my sins are such a hard
and heavy burden, but they are. Groans and
tears are often my lot, and I would give
all that I possess if I could know that
I am now forgiven and that God smiles

on me. I sometimes think that this is the
most important thing of all, greater than
my job or my pleasures or family,
or anything on earth that men can name.
Take the whole world, but give me a heart
that knows the sweet truth of forgiveness now.

What are success and enjoyment of things,
or the dearest ties of our mortal life,
or even life itself, if at the end
of all there lies God's frown and deep despair
and the dark pit from which no man escapes?

As David said, "Blessed is the man whose
transgressions are forgiven, whose sins are
covered." But is there mercy large enough
to cover mine, or grace willing enough
to do this thing, or love great enough to care?

I've seen my nature fallen beyond belief.
When I think I've reached the bottom of my
sin, I later find levels lower yet.
If I see still more I will die of grief.
My heart's a rock in a polluted ground.
Would that my beating fist could shatter it
and make it soft and ready to receive
one good word from God bringing hope and peace!

I cannot do much, but will now do what I can.
God be merciful to me, a sinner, is all
I can say. And may God in mercy now let fall
one drop of soothing balm to this unworthy man.

## The People of Nazareth
**(Matthew 13:53-58; Luke 4:16-30)**

No, we did not believe that he was the
Messiah of Israel. Remember,
we knew him well. In fact, did anyone
in this whole land know him better than we?
We knew his first baby words, saw his first
steps and year by year his growth to manhood.
We observed him in the carpenter shop
where he worked, often met him on the town
streets, and talked with him in the synagogue.
We knew him, his parents, and his way of life,
and all his brothers and sisters and kin.
As you may have heard, ours is a small town,
and here everyone knows everyone else.

Jesus was a good lad while growing up,
and became, as far as we could see,
a good man. This we will never deny.
But that hardly made him the one great hope
of the nation, did it? Yes, we knew him,
had not seen anything exceptional
in him, and had no reason to expect
anything exceptional later on,
despite the rumors that surrounded his
birth. He was a good carpenter, but need
we think that even the very best of
carpenters is necessarily good
for anything else?

Then he went away
and was gone for some time. We did not know
where, or why he chose to be somewhere else.
But not long afterwards reports reached us
that he had gone to the Jordan and had

met John and been baptized by him, and that
some strange, unexpected thing had happened
to him. We did not understand what it
was, but supposed we would find out when he
came here again.

Then we heard that he had
begun to teach in synagogues here in
Galilee. We could not imagine why
he started this, or what he might have to
say that people would ever want to hear.
We knew, of course, that he had not been trained
for this in the schools. But some people said
he spoke with authority, and backed up
his teaching with amazing miracles.

At last he returned, and we were all there
waiting with great expectation to hear
what might fall from his lips. But we must say that
all his words and acts disappointed us,
and did nothing to change a single mind.
"I am the true Messiah," anyone may say,
but never to us. We were not born yesterday.

## Boy Whose Food Fed 5,000
**(John 6:9)**

I'm just a kid and maybe a pretty
dumb kid at that but I was as happy
to be there as any big person. I
love to here Jesus talk. He don't talk like
other people I'll tell you that. He has
a lot of good stories. And they're not just
stories. They really mean something.
Sometimes
I know what they mean and sometimes I don't.
But whether I do or don't I like to
here 'em. He has such a way about him
I could listen to him all day and he
tells us things about God and makes me want
to love him a lot.
Maybe I don't git
all them what do they call 'em? them pairabulls.
They are hard but I even like them to.
It seems to me he's giving a pretty
good slap at some of them people who
think they're so high and mighty. I can see
they don't like 'em.
Grownups can be a pain
in the neck sometimes. They're always after
us "aren't you ever going to grow up"
"foolish boy" "why don't you ever listen"
"stop that this instant" we hear stuff like
this ever day of are life. We git sick
of it.
Jesus never once talks like that.
He's my hero. I'd do what he asked no
matter what it was.

I didn't wait a
sec when that man came around talking about
stuff to feed the people. My mom packed that
grub for us and I just ran up and put
it in his hands and wished I had more to
give. It made me feel happy when Jesus
fed that big crowd with it.
Wow! I'll bet not
many people can do a thing like that
I sure never saw it nowhere before.

When I git big I want to foller him
around and here everthing he has to say
and also see everthing he can do
I'll help him agin if I git the chance.

Now I don't git to go to school no more.
I'm sorry I can't talk good or spell right
and stuff like that. Maybe some day I'll learn

These are my thots and words. It's the best I can do.
To put it down like this my mother helped some to.

## The Woman of Canaan
**(Matthew 15:21-28)**

I was so desperate for help that I
was beyond humiliation. Nothing
anyone could say to me would change my
determination to find healing for
my little girl. Can you even guess what
she and I had to go through day by day?

Believe me, the attack of a demon
is a fearful thing. And if there could be
even the slightest chance for me to get
her healed I was going to go for it.
And what better chance would we ever have
in our whole lives than the one which then came
so near our door? Why, the Son of David
Himself suddenly appeared at our place.

Of course, I had heard reports of the great
things He had been doing in Galilee–
things which could not but be heard in our town.
I heard, too, of His compassionate heart.
They said that never once did He turn an
individual away, but always
heard the request of anyone for help.

Somehow I believed in Him before I
could see His face or hear Him speak a word.
And I dreamed that some day He would come here,
but could not really think He ever would.
But He did! And I resolved at once to
seize the time and prevail on Him to act
and heal our home.

You know my trial was
great when He did not speak a word to me.
But I would not so easily give up.
If He won't hear me, then surely He will
listen to His own closest followers,
I thought, and tried my best to gain their help.
But they cared not at all for me or for
my need. (Is this the way they always are?)
So back I went to Him. Now He did speak,
but His words gave me no encouragement.

But I was beyond discouragement too.
I was not going to leave without the
answer "yes." I would rather have died at
His feet than go away with empty hands.
And I was willing to be a pet dog
in His sight or anyone's, if my girl
could only be cured. And behind His words
I could sense a heart of love, and almost
see a smile in those penetrating eyes.

So I believed His heart and saw the matter through.
And my faith won the day, as faith will always do.

## Mark

**(Acts 13:13; 15:39; 1 Peter 5:15; 2 Timothy 4:11)**

I have always regretted how I left
my uncle and Paul at Pamphylia.
It was a big mistake with serious
consequences. It caused sad division
between those two men of God. I confess
the reason: inexperience and youth,
and a bad defect in my character.

For a long time Paul kept his distance from
me, and I don't blame him. I proved myself
unreliable once, and after that
he was bound to think that I might do so
again.

I will not say–or even think–
a critical thing about that great man.
No one could have higher standards than Paul,
and no one ever lived up to them more.
I regard him with the utmost respect
and admiration. But I do thank God
for Barnabas, the great encourager,
who thought if I were given a second
chance, I might then prove useful in God's work.

I am grateful to Peter too. He took
pains and opened up the way for me to
serve God with him in the ministry.
He taught me many things–things which our Lord
had said and done while He was still on earth.
And these the Spirit of God led me to
write down in my little book, the Gospel
which now strangely bears my name–it is not
my Gospel but His, and the words are His.

Not a day goes by that I do not thank
our God for Peter, who viewed me with more
understanding than Paul. Perhaps we two
share a similar weakness of nature.
When faced with difficulties, instead of
meeting them bravely head on, we both try
to escape. We are all but men with the
struggles and failings of men, and without
God's grace would not be good for anything.

So above all I give thanks to our God.
He is the God who gives a second chance–
and many more than two–as we can see
from the long history of Israel.
He is the divine Potter who remakes
the marred and misshaped clay until it bears
the form He desires. And He can repair
a shattered pot that brings despair to men.

I will praise Him for all time and eternity,
for I have felt His gentle hands at work on me.

## Father of demon-possessed boy
### (Mark 9:14-27)

Oh, my poor boy, my poor boy! How often
I have seen you suffer! And seeing it,
perhaps my suffering is even greater
than yours. Again I've had to pull you out
of the fire, and unconscious you lie there,
not knowing who you are or what you did,
but with new burns now added to old scars.
I'm afraid to leave even for an hour.
You may wake up and leap back in the flames,
or go to some dark pool, plunge in and drown.

How often I have consulted the priests!
And how many doctors have seen your face!
But I received only words–
"He is a
lunatic. The moon is working on his
mind in an adverse way. There's not a thing
that anyone can do."
Another said,
"It is some disorder of the brain that
is beyond our ability to heal."
Still they sold me some medicines, took my
good coin, and then said, "Try this. It can't do
any harm, and may do a little good."

One said straight out: "The boy has a demon.
Go to someone who knows how to deal with
that sort of thing."
I did, only to be
disappointed again. All I got was
some hocus-pocus, but no cure.

Some there
are who are healers by faith, or at least
that's what they themselves like to say. They said,
"You must confess your sin and call on God.
We will pray, and demand that the demon
leave your son." But all their much demanding
did not heal you, or help in any way.
Then they said it appears that I have no
faith at all. Don't they realize that I
went to them hoping they might have more faith
than I? They did not even tell me how
I was to believe God would heal you now,
when all my prayers and cries for years had gone
like wisps of fog into the silent sky.

Perhaps they would show some compassion if
they knew my groans and tears, the frequent nights
I lay sleepless on your behalf and begged
God to do His work, only to rise at
dawn with the same leaden weight on my heart.
I sometimes thought that I believed, but then
saw much unbelief mixed with little faith
in my struggling mind and heart. Oh, my son,
my son, if I could take your misery and
distress upon myself and set you free,
how gladly would I do it!
Today I
heard once more of that Galilean who
travels here and there, healing all those
suffering from any sickness or disease.
They say he can even cast out demons
with a word. When you're able to travel
I will take you and go to him, and find out who
he is and see what, if anything, he can do.

## Luke
**(Colossians 4:14)**

It is clear what the whole course of my life
would have been had I not met Jesus Christ.
Being a doctor, no doubt I would have
gone on giving medical treatment to
those in need of it, easing the pains of
the sick, and trying to help the dying.
And that would have been what everyone would
have considered a useful life.
At last
I myself would have succumbed to one of
the grim diseases I had been fighting,
and passed away. But passing away to
what and where I would not have been able
to say. And spending my whole life like that
I would have been less and less satisfied.
For at the very core of my being
there was an emptiness, an aching void
which I attempted for a time to fill,
until I despaired of all such attempts.

And even my work, which I loved, began
to seem more and more ineffectual.
Death always gained the final victory.
My doctoring could not prevail against it,
but only delay for a brief time the
day of its triumph.
Then also I thought
there was nothing at all in my life, or,
for all I knew, in anyone's life, which
inescapable death would not destroy.
Doctors do not save lives; all they can do
is postpone for only a brief time the

inevitable. Earth is a vast graveyard
pointing to the final failure of all doctors.

So then life for me was fast becoming
absurd, an almost impossible thing.
I was weighed down by its futility,
and could do nothing to turn things around.
My skill as a doctor could not reach to
the profoundest needs of my inner man.

And then came the day that brought a complete
revolution in all my thoughts and aims.
For I met Jesus, the Physician of
the soul, the One who knows all of our deep
necessities, the One who took up our
infirmities and carried our sorrows,
the One whose compassion brings Him near to
us to heal our inner man, the One who
truly saves lives, not for a brief time but
for eternity–and the only One
who can fill the vacant place in our hearts.
Mine He then filled, filled with Himself, and gave
me a joy and a satisfaction that
I never knew could exist.

Then, when I
entered into Paul's fellowship, I found
my life's work–serving the Lord Jesus Christ.
I consider the service of Christ as
the greatest privilege a human being
can ever have, either on earth or in
heaven, and the service of self as the
most foolish and empty thing possible.
And what people like to label service
to others is often the service of
self in disguise. Need we say that any
such service–serving one's family, or
the sick, or "humanity," or country–
without having the Lord first in one's life,

is a passing thing which may bring a small
satisfaction or reward now, but which
has no recompense in eternity.

Eternity–that is the one word which
defines the worth of what we do in time.
As for me (and I am far from being
alone in this), if I cannot live for
eternity, I no longer wish to
live at all. Only the everlasting
significance of what we can do on
earth makes life tolerable to me now.
And that is found only in God's service.
Therefore let me serve God or let me die.

For as long as I can remember I
always wanted to write, and while still a
boy sometimes tried to put pen to parchment.
One of the great privileges of my
life was to be able to examine
in detail the facts of the birth, life, deeds,
death, and resurrection of our great Lord,
and then by God's Spirit to write them down.

Later, He led me to record His acts
through His apostles in the first decades
of their truly heavenly ministry.
I was witness to some of that myself.

To serve Jesus any way pleased me well,
to serve in this way pleased me better still.
I am old now and soon will go to Him.

What a joy to know at death service is not done!
Our service then will be an everlasting one.

## The Good Samaritan
**(Luke 10:25-37; Matthew 25:31-46)**

If you would ask me why I helped that man,
it was simply because he needed help.
I thought not of his race or his beliefs.
I cared not for his place in life or work,
his attainments in education or
politics, whether he was rich or poor,
whether he was a good man or a bad.

He was a human being, and so he was
my neighbor. His wounds required binding up.
His battered thoughts reached out for my comfort.
His pitiable state cried out for kindness,
for a bed to sleep on and food and rest.
His necessity called out for action.

I am one who knows God and sees God's grace.
In all our deepest needs He does not pass
us by, but stoops to bless. So we must show
this grace of His to everyone we meet
who cry for help and cannot help themselves.

So do not ask me why I helped that man.
Instead ask why in a whole world of pain
most men pursue their selfish ways with not
a thought for other men, with no desire
to lead them to health, happiness, and life,
to bring them to God's blessed place of rest.

Ask why religious men will draw away,
scorning those not of their clique, leaving
the suffering to die in grief, and dreaming
that God is pleased with rituals, prayers and words,

in spite of what they do or do not do.

Ask why the hardened faces, the eyes which
glance and then look aside, the quickened step
away at sight of need, the callousness,
the withered souls, this selfish nonchalance
when faced with the disasters of others,
and all the thoughtless brains and heartless hearts.

Ask why many choose to destroy themselves
by ignoring others in deep distress.

Yes, you who read this now and wonder, ask.
To tell you why will be my willing task.

## The Friend at Midnight
**(Luke 11:5-8)**

I was desperate and it was midnight,
no time to cause trouble to a friend or
risk his anger and rebuke. But I thought,
(was I not right in this?) that if a friend
is not also a friend at midnight, then
he is no true friend at all.
                                        This other
friend had come to me, arriving very late
at my door, tired and hungry from his trip.
Of course, I was glad to see him, but my
heart fell when I remembered that I
had no food in the house, nor even a
scrap of bread. Showing hospitality
is important to me, and those of you
who feel like I do, and who have been through
something like this, will surely understand
my feelings, and my concern for my friend,
in fact, both of my friends.
                                        What should I do?
Let one go hungry? Or go and bother
the other? In the end the need to show
hospitality overcame all my
reluctance, so I went to my friend's house.
As I had feared, he did not seem at all
pleased to have me hammer on his door at
that late hour. He flatly refused to get up,
and showed no willingness to give me what
I asked.
                                I stood there in the cold night air
thinking about the next step. The stars looked
down at me, but gave no advice. What then?
Go back to my house and admit defeat?

Try some other friend? (But I really had
no other nearly as good as this one.)
Knock on the door again?
Fearing further
rebuff, but not wanting to return to
my place empty-handed and embarrassed,
I, somewhat timidly, I admit, knocked
again, and, from behind the locked door, heard
the same words as before.
However I
was fully committed now, and would not
give up. I knocked again, louder this time,
and went on knocking until my friend got up
and gave me what I asked. Much gratitude
is what I felt, and my love for him increased.

Prayer to God is the same. Here is my simple creed:
Keep on knocking in faith. He will give all you need.

## The Rich Fool
**(Luke 12:15-21)**

Once more I seem to have struck it lucky.
I've really never seen the like of it.
All I do turns to gold. What is the cause
of this? Just good fortune? Careful planning?
Hard work? I suppose some of each. Of course,
I've got good land, and can hire some good hands.
And wealth tends to breed wealth, and to begin
I did have some capital laid away.

My neighbor Asher says I ought to thank
God for good crops, that prosperity is
His gift. But I've never seen things that way.
He thanks God for everything, but look at
how he has to struggle to keep soul and
body together.
It seems to me that
the harder he prays the less he receives
(I admit his piece of land is quite small,
and is not of the highest quality).
He goes faithfully to the synagogue
every Sabbath, pays tithes on his income
–such as it is–and gives offerings on
top of that. And see what little results
from all this religious activity!

If poverty is piety's reward
I want nothing at all to do with it.
You would think he would see that it's time to
abandon a method which produces
such meager dividends. Perhaps he lacks
sense. I can't deny that he's a good man.
But for a long time I have observed that

our goodness, or lack of it, has nothing
to do with obtaining the things I want–
success and wealth and the comforts of life.
In fact, it seems to me that goodness may
even be a hindrance to that.
                                        This year
in my prospects I see a big step up.
Never have my fields produced more, never
have my barns been fuller. Now it's time to
expand. My storehouses aren't big enough.
I must tear them down and build bigger ones.
I might do something about this house too.
Fine as it is, it is not the proper
symbol for a man of my affluence.

And I won't have to work so hard now, so
why shouldn't I eat, drink, and be merry?
I'm still in good health, and there's no reason
why I should not live for many years yet.

Yes, after all this has been done, I think that I'll
put my feet up and take life easy for a while.

## The Shepherd
**(Luke 15:4-7)**

A brief time ago when I counted them,
he was gone. When there are so many to
look after, and when, by nature, each one
of them is lacking in judgment and has
a tendency to do his own thing and
to go his own way without thinking of
consequences, it is not as easy
as you might think to keep them safe from harm.

There are so many temptations to draw
them away–too many sheep trampling the
meadow in this one place, that patch of grass
looking more delectable than this one,
that clump of bushes over there exciting
curiosity, and so on. So they
are sometimes determined to explore all
that seems appealing to them, and they show
no apparent concern for the trouble
or peril that may be lurking there.
They seem to be unaware that there are
fierce wolves and lions in these hills who like
nothing more than to sink their teeth into
some sheep or lamb. One might wonder if they
altogether lack imagination.
However that may be I have found that
no animal on earth needs a shepherd
so much as sheep, and that constantly my
heart and attention must remain on them
to save them from disaster.
All can see
that they have no great speed to run away
from predators, no strength in themselves to

resist their savage and determined foes,
not enough brains to outwit them, and no
weapon of tooth or claw to defend their
own lives or the younger ones in the flock.
When it is seen that this lack is combined
with their tendency to wander, men could
well wonder that any of them are kept
safe to the end.

That is where I come in.
I love my sheep and I love my work, and
I am more determined to keep them than
any of their enemies can ever
be to destroy them. And so every one
of them will be brought safely to the fold
at last. They are mine. My name is bound up
with them, and their future depends on me.
My eyes are sharp, my shoulders and hands strong,
and it is the greatest of all my joys
to save the helpless from the lion's mouth.

So though it's true that now one has wandered away,
I'll go and bring him home before the end of day.

## The Rich Young Ruler
**(after meeting Jesus–Mark 10:17-22)**

I can't really say that I have much joy.
Great pleasure and delight in prestige and
wealth, privilege and rank, I have not found.
One wants more than fine clothing and good food,
and servants to fulfill one's every wish,
and the respect of upright fellow men.
I know God has made us for more than this,
and in our hearts has placed eternity.

And perhaps even yet I will find out
what must be done to gain eternal life.
Youth is on my side, and the question is
still of very great importance to me.
So even after my experience
with the Galilean teacher I will
go on searching. Surely someone will give
me a better answer than he has done.
Selling everything I have, giving it
away, and following him doesn't seem
to be the solution to my problem,
but rather to increase difficulties.
And I cannot see the least need for it.

Perhaps there's a slight chance that he is right.
But can one stake his all on such a chance?

My hopes were high that day I went to him,
and getting such an answer made me sad.
How could a reasonable man ever
require such a strange thing of anyone?
And suppose that I did just what he said–
would I not then become an object of

much ridicule to friends and foes alike?
This I would never be able to face.

Now I will spare no effort, no expense,
to learn everything I can about this.
Perhaps I will find the answer in books,
or in the words of another rabbi–
though I have to admit I don't know one
who speaks with such authority as he.

There is certainly no need for me to
give up adherence to the law of God,
or what comfort my religion may give,
because I did not follow his demands.
Can we think that no one has eternal
life who does not obey his every word?
Thinking that would be like rejecting all
of Israel's great scholars and wise men
who do not follow him, and limiting
eternal life to the small ragtag band
that he regards as his true disciples.

Now this is most unlikely to be true.
So I'll ask God to show me what to do.

## Three Views of One Event
**(Luke 15:11-31)**

### The Prodigal Son Returning Home

Leaving was easier than coming back,
far easier. Then I was all glowing
with excitement, and visions of pleasure
and success were drawing me from home.
My feet went dancing in the sunny air.
Now with unsure steps I go on, and stop,
and then go on again, and feel I can't
go on, and know I can't go back. Hard as
it is to look my father in the face,
the thought of returning to what I have
just left fills me with dread.
                There my poor ship
was wrecked on rocks of selfishness and lust,
and left me without life or hope. Ashes
in the mouth, the gnawing worm of remorse,
a conscience defiled, a mind all adrift,
my wasted strength, and all those wasted years,
and the remembrance of that look of pain
on my father's face when I said goodbye–
these are the things I purchased with my wealth,
and corn husks in the sty.
                Where was my sense?
What demon drove me to such lunacy?
No! Blame no vile fiend, but your own vile heart.
Take the guilt yourself or not one step more.
But I can't stay here, and turning back is death.
So I go on for what wealth cannot buy–
mercy and the chance to start life again.

But now there is the house, and I can see

dimly the figure of someone, a man,
and running hard and coming on this way.
It is my father's form, my father's face!

Recall your theme, O tongue, make no excuse
for wicked deeds, but tell things as they are.
He may receive me as a slave. Better
to be that here than enslaved in that far
place to all that's false and wrong. Prepare now
your mind and heart. Rehearse the words to speak.

He draws near. Fall in the dust at his feet!
But what is this? No curse, no blow, no frown–
a huge smile, and tears of joy flooding his cheeks,
and blessed words of welcome with arms wide apart,
now raising me up and drawing me to his heart!

**The Waiting Father**

My boy has gone away on his sad quest.
That day I saw in his eyes that I must
let him go, that no attempts at constraint
could now tame that reckless, determined look,
focused as it was on a distant land.

It was not that life was unpleasant here.
He could not say I did not show him love.
But I am sure he thought that I was strict,
and hedged him in with rules he did not like,
that I was an unceasing threat to his
liberty.
He did not understand that
true liberty is found in obedience
to the laws of love, that living freely
for self is hard slavery.
And wisdom's
words could not move that unsurrendered heart.
A flaw in his nature until then hid

from himself now produced its grim results.

So crying independence off he went
in swift and ignorant pursuit of those
pathetic pleasures of this fallen world.
He will learn yet that sin is the thief of
life and peace, that love and joy are found in
just one place, that at God's right hand are true
pleasures forevermore.
                    My heart is pained.
What would I not give to look on his face
once more, and, if he would permit, for a
moment, hold him close in my arms again!
With my whole soul I want to do him good,
and show him kindness as long as he lives.
Not a day goes by that I do not look
down that long road that took him from our home,
as I am doing now.
                    And who is that?–
that weary traveler, covered with grime,
coming on alone, with ragged clothes and
faltering step, with that gloomy face, and–
that face! It is my boy, my boy! My son!
Coming home again! Now for strength to run!
May not my pounding heart burst in my chest
before I get to him!
                    Now let us kill
the fattened calf! Bring the ring and the best
robe, and dance and sing! This my son was dead,
but now he lives, was lost, but now is found.

This is the one great joy that I have lived to see–
my poor repenting boy coming home to me.

### The Prodigal's Brother

When he went away my one thought was, good,
at last he's gone. He was a selfish clod,

lazy and inconsiderate. His mind
was never on the job at hand, but was
always running here and there through the earth,
thinking of some pleasure or other he
might go and enjoy. And now that
he has returned, my one thought is, the trash
is back to bring grief to our lives again.

"Kill the fattened calf! And let's dance and sing!"
–no, no! Sing and dance for what? For one more
useless mouth to feed? For having that lewd
fornicator staying on here again,
that crude waster of hard-earned property,
that cold destroyer of my father's peace?

And speaking of a "fattened calf"–is it
because I am good that my father has
not once killed one for me? Then the penalty
for my goodness is more than I can bear.
So should I start plotting how to waste his
money, bring dishonor on his home, and
break his heart, as my young brother has done?
Then perhaps I too will get a gold ring,
and splendid robes to wear! And at least one
embrace and kiss of love, and one kind word.

I will not go in. I would rather die
than enter and hypocritically
smile, and dance their insane dance, and sing their
song of welcome to such a one as that.

My father pleads, but he is a father
and has a father's heart, and I do not,
and do not wish to have, if it inspires
such unjust ways. Perhaps I'll go away.
That is, if my brother stays. There can be
no place for me as long as he is here.
But more than likely he will try to get

money from father, and go off again.

One thing is sure: I never want to see
my brother's face and have him smirk at me.

## Rich and Poor
**(Luke 16:19-31)**

### The Rich Man

Here in Hades I raised my eyes and saw,
of all people, the beggar Lazarus
with Abraham and all the saints of God,
across that chasm, there in Paradise,
the only one that I could recognize,
for all my dead friends are imprisoned here.

These flames torment me. Perhaps, I thought, he
would be so kind as to bring water in
a cup to cool my tongue and help to quench
this raging, never-ending thirst. I hoped
one drop would do me good–more good that I
ever did him while we were still on earth.
I drank wine from golden chalices. He
longed for a glass of water from my house,
and longed for it in vain. I closed my heart.
Now I am here and he rests in that place.

I believe that he volunteered to come,
but was stopped by the just laws in force there,
and this deep abyss that kept him out and
keeps me in. And, as to that, will always
keep me in, forever condemned and lost.
The fearful mandates of justice will hold.
I abandoned hope when I entered here.

There is no bail that can provide release
from this grim prison house, and no appeal
to some higher court, and never pardon
here for sins done up there. Despair, my heart,

of ever overturning your lost case.
The gnashing of teeth, the worm and the fire,
and the ceaseless wailing are what you've earned
and what you have received. If I had it all
to do again–but why this vain regret?
Nothing can be changed, and remembering
does no good and adds only to my pain.
My opportunity has come and gone.
I worshiped wealth, not God. No chance will come
again, so forget now, if forget you can.

I am sure now that each desire and hope
I have will fail to be fulfilled, that now
my prayers fall on unresponsive ears.
Even my wish to give my brothers help
came to nothing. They will follow me here.

For the righteous God has done just as He said.
And He hears no pleas in this world of the dead.

**Lazarus the Beggar**

This place is not at all like I thought it
would be–better by far than all my best
conceptions. Fear of death for a man of
faith is foolish and unnecessary.
This is like a great banquet of good things
to a man who's long eaten thrown out scraps,
and crumbs fallen from tables of the rich.
Absolute delight are words that faintly
describe what I feel here, and peace and bliss
such as I never imagined could be.

I knew Abraham immediately,
I really don't know how. And he seemed to
regard me with a special interest
and a quite remarkable affection.
I say remarkable, for he was a

very great man on earth, and I was less
than a nobody, disgusting to all
who looked at me. I recognize a few
people here who had been poor on earth, but
hardly one among those who had been rich.

I fear that those who are pursuing wealth
and earthly possessions will sadly find
they have lost all when they arrive in this
unseen world of the dead, including their
souls. What they love so much will overwhelm
them in ruin and destruction at last.

There across this wide chasm that exists
between Sheol and this place I can see
a very fearful example of this–
the rich man whom I often saw on earth.
Then he dressed in costly clothes, lived in a
mansion, and dined only on the finest
of all fine foods. He spent more on trifles
in a month that I had to live on for
an entire year. And when I lay for days
there in misery and hunger at the
grand entrance of his estate, never once
did he give me so much as a clean crust
of bread.

But now his time for good things is
over and he suffers there in those flames.
I would be glad to carry water to
him but no path exists from here to there.

What a proof he is of the folly of
a life lived for material things and
not for God. On earth I had scant fare,
but God enabled me to trust in Him.

Though I was poor, my faith brought me to Paradise.
He chose unbelief and now pays the dreadful price.

## Zaccheus
**(Luke 19:1-10)**

Though I was quite short in stature, I was
tall in desire to see and know the Lord.
I knew some would laugh when they noticed me,
a rich man, climbing that tree, but I laughed
at them laughing at me–laughed at myself
too. If we don't sometimes find ourselves at
least a bit amusing we will have a
hard time in life.
I well knew, of course, that
because of my profession I was not
popular with the people, and I had
no great care what they thought of me.
And in my hunger to see Jesus I
was willing to risk a few jeers to feast
my eyes on Him as He passed through our town.

Well, there I was up a tree with the crowd
walking in the street below, and He in
the middle of it. So I gazed and gazed,
and listened to all that He had to say,
loving every single moment of it,
but little suspecting that my life was
shortly to be turned completely around.

For He knew I was there and knew my heart,
and glancing upward to me on my limb,
He spoke those words I can never forget:
"I must stay in your house today." O Lord,
stay forever! Now let my home be yours!
Salvation has come to my house this hour.
The poor get half of what I've got. Dear Lord,
take all the rest for yourself. For your one
look, one kind word have won my heart for good.

Yes, He looked and lovingly said to me "Come down"–
to me, who was, I believe, the worst man in town.

## The Poor Widow and Her Offering

**from two points of view (Luke 21:1-4)**

### The Widow

I believe I truly love God, though my
love is a poor weak thing compared to His
love for me. So much so that I sometimes
wonder if what I have is love at all.
However that may be, I know I want
to give an offering that pleases Him.

But what do I have? I think there must be
few in this whole city poorer than I.
For me it's a day's work for a day's food,
with nothing much left over for other
things men usually regard as needs.

Two small coins I have in hand, reward for
hard work. I can hardly bear to think of
giving an offering so small to the
great God of the universe.
I see there
the rich in their fine robes putting into
the box such huge donations that I feel
I should hide my face, go quickly, and give
my two mites and then as quickly be gone.

O God, because of your great love I now would part
with all I have, and giving, give again my heart.

### Jesus

You see them there, those men in their rich clothes
come to tread my courts, hardly knowing what

I desire to see. What homes they live in!
What big amounts they spend on luxuries!
The money that goes from their pockets for
trifles is more than that poor widow can
ever hope to earn by her constant toil.

They are pleased with their offerings, and think
that God is too.
Men look on outward things,
but God looks on the heart. So what really
matters to Him is not how much one gives,
but how much one keeps back to use for self,
and what the motive is which prompts the gift.
So to the Father this poor widow's coins
is worth more than all those rich men's gifts combined,
For out of love she gave Him all she had.

Listen to these words of mine and learn what and how
to give to God. Make this woman your teacher now.

## Nicodemus
**(John 3:1-16)**

I was an old man when I went to Him,
old and experienced and instructed
in all of our religion's sacred books.
And I was a teacher of God's great law
to my people Israel, and always
tried to practice what I preached. But in spite
of my knowledge and experience I
was puzzled by Him.
I was sure that He
was a teacher whom God had sent to us,
but His teaching was quite different from
the things we usually taught or heard.
If it had not been for His miracles
perhaps I would have regarded Him as
just another itinerant preacher,
though He spoke out with great authority.
But because of those mighty miracles,
the evidence for which I could not deny,
I did not doubt that He was a special
messenger from God, at the very least,
and wished to hear more words from His own mouth.

Going to Him at night seemed the sensible
thing to do. He was more likely to be
free from the crowds which pressed around Him in
the day. And, to be perfectly truthful,
I would add that I thought by going then
there would be less chance of my being seen
by those who might raise objections to my
going, or even jeer at such a thing.

His first words filled me with astonishment.
I had never before heard of being
born again. Yes, I confess that I was
completely ignorant concerning this.

Now, while reading the Scriptures again with
understanding, I see His teachings there–
sinful human nature can never keep
God's holy law as it ought to be kept.
It has never done so and never will.
And we are all sinners by birth and deed,
and so come short of what God wants of us.
"There is none righteous, no, not one" are words
God Himself has spoken of our whole race.
And through the prophets He spoke of a day
when He would take away hearts of stone and
give new hearts of flesh and write His laws on them.
A new nature, a new heart–these we must
have, or forever perish in our sins.

I believed Him that same night, bent my grey
head to obey the heavenly truth that
His mouth spoke, and became a little child.

In that life-changing hour God's Spirit entered my
humbled, trembling heart, and I was born from on high.

## Woman at the Well
**(John 4:4-42)**

What I went out for was just a pot of
water and now my whole life has been changed.
And my secret has come out. Now the world
knows that I, this senseless woman, was keen
on men and went from one to another
hardly without a break.
It didn't take
long for me to discard one, if I saw
another I liked better. What else did
I have to do? My whole life was empty,
and I wanted to fill it with something.
In my great ignorance, I turned to the
one thing I had tasted that seemed to ease,
for a time at least, that awful feeling
of emptiness. Of course, I mean pleasure.
Having no God, it was either pleasure
or hard work I had to choose, and who wants
hard work? I hope you don't mind my being
so frank. I learned from Someone to tell things
as they are. Or, I should say, as they were.
For that same Someone revolutionized
my life, and filled up the hole in my heart.

Filled it with what? With real love, the kind that
lasts forever and knows no change, except
to grow more dear, God's love. And how did God
get into all this? The Jews' Messiah
brought Him in, that day when I met Him at
the well. Now living water always springs
up in me, and my dry well overflows,
and life, eternal life, and love are mine.

Afterwards I had a time deciding
how to sort out my life and still please God.
What can one do about five previous
husbands (yes, I had five), and about the
man not my husband I was living with?
I will let you guess how I worked things out.
You know enough already about me,
and I don't wish to tell you any more.
Every woman likes to keep some secret.

But there is no secret in how the Lord
fills up the empty place and gives us joy
and glorious freedom. Go straight to Him.
If He received me with all my sins, He will you.
Raising up the fallen is what He loves to do.

## The Paralyzed Man
### of John 5:1-15

"Do you want to be healed?" he said to me
in my total helplessness and misery,
there by Bethesda's pool, with the milling
crowd around, all bent on getting in the
water first, and all unconscious of me.

Did I want to be healed? What sort of question
was that to ask me? I've been a cripple
for 38 long, long years, and have come here
often. Why did he think I was here if
I didn't want to be healed? Maybe he
wants to mock me, or at least suggest how
meaningless is any such dream of mine.
Or could he imagine I was a mere
spectator, there out of curiosity?
Was he a doctor with a partial cure,
or at least wanting me to think he was?

These were the kind of thoughts that raced through my
brain as I sat there and looked up at him.
But something in his tone of voice and in
the look on his good face gave me some hope.
I could see he was serious, and so
I spoke very politely to him and
explained the case.

Again he spoke to me,
"Get up! And take up your pallet and walk!"
My first thought was, I am a cripple and
I can"t get up or walk. Is he some sort
of madman? But closely gazing at him
I could see nothing but compassion and
a calm authority.

And all at once
I got up, and I stooped down and picked up
my pallet and I walked, and I stared at
my crippled legs and they were no longer
crippled. And I didn't even know his name.
I don't fathom everything to this day.
All I know is this: faith suddenly came
to me that I could do just what he said
and that his power would enable me.

He met me later and said something I
didn't much like, for it worried me a lot:
"Stop sinning, or something worse may happen
to you." So am I such a sinner then?
And was I crippled because of my sin?
Which sin exactly? Or was it all of them?
And what did he mean by "something worse"
than being lame? Maybe some day I'll know.
I'm always thinking now about his words.

That's my story–no stretching the truth, not a bit.
And you say you cannot believe it? Believe it.

## The Blind Man
**of John chapter 9**

I did not know why I was blind from birth
until the Lord Jesus Christ explained it.
The disciples too did not understand.
I heard them inquiring about it all–
without, it seems, any wish to help me.
Their problem was just theological,
untouched by a feeling of sympathy.
I wonder if this is normal with them.

It was not a reason that one could guess.
How could my blindness bring glory to God?–
this was no easy question in my mind.
The blind alone can know what I went through.
I did not know what was meant by "seeing."
When people said to one another "Look
at that" I could never know what the "that"
that they looked at looked like.
I could hear words
like "breathtaking," but those things never took
my breath. Exclamations such as "Beautiful!"
and "Magnificent!" left me in the dark.
Once they spoke of how lovely were the stars
at night and the soft moonlight falling on
the hills around our home, but when I asked
them to explain, they could not enlighten me.

I learned to walk without bumping into
things or falling in a ditch, and could even
grope my way on unknown ground. But the faces
of my dear parents I had never seen.
I never read a book, or studied in
a school, or even learned the alphabet.

But in spite of all this I had a mind,
and, I dare to think, a logical one.

My parents (how I thank God for them) taught
me many things, including some great things
from our Holy Book. Though one has no eyes,
if he has ears he can make use of them.
So I had some precise thoughts about God,
which were made clear by His revelation
to my spirit, which has eyes of its own,
not dependent on any outer sight.

Then, as I said before, the Lord came by.
He did not tell me what He meant by God
being glorified through me–He showed me.
Can mud on the eyes give them sight? Can the
water in Siloam's pool where I went?
Yet when I washed them there quite suddenly–
praise His holy name!–just like that, I saw.

For instantly light streamed into my eyes and mind.
What but God's power could ever heal a man born blind?

## The King Who Gave a Feast
**(Matthew 22:1-14 with Luke 14:16-24)**

I wanted my citizens to feast on
good things. And so all that a heart of love
and a mind inspired by benevolence
could ever plan, and a lavish hand could
prepare, I planned and prepared for them in
that great wedding banquet for my dear son.
And to the invited I sent my men
to ask them to come.
                    What was the result?
Something hard to imagine or believe–
utter indifference.
                    Again I showed
my genuine desire to have them come
by sending servants different from the first
to speak with what I thought were clearer, more
persuasive words: "My oxen, my fattened
cattle have been prepared, and all things are
ready. So now come to the wedding feast."

But they met with arrogance, defiance,
and hostility. For this offense of
inviting others to my banquet hall
they were despised, cursed, beaten, kicked, tortured,
and jailed. Some were killed by stoning, and some
beheaded by the sword or sawn in two.
And some had to roam about, far from home,
persecuted, afflicted, destitute.
And all of these were servants of the king!
And their tormenters were my own subjects
whom I had always treated with complete
kindness and love!

So rage is justified.
Judgment must now fall on such wickedness,
or else rule of law in the universe
falls. Clear-sighted justice calls for action.
This city will be given to the fire.

And my banquet, prepared and waiting here?
Must my dining hall now remain without
diners? I will send other servants now.
And my word to them is this: Bring all you
can find, I care not who they are or what
they have done. Bring both the good and the bad.
Bring the poor, the foolish, the weak, the lame,
the sick, the hard and ignorant.
Bring the
liars, the unchaste, the drunkards, the thieves.
Pull them from their hiding places in the
hedges, from behind high and stony walls.
Drag them from the gutter dripping with filth.
Bring them in if they are eager to come,
or careless; yes, even if at first they
kick and scream. Speak kindly and bring them in.

Believe me, my house must be filled with guests.
And I will show them love, and see that they
are fully washed, and give white robes to wear.

Hear now this narrative and learn, if learn you can,
some defining qualities of both God and man.

## The Household at Bethany
**(Luke 10:18-42; John 11:1 - 12:11)**

### Martha

True, I am a worker, always wanting
to keep busy. If I sit when some task
is waiting I feel a fire in my bones.
Always there is so much that needs to be
done, and I never seem to get caught up.

I do sometimes wish I had more time for
prayer and meditation, but the work
so presses on my heart I can't relax
and let it go until some other day.

Mary is quite different. The house may
be turned upside down, and every dish and
pot in the kitchen may be dirty, and
she can sit for hours listening to
Jesus. Her behavior can be very
exasperating.
I said something once,
but was rebuked for my attempt to get
her to do some chore that was crying out
to be done. I was informed that she had
chosen the better thing. All very well,
but someone had to see that there was some
food put on the table.
That sounds a bit
bitter, and this is something I do not
chose to be. Jesus is the Lord. He knows
better than I what the better thing is.
Yes, He knows, and I will really try to
make more of an effort to sit down when

He comes again, let the work go, and just
listen to Him. I will not be upset
if Mary takes the whole day off to do
the same. And I will not worry even
though things remain undone and we have to
eat late and have only cold leftovers.

At least, I promise myself that I will
act like this, but I know how difficult
it is to go against one's own nature.
But this I will try, really try, to do.
And I will pray that God will help me too.

**Mary**

Our home was His, and our hearts too were His.
We all loved Him, Lazarus and Martha
and I. So it came as a complete shock
to learn that some people in Israel
were demanding His rejection and death.

When it appeared that He was facing this
I wished to show all that was in my heart,
and I thought of the perfume I had there,
the best and most costly thing I possessed.

Often to Him I had poured out heart and soul.
Martha sometimes thought I was shirking work,
but I was only choosing one of two
good things, and chose the better of the two.
For I loved to sit at His feet and hear
the gracious words that issued from His mouth.
Now on those feet I poured the fragrant oil–
thus preparing Him for burial–
then dried them with my hair.
We all know this:
No grave will long have power over Him.
He is the resurrection and the life,

and He will rise triumphant over death.
I believe this, and in my heart's deep grief
can rejoice too in what the future brings.
His mortal sufferings will shortly cease,
and Paradise will claim Him as its own.

In our home here He always had a place.
There, through grace, I know we will have a place
in His. Here we gladly welcomed Him and
showed Him our love. There He will welcome us and be
loving toward us throughout all eternity.

**Lazarus**

I had never been more ill in my life.
Martha and Mary sent for Him, but He
didn't come in time to save me from death.
Quite suddenly the angel drew near and
I heard a wail from someone, and, just like
that, I was gone. I remained nearby for
a time wondering what would happen next.
I kept looking down from–from where I was.

Jesus did not come for three or four days.
By then my body had been bound in grave
clothes and placed in the tomb. It had begun
to decompose, but there was nothing I
could do about it. So I just watched and
waited–it was clear God wanted me to.

At last the Lord Jesus Himself came there.
I knew He was there, and I heard Him speak
to the Jews and to Martha and Mary.
And He wept (and this almost broke my heart).

Then He prayed. And as always His prayer was
direct, earnest, and simple in language.
Of course, I had no idea at all

what He would do next. You can imagine
how astonished I was when He called out
with authority,
"Lazarus, come forth!"

No one could resist a command like that.
My spirit (that is, I myself) entered
my body, which then became fresh and new,
and I came forth alive, raised from the dead.

I was prepared and happy to go when
I went, and prepared and happy to come
back when I came back. I had learned before
that God's will is best, and for a long time
I had been ready to live, or to die.
And I still am. Again. All praise to Him.
Like this He conquered the grave and delivered me.
You should believe the One who showed such mastery.

## Caiaphas

**(John 11:47-53–the day after the death of Christ)**

You must first understand that I do not
really believe in messiahs. Not that
one at any rate. My head is not in
the clouds and my eyes are not fixed
on the beyond.
I am a pragmatist.
The here and now is what interests me.
I believe in getting the most from good
situations, making the best of bad ones,
and getting on with my job whatever
may take place.
As for this recent matter:
My situation was quite difficult.
It seemed that a revolt was imminent,
a rebellion that would soon have brought down
the might of Roman arms on our poor heads.
So, as high priest, I had to be concerned
with the good of the whole of Israel.

It is far better for one man to die
than for this nation to be crushed again.
I do not like to condemn any man.
But at this time it was expedient,
the one way I could see to save us all.

And we were all aware of God's just law
that blasphemers do not deserve to live.
Sad it is to end one's days crucified,
and I could never wish such a thing on
any man. But certainly the world will
be a far better place without that one.

For now at long last with him gone I can be sure
that the nation, and my own place, will be secure.

## Judas Iscariot

**(on his was to betray Jesus–Matthew 26:14-25)**

I hardly seem in control of myself,
yet I'm doing exactly what I want.
I must look back in this decisive hour,
and try to comprehend just what I do.

Going about with his appointed group,
and performing miracles just as they,
I have felt elation at it all, but,
my heart, I must confess I never have
understood either you or those events.
I am not much devoted to the Lord,
but yet I could do those miracles. This
is a puzzle. Or does it simply prove
that a man need not be a godly one
to do some astonishing feats like those?
For godly was never the word I would
have used about myself–not that I think
that I am all that terrible a chap.

And I could never really believe
that he is the Messiah, although he
certainly did some very striking things.
He healed lepers and multiplied the bread;
he walked on water and he raised the dead.
All this I saw with my own eyes. He is
more than your ordinary sort of man.
But I've never received him in my heart,
and never wanted to obey his words.

At times some force in my nature made me
daring in my acts–I stole from the purse
even when I knew it was dangerous.

Not much could ever be concealed from him;
he knew what sort of character I am.
I could fool the disciples, but not him.
With them all at this Passover he knew
it was me. And then a dark shadow came
hovering, and I entered it. Or did
the shadow enter me?
                                        Perhaps now I
am not acting in a rational way.
But, of course, a man has to look out for
himself, and acquire as much as he can,
if he wants any real security.

Do I hate him? Sometimes I have thought so.
At least I know that I do not love him.
I don't know what the priests will do to him,
but why should I care about that, as long
as I get the hard cash? That's the big thing.
And I do wish I had demanded more to come
to an agreement. I asked too small a sum.

## Pontius Pilate
### (Matthew 27:11-26. Many years after Christ's death)

I know what you will want to say to me–
I should have dealt with that case with far more
skill and sensitivity than I did.
I know I let those fanatical Jews
pressure me into action some will think
unwise. But try to see it in this way:

Religion has never meant much to me,
and the passion, the fierce intensity,
it arouses in people has always
surprised me. In this case, because of it,
sensing a real threat to order and law
(also, I should add in all honesty,
to my own position as governor),
and not wanting to provoke the large mob
to any more disturbance of the peace,
I was forced to listen to their demands.
I confess that I was not prepared for
their frenzied zeal, and so was swayed by it.

Nor was I prepared for the one they brought
before me to judge–a strange man indeed.
To this day I regard him as unique.
He had quite unearthly serenity.
His eyes, his face spoke of secret power.
Facing a possible sentence of death,
he showed no flicker of alarm or fear.

It almost seemed to me that he felt he
himself was the one appointed in charge
of matters, that all must take place as he
had already considered and approved.

He did not try to flatter me at all,
or to tilt any judgment I might make.
It seemed that he was more concerned for me
than for himself or what might happen next.

I knew that he was not guilty at all
of the charge that had brought him there to me.
And I firmly refused to condemn him.
I would never condemn the innocent.
You say handing him over to the Jews
to put him to death was the same as my
condemning him. But look at the record.
The truth is, I did my best to save him.
And I forcefully declared both my own
innocence and his. Washing my hands said
this better than even my words could do.

Of course, I doubt you will listen to me,
but, believe me, my conscience is quite clear.
So go on, make your accusations; you will find
nothing will disturb me, or ever change my mind.

## Barabbas

**(Matthew 27:15-26–shortly after Christ's crucifixion)**

It was very hard to believe they meant
it when they came and said "You're free to go."
I knew that I was guilty of murder
and rebellion against the Roman state.
I also knew that those caught as I was
were not given their liberty. Quite the
opposite. I had only one prospect
as I waited in that foul prison cell–
agonizing death on a Roman cross.

Before they came I had heard some shouting
of my name among other cries from near
the governor's palace, but could not think
what was meant when the mob roared with one
voice: "Barabbas! Barabbas!" Now I know.
It meant my freedom and another's death.

I followed them all the way to the hill
of Golgotha to see what person the
roaring mob thought more worthy of the cross
than I myself. He certainly did not
look like such a man, but seemed a meek and
gentle sort of person. On his face there
was nothing indicating cruelty,
no evidence of depravity or vice.
Patient suffering was all I could see.
He uttered no blasphemies, no curses
on his enemies. In fact, until raised
up on the cross He hardly spoke at all.
I could not imagine what threat he could
ever pose to the iron rule of Rome
that should cause them to treat him as they did.

But I was glad enough that he was there
to die in my place.
                                        Then I heard him say,
"Father, forgive them. They do not know what
they're doing." These words did not strike me as
being those of a vicious criminal.
He went on to say other things, which I
don't now remember. But the impression
I received that day remains with me now:
He was a good man somehow caught up in
something both Romans and Jews considered
dangerous to them all. I don't see how.
As for me, from now on I will take care.

For to be caught once more means death. It's very plain
no other substitute will die for me again.

## The Centurion at the Cross
**(Matthew 27:54)**

I was there when they brought Him in to be
whipped. I wasn't pleased to see Him, for I
am always uneasy when this goes on.
I know some soldiers who actually
seem to enjoy it, and try to inflict
as much distress and damage as they can.
And I wondered how this man would endure
a beating with one of those barbaric whips.

I say "barbaric" for that's what they are.
Call me soft, but I've never liked to see
them used on a fellow human being,
no matter how degenerate he might be.
Too often I have seen those metal bits
bite to the very bone, tear away the
skin and flesh from the back, and expose the
body"s vital organs through the rib cage.
I'd seen men die from shock and loss of blood,
and had no wish to see it again now.

He took it well–far better than I had
ever seen. Not a curse, no begging words
to stop, not a cry for mercy escaped
his lips, In fact, He said nothing at all.
Did this cause those doing the work to be
more determined to make Him scream and plead?
But He did not, even though the beating
they gave was quite savage and pitiless.
One could see even His strong frame grow weak.
When it was over I was surprised that
He was still able to walk, and later
on carry His cross for a little way.

I was there on the hill when they nailed Him
to that cross–another barbaric and
brutal custom I wish we Romans would
bring to an end. Maybe I have too much
imagination, but I could almost
feel the spikes go through my own wrists and feet,
when they went through His.
And afterwards I
saw His agonizing attempts to thrust
Himself upwards by His tearing feet to
draw deep breaths, and avoid painful death by
suffocation. The bones of His shoulders
and arms were out of joint, all the muscles
and ligaments stretched to the full. And still
He spoke not a single word of complaint.
He seemed much more concerned for others than
for Himself, and even prayed that God might
forgive those who were crucifying Him.
Such love, such meek patience, such dignity
I'd never seen before in dying men.

Then that mysterious darkness that fell at noon!
And at His death the quaking earth and splitting rocks!
So when His final drops of blood fell to the sod,
I spoke (and meant) those words:"This was the Son of God."

## The Two Crucified Thieves
**(Matthew 27:44; Luke 23:39-43)**

### The Unrepentant One

The only thing I'm sorry about is
this: I got caught. It's too late for me to
deny that I did what they say I did,
so I won't bother with that. The fact is
I know, and I know that my accusers
know, that I broke those man-made laws of theirs.
But they do not know, and I'm sure do not
even care to know, that when I broke those
laws, I felt they were not my laws, and that
breaking them had no importance at all.

One more thing–if I had my life to live
over again, being in the same sort
of situation I was in, I would
do, more or less, the same things as before.
But I'd be more careful not to get caught,
and so, perhaps, escape this unjust death.

Not for one moment do I believe this
punishment fits my crimes, if crimes they were.
It never struck me that taking from those
who have plenty, to fill needs in my life,
was something to be condemned. My conscience
never troubled me then, and does not now.

As for the idea of sin, I can't
really believe there is such a thing.
If there is a God at all (something a
reasonable person is bound at times to doubt)
I don't think He is much concerned with

what we do, or makes any laws for men.
And if He makes no laws for them and I
make no laws for them, why should they make laws
for me?
I am convinced that we can do
anything we need to do to survive.
Life is far more important than man's laws,
and all things we think to do for a good
life, are lawful. This has been my motto
for years, and I see no need to change now.
For at last we all come to the same place.

Look at this weakling who says he's the Christ–
feeble and pathetic and crucified.
Some Messiah! His religion, faith and
high-sounding principles have brought him to
a cross, just as my own ways have brought me.
Such things are useless. I will not give up
beliefs I've long held because of these pains.
Certainly no fear of hell, no thought of
paradise can change my mind. There will be
no so-called deathbed repentance for me.

**The Repentant One**

At first I thought the same as my friend there
on the far cross–that the one crucified
between us was like us in character,
but with a thin veneer of righteousness,
which the officials concerned with His case
had seen through. This amused our darkened hearts,
and we opened our mouths in ridicule.
Religious pretension we could not stand.

They read it out–the sign above his head:
"This is Jesus of Nazareth, the King
of the Jews." And the rulers sneered at him:
"If this is the Christ of God, the Chosen

One who saved others, let him save himself."
And the chief priests and teachers of the law
also mocked him: "He said, 'I am the Son
of God.' If he is the King of Israel,
let him come down from the cross and then we
will believe."

And so I began to think,
hanging here in my pain, that He is not
really like us at all. The soft words He
spoke we certainly never would have used,
His patient conduct was foreign to us,
and His face when He turned to look at me
was not the hard face of a criminal.
I saw there, not hate, not arrogance, not
deceitfulness, but humble love, and light,
and, strangest of all things, concern for me.

It's hard to explain what's happening now.
Those rumors I heard about Him, that He
did those awesome miracles, and that He
always showed compassion to everyone–
maybe it's all true. And those teachings I
learned at my mother's knee, and believed then–
how strongly now they come back to my mind!

A strange warmth possesses me, and new hope.
It seems that God Himself is around us,
and beginning to work in my hard heart.

Now I think I believe this impossible
thing–that He really is the Son of God.
Yes, here is Christ, the Lord, the promised King,
and Savior of bad men! And I am a
bad man, a thief and a robber, and one
who has just now scorned and insulted Him.
And thieves go to hell, not to Paradise.

Will He hear my prayer? Once more He looks my way,
and His eyes tell me what I need to know:

God's grace ignores our deserved destiny.
So I dare to speak: "Lord, Remember me."

## God the Father
**(as Christ hung on the cross)**

There He hangs now, my only Son, my heart,
rejected, despised, condemned, crucified,
calling to me in misery and pain,
"My God, my God, why have you forsaken me?"
And I? I have had to leave Him there and
bring this anguish on both myself and Him.
I am the Father and have a father's
heart, and I am all-powerful and can
with one word save Him now from evil men.
And yet I cannot, even though my heart breaks
with His.
In accordance with the ancient
purpose of the Trinity, our plan to
save men in this way, made with all wisdom
and foreknowledge, I must let Him suffer
there, desolate, forsaken, and bearing
the crushing weight of the world's sins and crimes
committed against Him and me. I had
to let mad bulls surround Him, raging and
roaring lions open their mouths at Him,
wicked men encircle Him and pierce His
hands and feet.
My own hand had to fall on
Him to punish the evil deeds of men,
to strike and afflict and wound Him to death.
It was my will to bruise Him, to put Him
to grief, to make His soul an offering
for sin. Yes, my hand had to fall on Him.
Am I not free? Am I not God? But love
has compelled me, love for the human race,
love for the fallen, the sinful, the lost.

And I can see the dawning day, when His
sufferings will end and He, risen from
the dead, will stand in my presence with men
redeemed by this one sacrifice, sinless,
justified, glorified eternally.

How I long for mankind to know me and
my ways! With my powerful word I made
heaven and earth and all that in them is,
and by these things gave revelation of
my eternal power and divinity.

And I spoke through all my prophets of old,
rising early and sending them, giving
them my own Spirit, inspiring them to
write my very words, so that all mankind,
wherever they may be, might truly learn
what I am, what I do, and what I want.

But here at my Son's cross I speak more clearly still.
See my grace and mercy displayed toward you. See
my nature, my mind, my heart. Look and learn of me.
Repent, believe my Son, accept my righteous will.

## Joseph of Arimathea
**(Matthew 27:57-60)**

He lay there on the hard ground of the hill,
His sad lifeless features relaxed in peace,
His brow marked with the wounds from the tearing
thorns and his whole face with the streaks of dried
blood that had formed twisting rivulets like
crimson tears down His gentle countenance.
His lacerated back lay in the dirt,
and His eyes stared sightless into the sky.
The holes in His wrists and feet and side tore
at my heart, and his bones all out of joint
made my own ache.
Our Teacher, our Messiah
was dead, impossible as that had seemed
to us. Could He not have, by one great act
of power, by one divine miracle,
escaped the cross and overcome His foes?
For some reason He did not. But what that
reason was we could not then understand.

I had a tomb, newly cut from the rock,
in which I thought my own body would rest
in death one day. Now I knew that it was
His body and not mine which must rest there.

Pilate the Roman governor was an
ungodly, haughty, egocentric man,
and it took some courage for me to go
and ask him for the body of our Lord.
After making sure that He was really dead,
He agreed.
So my friend Nicodemus
and I took His body away and with

a great weight of myrrh and aloes wrapped Him
tight in strips of linen cloth and laid Him
in my tomb. After seeing its large stone
rolled in front of it, so the place would be
undisturbed, I went straight home.

There I stayed,

broken in spirit and in heart until
the third day. Then resurrection from the
dead raised my hopes again to heights till then
unknown. Jesus lives! His mortal body,
made immortal now by power from on high,
came through the rigid stone to walk our streets again
and give eternal life in place of death and pain.

## Mary Magdalene
**(Mark 16:9)**

You, you normal people, can never dream
what it is like to have demons living
in your own body, and making you their slave,
and each day working out their will through you.
I know, for that was my life all too long.
I was possessed by malignant powers,
and their thoughts often seemed like my own thoughts,
their evil goadings like my own desires.
Their fear was my fear, their desolation
was my desolation.
                    I was caught in
a trap of my making. I let them in,
and later could not get them out again,
weep and wail and rage as I might, and did.

One day the Lord Jesus came, my Savior
came, the one with complete authority
over demons, yes, and everything else.
He spoke just the one word, and I was free–
free! Free to think His thoughts and do His will,
and now to follow Him along life's road,
and to love Him now and forevermore.

This glorious freedom of the children
of God! Who can describe it? Who can feel
it but those who've known their own slavery?

He who has been forgiven much loves much,
He once said. Who, then, should love more than I?
The worst of sinners, once redeemed, must then
adore Him even more than others can
who have not known the depths that some have known.

I give Him the gift of my love. My tears
flowed for His pains, my heart now rejoices
in His victory over sin and death.

I stand here alone at the empty tomb
and know that He has risen from the dead.
And never again will I belong to
anyone else, anyone else at all.
Nothing and no one else will ever reign in me,
for my heart is His, now and for eternity.

## The People of Jerusalem
**(after Christ's resurrection)**

Why don't they give up–those disciples of
that false messiah? We thought that when he
was crucified that would be the end of it.
But, no, now they have invented one more
strange tale, and this one wilder than the rest.
Risen from the dead indeed! How can men
believe old wives' tales like this? But there are
some who do. Rumors floating around put
the number at several thousand now who
profess to be his followers here in
Jerusalem alone–a figure which,
of course, is highly exaggerated.

We predict that before too long, in spite
of these attempts to create fables and
rewrite history, this nonsense will come
to an end, and the wide world outside will
never hear the name of Jesus or learn
of how he met his death as a condemned
criminal on a Roman cross–a death,
we might add, that he fully merited.
To be eternally forgotten is
what he deserves and what he will get.

For on the whole we still stand firm against
such madness as he and his followers
exhibited, and cling to the teachings of
the law of God, and the traditions of
the scribes and Pharisees.
And in this we
will find our safety, just as our great high
priest has said. With their leader dead and gone,

the revolt has been squashed, Rome's armies have
not marched, and we look forward to a long
and prosperous reign under the king we
reluctantly chose, Caesar (certainly
he was a better choice than the one whom
Pilate mockingly presented to us).

Now we will wait in peace and hope that soon
the real Messiah will come, rescue us
from our enemies, and set us free from
all bondage to anyone, anywhere.

He will not be some meek carpenter from
an unimportant place like Nazareth,
not some rabble rouser who gathers to
him some poor weak specimens of mankind,
not a mere talker who does nothing to
throw off the Roman yoke, but a man of
war whose credentials will be the proper
ones, whose right actions will fulfill right words.

You may be sure that He will not be at a loss
to know what to do, and will not die on a cross.

## The Fool
**(of Psalm 14:1, full of words)**

There is no God. If God there were, He would
not make a world like this. Stop now and look
out there for yourself. Put aside for a
moment, if you can, all the religious
brainwashing you have had, and for this once
look reality in the face. If you
want the truth, view things as they are, not as
you hope they are. For beliefs must be based,
not on whims, but on unbiased probing
of the evidence we have.
So now look.
In this whole world do you see anything
appealing to wise and sensitive minds?

Look at all the suffering life of beasts,
the unchangeable law of the jungle
where each cruelly feeds on those weaker
than itself, and terror, pain and blood, night
and day, cry to the heedless sky.
See the
lion's savage claws, the startled fear of
the tender fawn, and the beast's hot fangs on
its delicate throat.
Look at the tearing
teeth of the crocodile as it lurks near
the edge of the stream waiting for some child
to come to the edge. And now hear that child
give terrified screams as it disappears
beneath the water's surface, and then see
how his innocent blood comes swirling up.

Then tell me, is your loving "God" behind

that? Is this the best world that an all-wise,
all-powerful one can cause to exist?

Now look at man, the presumed crowning work
of your presumed creator and great God.
Time and again they show themselves far worse
than any beast. Lions and crocodiles,
which kill to eat, are soft compared to them.
Among mankind what frightful homicides!
What senseless crimes against their fellow men!
What wars! What genocides! What holocausts!
What abuse of infants! What rapes of the
innocent! What groans and tears in the night!
What unheard prayers and cries to the still sky!
What woeful suicides in sheer despair
at such a vile, uncaring, and senseless
world as this!
Will you say that the one who,
according to you, made the world and now
rules it, is not responsible for this?

Let us come to earthquakes and volcanos,
tornados, hurricanes, famines and floods.
I suppose that some of you will think
it is perfectly all right for the God
you insist you believe in to go on
drowning the old and the helpless, the young
and innocent, or starving them to death,
or pouring out burning ashes on their
heads and molten lava on their poor homes,
or violently shaking the ground under
their feet, so that they and all they have and
their pathetic cries are forever gone.

If men did such things you would brand them as
monsters, and worthy of the lowest hell.
But when "God" does them you are strangely quiet.
Tell me the truth. If creator there be,

is he not responsible for this too?
Is he deaf? Blind? Or simply unconcerned?
Or is his heart filled with malevolence?

Is it not far more sensible to think
that no kind of good God is possible?
And the thought of a bad God is not a
thing we can bear.
Lastly, take a long look
at religion. Should we not think that since
believers in God are what they are, the
God they say they believe cannot be real?
Should we not judge whether there is a God
by those who profess to be his children?
But can I, can you, can anyone, see
any great difference between those who
profess this and the many who do not?
Do not all men have the same faults and "sins?"

Or, to say only the truth, are not those
known as religious people guilty of
worse crimes against each other and against
mankind as a whole than anyone else?
Persecutions, tortures and murders in
the name of God are all too common things.

Yes, look well at religious men and see
the veneer without, the venality
within, the shameless lust for wealth, power,
and fame, and all the brazen hypocrisies
with which the so-called righteous people of
their "righteous God" have made their profession
a mockery and burlesque.
The wanton
behavior of men with high-sounding creeds
makes honest unbelievers feel contempt,
both for them and for the God they proclaim.
There can be God, or all this, but not both.

Oh, there's beauty out there, we all know that,
but not such beauty that could not have come
by itself, as matter formed together
in an orderly way, without any
supervision from anyone. I say
matter has this innate ability.
Can you ever hope to show it does not?
Or prove that matter is not eternal?
There was never any need for a God,
and no more reason to believe in one
than to believe in matter's own potent
capability.
                    All that I've described
above could result from matter itself,
but not from any kind of good God that
intelligent people can conceive of.
But why go on? I've surely said enough.

Nothing I say will change your minds before the dawn
of clear thinking in you. Until that day, dream on.

## The Believer
**(2 Corinthians 4:13)**

Once my mouth too was filled with arguments
feeding atheism and unbelief.
In the days of my ignorance I too
attributed all the worst events on
earth to a God I denied, and ignored
all the good that we meet with day by day,
always grumbled about what displeased me,
never gave thanks for anything at all.

I did not then comprehend that the real
destroyers of the world are the sinful
human race and its unseen enemy,
the devil, with whom mankind sides in
his mad revolt against heaven's King.

I did not know what now I understand–
that even the very worst disasters
which afflict us are less than we deserve;
that before man turned his back on God
no tooth or claw ever came against him,
no tempest, fire or flood endangered him,
no sorrow, pain or death entered his home;
that by acting against God's nature man
turned nature against himself and so brought
destruction to what had been paradise.

Nor did I even guess that, if He wished,
God could conceal Himself from sinful eyes
behind the material worlds our eyes
can see, or that there was such a thing as
spiritual sight which can discern Him there.
Sightless myself I foolishly supposed
that no such sight could be.

In mercy God
came to me, and in the light He gave I
began to see that atheism is
a kind of madness, a withdrawal from
spiritual reality. Without proof
of any kind I had been forward to
deny those things which people now made sane
know to be true.
An easy task had the
sly, exhausted Sisyphus compared with
that of atheists, who try to prove the
unprovable, saying that God does not
exist, as if their saying so would make
it so, and, for the dreadful arrogance
of their unbelief, must push their stony
thoughts on to eternity, staking their
all on false suppositions and empty
conjectures without a hope in the world.

There came that day when I no longer could
pursue with grim determination my
own way. I called out to God, believing
that if He could not hear, nothing was lost,
but that if He could, there would be great gain.
A presence came which I could not mistake,
and a voice to my heart I had never
thought to hear. Willingly I listened and
so came to learn that what Jesus had once
said about the Father and Himself was
true:
*"If anyone is willing to do
God's will, he will know whether my teaching
is of God, or whether I speak on my own."*

So, having been made willing, I came to
know the living God, and to believe in Him,
and at once could see that none so honest
as Jesus Christ has ever walked the earth.

And what is the foundation for my faith?
His authoritative words, His character,
His sacrificial death in love for us,
His glorious resurrection from the dead,
and all those many prophecies fulfilled
in Him, His Spirit moving in my heart,
and a continuing experience
that all He taught concerning God and man
accords with the deepest reality–
God's unique holiness, mercy and love,
and my own utter sinfulness and need;
my dullness of mind about God's deep ways,
His delight to teach those who look to Him.

Now try this for yourself and learn it all,
for God still hears the voice of those who call.

## Stephen
**(facing the stone-carrying mob–Acts 7)**

Should I think my denunciation was
too strong, or that I was too bold or rash?
With my courage should I have shown caution?
I thought that strong opposition to truth
demanded strong measures to oppose it,
that soft words would have been betrayal of
my Lord who died strongly denouncing men's
lies and their whole deceiving way of life.
And then His Spirit welled up in my heart.

If I could have the opportunity
to relive my brief life, another chance
to stand for Jesus and for His sweet truth,
I would speak out again in the same way,
without hesitation, without regrets.
What are all the honors the world can give
compared to this way of showing my love
for Him who showed me love to pain and death?

I am in an ancient line of faithful
men and women who were willing to die
for the sake of God and His righteousness.
Do you think I could ever regret that?

They were hounded by fierce persecutors
into desert sands and desolate hills,
to lonely caves and dark holes in the ground;
were flogged and tormented and ridiculed;
were imprisoned and bound with iron chains.
They braved the sharpened sword, the lion's den,
the flying stones, the consuming fire.
All this because of love for God and truth.

There is no nobler way to live and die.
Better to depart young standing for the
Word of God than to live on compromised
and fearful to an unhappy old age.

Do not grieve for me, but rather for those
who stop their ears at truth and hurl their stones.
Theirs is the mournful condition, not mine.

Theirs the condemnation and the fiery abyss;
mine the welcome in heaven, the eternal bliss.

## Philip the Evangelist
**(Acts 6:5; 8:5-40)**

I was appointed to wait on tables,
and see to the equal distribution
of provisions, along with Stephen and
some others. We were glad to do this work
because it freed the apostles for the
ministry of the Word of God and prayer.
I tried to do my job in a faithful
manner, and never asked for a higher
place, or what the majority of men
think of as a more spiritual work.
But God had plans for me which I had not
ever guessed at, or even dared to dream.

What a stir in Samaria, and what
miracles the Lord did there, and what a great
number believed in His name! I would not
have thought it possible for me to have
the privilege to engage in such work.
There I was serving at table and then
suddenly and surprisingly I found
I had the gift of evangelism
(from the start I had a true heart for it),
and saw large numbers turning to the Lord.

Further surprises were awaiting me.
For one day in the midst of my success
and joy, God's Spirit said, "Arise and go
down to the desert highway that leads to
Egypt." And at once I arose and went
not knowing why, but knowing that I must.

And just one man came traveling that way,

coming from Jerusalem where the Church
was strongest and where the apostles were.
Yet–think of this–God did not have this man
meet with them, but called me from the thriving work
in Samaria to the wilderness
to speak to him alone. Are not God's ways
past finding out, and strange to our poor minds?
And speak to him I did. The good seed of
the Word of God planted then in his heart
will surely now bear fruit in distant soil,
producing harvests only God can know.

When we obey and place ourselves in God's great hands,
our simple ministry can reach the farthest lands.

## Simon the Sorcerer
**(Acts 8:9-24)**

I know a thing or two about occult
matters (I am not called "The Great Power
of God" without reason). This was not that.
Philip did things that I had never seen,
never even imagined could be done.
And took no credit at all, but gave it
to God. This is no sorcerer with his
bag of magic tricks. This is something else.

He exorcized evil spirits with a
word. Paralytics and cripples were healed.
I myself saw limbs that were twisted and
deformed becoming straight and strengthening
before my eyes, and the lame leaped for joy.
And there is no magic that can do that.
And he did not try to promote himself
as some great one, as magicians and their
like always try to do, but preached only
Christ, not himself.
                    Then came Peter and John,
very powerful men–just by putting
hands on others God's Spirit entered them.
For such power I would give all I have.
I even offered what I had with me,
but they scorned it with some vicious remarks
(something about my being in the bonds
of iniquity, whatever that means).
I confess I don't understand these men.
All these miracles and no desire for
reward of any kind? Or even fame?
Such amazing power and no thought of
financial gain? Please explain this to me:

Why do they travel about doing what
they do? What benefit is it to them?
In all my life I've never seen this sort
of thing.
They all look like poor men to me.
Their clothes are old, they traveled here on foot
all the long, slow way from Jerusalem.
They eat plain food and stay in simple homes.
I hear they are in constant danger from
leaders of their own nation. What moves
these men? What secret motive drives them on?

I was baptized with all the rest, but still
they want no part of me. I don't know why.
I have always been a much honored man.
I am frightened of them. What do I lack?
Well, if I must go my own way, I will.
If I cannot serve their God in their company
I'll serve the magic arts which have been good to me.

## Cornelius
**(Acts 10:1–11:17)**

Something was always lacking in the gods
of Rome. To me they always seemed more like
fallen human beings than any Supreme
Being that I could picture in my mind.
So, although my own nation worshiped them,
I was not satisfied. My heart was filled
with longing for a greater One than all
the idols made by men could ever be.
Now I am sure that it was God Himself
who put this good desire in me.
Living
in Caesarea I met some godly Jews
who taught to me their way, the way of law
and works, to lead me to Israel's God,
the one Creator of the universe,
the God who is fearful in holiness,
and worthy of all men's exalted praise.

And I at once began to worship Him–
my heart, my voice I raised to Him alone.
His Word became the guidance for my acts,
His will my study and my deepest aim.

If someone had then asked me, "Are you saved?"
my answer would have been, "I think so, yes.
The true and living God I now revere.
And I have joined myself to His own flock
and do my very best to follow them."

I come now to the vision that I had
which changed for good my thinking and my life.
I could not misconceive the angel's words:

"Send to Joppa for Simon who is called
Peter. He will bring you a message through
which you and your whole household will be saved."

I understood "will be saved" could only mean
that then I still was not. And now this great,
this fundamental truth I have well learned:
All my respect for God, my giving alms,
my devout way of life, my many prayers,
brought me to God's notice, but never could
bring me to His place on high. The end of
works of the law is not salvation, but
eternal loss. One's best can never be
good enough. And so God must intervene
and bring us to the truth of Christ His Son.

But if with willing heart you seek for Him
He will move both heaven and earth to bring
the truth to you, just as He did to me.

See the kind acts of God fulfilling His sweet plan,
sending an angel, then Peter, to teach a man.

## Gamaliel
**(Acts 5:34-39; 22:3,4)**

I thought I knew him well, but now have doubts.
For some time I watched him with disquiet
and, sometimes, considerable alarm.
Saul seemed so fanatical, so intense,
so severe in his judgments, and almost,
I should say, murderous.
Zeal for God is
a very good thing, but it should be
in accordance with true knowledge and that
humbleness of mind that can come only
by more understanding of life and a
deeper awareness of one's own defects and
limitations than Saul ever showed.
The hot extremism that he displayed
I have always deplored, and do so now.

I was afraid that his intemperate
behavior would be traced clear back to the
teaching he heard from me when he used to
sit at my feet, and at times I myself
wondered if I had unknowingly helped
to produce some kind of monster.
He was,
(and still is), a man of real intellect.
But unlike many men of intellect
he was willing to take firm action when
he once thought the truth was under attack
(as all of you have come to know quite well),
and not merely sit and think.
And he was,
(and still is, I doubt not), a deeply moral
man who, above all the disciples I

ever taught, labored to obtain that true
righteousness of the law that Pharisees
are known to love. I don't believe that he
would ever knowingly violate his
conscience or perform an act he thought was
against any word of our Holy Book
(surely my teaching had that much effect).

By many I am regarded as a
wise man (I think I may be wiser in
the eyes of others than in my own eyes),
but in the case of Saul there is now a
man I confess I don't much understand.

What has happened to him? How can there be
this complete reversal in his outlook
and conduct? I gather that he now seems
a person altogether different.

And I have heard of his testimony
concerning that strange experience on
the Damascus road, and the witness too
of others that something remarkable
happened there.

But what are we to believe?
Can we think that in fact he saw Jesus
risen from the dead? Or was it a fit
creating some disorder of the brain?
(But those who were with him at the time speak
of a sudden blinding light from the sky.)
Or is this Satan at work to destroy
all those things which Saul once defended and
maintained with such fearless tenacity?

But if the things I'm told of him are true
there is nothing at all which indicates
a mind that is diseased. And his calm and
loving demeanor, and willingness

to deny himself and live for what he
considers the good of others (I hear
these things) strikes me as more angelic than
Satanic. He seems a much better person
than before. And my experience has
instructed me that good results like these
are not produced by causes which are bad.

And this is puzzling. For if we are not
willing to accept his word about what
happened then, how can we find a reason
robust enough to account for this great
change in him? And so should we believe him?
My reputed wisdom, I must say, seems
to me wholly unequal to this task.

I will wait to see how things turn out, and pray for light.
For against the Most High God I do not wish to fight.

## Paul
### (toward the end)

During the long course of my ministry
the Lord Jesus sometimes directed me
to speak or write of myself, my life and
work, all for other people's benefit.
He taught me that He had set me forth as
an example of His grace, and of how
a servant of His should behave and serve.
It may be a help to some if I speak
again about matters concerning me,
though I know that I am less than the least,
worse than the worst, unworthy of His Name.

I will never forget what I once was,
or how, when in mad haste to persecute
the Prince of life and all who followed Him,
I saw that blinding light, fell there in the
dusty road and heard the astounding words
of Jesus Christ, Son of the living God:
"Saul, Saul, why are you persecuting me?"

That incandescent hour changed everything,
and my life now is proof that Jesus lives.
If it was not His great transforming power
that changed my course, what did? Would I give up
my ambitions and aims, reject my self,
defend what once I was fierce to destroy,
face constant death, and love through suffering
One whom I had rejected and abhorred,
without sufficient grounds? Changes so great
require great causes. I met the Lord on
the Damascus way, heard His loving voice,
and saw that He was alive again,

and this is what has made the difference.
His astounding grace lifted me above
the hard cold rock of my depravity.

Now He fills my life and every waking
thought, and is as real to me as my own
self. The life I now live I live in Him–
indeed, His life it is that lives in me.

I have learned well through many inner trials,
and through clear revelation from above,
that God's grace is the doer, not myself.
It was grace that undid me, remade me,
then gave me the exalted privilege
of preaching the pure Gospel of God's grace.

For this I am content both to live and
die for Christ, willing to meet with dangers,
go anywhere, do anything He says.
For Him I can face any obstacle
or meet any fear with peace in my heart.
I am prepared for any discomfort,
ready to experience any pain,
to tolerate any indignity,
to suffer in chains, despised as He was,
and to pour out all that I have for Him.
Long ago I renounced this corrupt world,
and counted all as loss for His dear sake.

From the day I knew the Gospel of our
glorious Lord and Savior Jesus Christ,
prepared for us all by the Triune God,
and God's great program for this age of ours,
one aim, one supreme goal, has led me on
–to preach His truth where He was never known.
What is an ordinary life to me,
having a wife, a family, working,
playing, buying, selling, compared to this

work which reaches into eternity?

So now I would finish my ordained course.
My life is not dear to me if only
I can delight my Lord and reach the goal,
and then with loving words of welcome hear Him greet
me, and then prostrate myself at His wounded feet.

## Barnabas
**(Acts 4:36,37; 11:22-26; 15:36-39)**

I have no wish to be noticed by men,
and am reluctant even to write this
for fear it might bring unwanted regard.
But if what I have to say can be of
encouragement to those in the ministry
I am willing to go ahead. For this–
encouraging others in God's work, and
seeing them succeed–is one of my chief
delights. In their encouragement I find
my own.
I always rejoice to see God's
great grace at work in other people's lives.
In Antioch I saw much that stirred my
heart to praise. And while there, our brother Saul,
returned to Tarsus, and now engaged in
I knew not what, often came to my mind.
Grace is at work in him, I thought, and so
perhaps now I can be an encouragement
to him. So off to Tarsus I went and
brought him back. The results you have all heard.

And Mark. If ever a young man needed
encouragement it was he. After that
rash and ill-considered decision of
his to leave Paul and me at Perga, and
then Paul's refusal to take him along
again, the poor lad was really crushed.
I risked my fellowship with Paul to see
if I could recover Mark's life for Christ.
My efforts, as you know, were not in vain.

Now if I were asked for advice about

the Christian life, I would say to you all:
Let Christ's love win your heart, then set to work.
Give Him all you have and see Him use it
and you for the glory of His great name.

You may have many duties toward your
family, or in your profession,
but invite the Lord into all of that,
and do not let your own affairs so grip your
mind and so control your activities
that you forget the really important
thing in life–serving our great Redeemer.
And if opportunity comes to serve
Him with all your time, mind and strength, seize it.
And learn to resist all discouragement.
Remain true to the Lord with all your heart.
And if you fail or fall, get up again.
All is not lost. The Lord will not leave you.

Never give up. For any service for the Lord,
even the smallest thing, will have a sure reward.

## Silas
**(Acts 15:32-40. Old and looking back)**

I seem to be remembered, not for who I am,
but for going about with someone else–
small wonder, when that someone was Paul.
And I don't mind that at all. Silas did
nothing to stand alone in history.
And since I cannot be Paul, I will be
content as Silas, a servant of God,
companion and friend of a greater man,
and glad to share with him in ministry.

And what a ministry it was! We saw
God at His work in ways so wonderful
there are some people to this very day
who have thought it far too much to believe.
But I was with him when it all took place,
and the exact truth was written down by Luke.

Later on I had the great privilege
of serving with Peter–I am that man
Silvanus who once helped him to write his
letter, his first one, for he did not feel
at ease writing in Greek and asked my aid.

Giving help to two great servants of God
has been an honor and a rare delight.
But service to my Lord is best of all.
Remarkable opportunities were
given to this unremarkable man–
what a God we have to serve and adore!
Love Him, you saints, love Him forevermore!

## Elymas the Sorcerer
**(Acts 13:6-12)**

I've had a very good thing going here.
And now this itinerant preacher Saul
turns up and threatens my place with the chief
Roman official of this pleasant isle.
For Sergius Paulus is listening
to this man and drawing away from me.

It appears that Saul is opposed to all
magic, and sorcery, and to all those
occult ideals and practices which make
life much more interesting and liveable
for most men who know there are unseen Powers
out there to be contacted and then used,
if possible, for our own purposes.

Who is not intrigued by the mysteries
of existence? Who does not want to know
what benign spirits, what shining Beings
are active behind the deceptive face
of the material world, who can be
called to our help? And how to make them all
kindly disposed toward us? And who does
not need to know what evil Forces there
are who would lead us astray and plunge us
into nightmares of suffering and loss?
And how to propitiate them when they
are angry, and keep them far from our doors?

And should no one search out the magic words
that help unlock those spirits' secret world?
And gain the expertise to read the stars
and mark well their influence on all we

are and can become? Who does not need to
know which days are auspicious, and which are
not, and when we may safely do one thing
and when not? And who does not long to find
the hidden path to immortality,
to becoming gods ourselves?
Saul would do
away with all this and make the world a
far more dangerous and frightening place.
And certainly a poorer place for me.
And what does he offer instead of this
ancient way of wisdom and well-being?
Incredible stories about some dead
man or other who, Paul says, came to life
again and afterwards appeared to him!

I for one will resist him with all my
strength and wiles. What this poor world needs is not
some new religion, but more sorcerers
and astrologers and enchanters and
wizards to bring the occult truth to bear
on all of mankind in general, and on our
well-known leaders and rich men in particular.

## Timothy
**(1 Timothy 1:2)**

Christ is the incarnation of the truth.
Every religious teaching opposed to
Him is false and deceptive and comes from
man's sinful way of thinking or else from
the dark world of evil spirits where snares
are devised to trap the unwary.
                                        Christ
is the standard by which we all should test
every thought that comes to us or that is
abroad in the world.
                                        A man who ignores
Him and the heavenly truth He taught is
like a ship with mutinous crew sailing
through a cloudy night when no star appears,
with no compass to guide them on the way,
tossed about and in danger from all the
waves and currents in the sea, and with a
very dangerous captain at the wheel.
When the devil steers a man should be alarmed.

Paul taught me this, just as Jesus taught him.
I think that no one but Jesus ever
emphasized the importance of truth more
fervently, more diligently than that
great man of God, my father in the faith.
And except Christ Himself, who is the Captain
of our souls, no one ever encouraged
and motivated me to the highest
in my life and ministry more than he.
I am sure that our Lord led Paul to me
and me to Paul to equip me for His work.

So I praise God for Jesus first of all,
but I praise God for Paul too, who under
the authority and teaching of the
Lord, taught me those things I needed to know,
so that I might teach others too, and they
still others, till the glorious Gospel
of the Lord Jesus Christ resounds in all
the distant and dark corners of the earth.

Now Paul has gone, but Jesus is among us still,
always delighting to teach those who choose His will.

## Epaphras
**(Colossians 4:12,13; Philippians 2:25-30)**

My name, I think, is not much recognized,
but I am not concerned in having men
know my name at all. On the contrary,
my passion is lowly service to them,
and that highest of all secret service–
one done where only God sees. I mean prayer.

What higher privilege can come to us
than, nameless, except for His own dear name,
to bow before the holy throne of God,
and speak to Him as Father and as Friend,
and lay our cares and burdens at His feet,
and intercede for blessing on all men?

But why prayer? Does not God know what He
desires to do and what to grant or not,
without our asking Him? Send such vain thoughts
back to the evil source from whence they came!
Has not our Lord Himself commanded prayer?
And is this alone not sufficient ground
to bring us always to the throne of grace?

Do we not have in God's own Word enough
example of what prayer can do to make
us spend our lives before Him on our knees?
By believing prayer what victories have
been achieved! What mighty foes put to flight!
What occasions of sadness given way
to joy, sickness to health, weakness to strength!
How many wandering souls brought to the fold!
How many families saved from their sins!
How many laborers sent forth into

the vast and needy harvest fields of earth!
How many times a people there has been
moved toward God and righteousness and truth!
How many blessings brought down from above!
And how often the Lord been glorified!

And so then shall we sin against our God,
against His truth and against His saints, and
rob ourselves of arms in this great war
that rages everywhere in this dark world,
by ceasing to pray? Shall we let our foes
now teach us that all our praying is vain,
and so fail both God and man, and plunge our
lives into defeat? Shall we, caught in our
own concerns, forget to pray? Or fall by
our shameful spiritual laziness?

I have been ill in this service and thought
I would die. But death is nothing to me,
only a veil I pass through to see Him
whom my soul loves, and to be forever
in His presence, where no ill comes to mar our days,
where all our deepest, truest prayers turn to praise.

## Demas

**Justifying himself. (2 Timothy 4:10)**

Paul has written that I left him because
I loved this present world. While there is some
truth in what he said, I know that his words
can be twisted to my disadvantage,
and cause some to think that by leaving him
I have forsaken God and Christ and truth,
and want them no more. And this is not so.

Let me give you my side of this matter.
I did not leave because I had suddenly
developed a love for this world. I loved
it before I went to Paul, and loved it
while I was serving God with him. Now don't
jump to conclusions. If you give me a
chance I will try to make my meaning clear.

When I say I love this world I don't mean
the corruption and follies of the world,
the lamentable ignorance of God
and the detestable idolatry
one sees in the world. I mean those things that
are attractive to intelligent and
sensitive people who can love beauty,
and admire fine ideas and good things
and pleasures wherever they may be found.

The reason I left was that Paul's views are
quite different from mine on this subject,
and, great man though he certainly is, he
is not very tolerant when it comes
to opinions that differ from his own.

To him everything is black or white, with
no areas grey, neutral, undefined.
With him you are either in or out, and
so I decided that "out" was better
for me than remaining on in that cramped
and narrow world of his.
                                        Don't mistake me.
I don't mean out of the kingdom of God.
I still consider myself a Christian.
You should not ever think that leaving Paul
is the same thing as leaving Jesus Christ.

What I want is the best both of God's great
kingdom and of this world, and see no good
reason whatever why I shouldn't have it.
For God has given both of them to us,
and with them all things richly to enjoy.

This does not mean that I am now resolved
to indulge my fleshly appetites, and roll
in the mire of sin. I've no mind for that.

For I still want to serve in some real place of need–
serve in my way, not Paul's, and see how God will lead.

## The Judaizers
**(Acts 15:1-5; Galatians 1:6,7)**

This fellow, this Paul, a renegade Jew,
and lover of Gentiles more than his own
race, makes the law of Moses null and void,
teaches things fit only for libertines,
and brings great peril to the truth of God.
And then he has the dreadful arrogance
to say that Jesus Christ has sent him forth.

We believe his teachings come from his own
overheated brain, or some demon source.
For those sent forth by Christ will preach the truth
Christ taught, and practice the law just as He.
And anyone who tries to overthrow
a jot or tittle written in the law,
and who proclaims to every man he meets
that he can now be saved by grace alone
without joining himself to Israel
and following Moses in all he taught,
can only be a villain or a fool.

What? Renounce circumcision and all the
commandments, regulations and decrees
inscribed forever in our Holy Book,
and ignore the eternal covenant
God made with us there in the holy mount,
and still be saved? This is rank heresy.
Believe us when we say to one and all
that without circumcision and the law
you cannot be saved and have peace with God.

Wherever on earth Paul may dare to go
we will be there to fight him every step.

We care too much for what God has revealed
to let him propagate his lies, seduce
uninstructed men to pernicious ways,
and bring reproach upon the law of God.

This is truth: Apart from the law of Israel
all that remains for any man is death and hell.

## The Jailer of Philippi
**(Acts 16:22-34)**

Never before in this work had I seen
anything like it. This is not a place
where one meets the best people. Once in a
while a decent, innocent man gets put
in here, but on the whole they're a rough and
hardened bunch, and be sure you wouldn't want
to keep your back turned to any of them.

You don't see much joy here, I'll tell you that,
and singing is as rare as hen's teeth. I
don't remember ever hearing it before
that night, except for some mad fellow with
his wild lament which no one understood,
or some drunkard not knowing what he sang.
Being beaten, clamped in the stocks, and then
locked in a dark and filthy cell does not
usually cause men to lift their voice
in song. When they lift their voices at all
it is only to hurl curses at the
universe, and sometimes at God.
I did not
expect anything different when Paul
and Silas were brought in. It is true that
they did not bear the usual marks of
criminals we see in here–the darkness
in the eyes, the sullen looks, the uncombed
appearance. Some of them act almost like
animals. By comparison, Paul and
his companion appeared intelligent
and civilized. No matter that, I thought,
for a nice face can hide a nasty heart,
and a bright mind plot dark deeds.

When the sharp
whip bit into their naked backs I felt
some surprise that no curse fell from their lips.
They took their beating like real men, and then
endured the stocks without a word.
But now
how can I describe that night, that night that
forever changed my life? I tried to sleep,
but prayers and hymns to God rose from that
inner cell where these new prisoners were.
With bleeding backs, and arms and legs held fast
in the hard wood, what can they possibly
have to sing about? This was my last thought
before I fell asleep.
I did not sleep for long.
Midnight came and with it the quaking ground,
and my quaking heart. What was God doing?
I was responsible for those in jail.
If any escaped, the authorities
would inflict severe punishment on me.
And so I drew my sword to end my life,
but dear Paul called out reassuring words.

Then, all at once, in a way I still don't
quite understand, I felt my many sins,
and deeply feeling them, began to shake.
I rushed inside and fell down at Paul's feet.

"What must I do to be saved?" was my anxious cry.
"Believe in the Lord Jesus Christ" came the sure reply.

## The Athenians
**(Acts 17:16-33)**

We're proud of our city, home of the arts,
fountain of democracy, teacher of
the whole world, and seat of philosophy.
We love to speak of the highest things, and
can never bear with fools gladly, never.

The metaphysical is our delight.
We are the children of Epicurus
and Zeno, Plato and Aristotle,
and truly a host of other great minds.
And we are stimulated only by
intellectuals. Perhaps we've been spoiled,
but with no new notions to talk about,
life is so boring we could almost die.

Recently there was a small stir which held
our attention for a little while. Some
traveling foreign preacher came by and
thought he could convert us to some god called
Jesus, we think he said. Or did he say
Anastasis? Perhaps he meant two gods.

Convert us, ha! As if we had any
lack of gods in Athens! With our skill in
reasoning and debate, to convert us
would take far, far more than he had to give.
Actually we didn't make much sense
of his strange discourse, so much like babbling.
Certainly he was no Demosthenes.

More for amusement than anything else
we went up Aries Pagos to listen
to him, though it seemed he cared little for
philosophy.
He spoke with what appeared
to be earnestness–we can give him that.
Or should we? He may be merely a good
actor who can simulate earnestness.
We can't be sure of this, but we do know
all that he said was hardly above the
mental level of schoolboys. So whether
or not he was an actor, we're sorry
to say we were not much entertained. Why,
he even dared to suggest that we–we!–
are ignorant. His speech got what it deserved–
our contempt.
Well, we can hardly hope that
all who speak here will truly stimulate.

The man put forth nothing that we could label bright,
only some foolish remarks no wise man believes.
There's greater amusement than this for us tonight–
they're restaging a play by Aristophanes.

## Gallio

**(Acts 18:12. Writing to his brother the philosopher Seneca)**

Recently some religious fanatics
among the Jews brought a case to my court.
Imagine my surprise when it turned out
that no one had perpetrated a crime.
The whole matter was nothing more than a
mad dispute about something in their creed!

I could not imagine what all the fuss
was about. Could you please enlighten me?
Why do so many people get worked up
concerning their own brand of religion,
and fight about dogmas and words and names?
How can they think all this is meaningful?

I believe, brother (great philosopher
though you undoubtedly are), you will find
a solution to this hard to come by.
Even the great deity in heaven–
if there is a deity in heaven–
must wonder at so much fierce commotion
about such very unimportant things.

I do not care at all if people want
to worship this god instead of that one,
or choose to practice certain meaningless
rites and rituals instead of others.
What possible difference can it make?

All this religious rage, violence and
hatred certainly indicates some strange,
perplexing fever in human nature.
People seem willing to pay any price,

even their very lives, for things like these!

No doubt such blind fanaticism and
frenzy have cost mankind far more than you
or I could ever hope to estimate.
And in our day, too, they could bring great harm.

Compared to the past we live in an age
of culture, wisdom, and enlightenment.
Surely now men can be freed from all such
ignorance and religious bigotry.
I wonder if something more can be done
in the way of good basic instruction
for the poor uneducated masses.

Perhaps this is our one and only hope
to bring harmony and peace among all
the tongues and nations in the Roman world.
When I see Caesar I will speak of this.

You know me, and how I always rejoice to find
any indication of a liberal mind.

## Priscilla and Aquila
**(Acts 18:2,26; Romans 16:3-5)**

Whenever Luke and Paul wrote of us we
were always linked together. This pleases
us. We are not only husband and wife,
we are united in purpose and heart
in the work of God, and we always serve
together.

We give instruction in our
home to those who come to us, and, while one
of us is speaking the other lifts his
(or her) heart to the Lord that the spoken
Word of God will be honored and bear fruit.
And when one is speaking, the other, who
is praying, may be inspired to insert
a thought or a verse of Scripture or a
word of advice or warning as seems to
fit the occasion.

One of our chief aims
when we are ministering the Word
of God to people in this way is
to be filled with His Spirit and to speak
what and as He leads.

Very recently
we had the honor of having a man
of great zeal and distinction in our home.
We have high hopes that he will bear much
fruit for God. He is an eloquent man,
well educated, and speaks with fervor
in the synagogue, and what he speaks is
true. When we heard him at first it was plain
that he had a thorough knowledge of the
Scriptures, and what he taught about the Lord
Jesus was accurate (by the way, he
is a Jew named Apollos).

But he knew
only the baptism of John. Let us
tell you what this meant. He had repented
of his sins and was prepared for the One
whom John said would come after him, the great
Messiah of Israel. And he knew
that He had come, and knew some of the facts
about Him, but not all. Nor had he been
baptized in the name of the Father, Son,
and Holy Spirit, the baptism that
signifies union with Christ in His death
and resurrection. And his knowledge was
limited of how believers now are
members of Christ's body, the true Church, and
have His very own life in them, being
born from above and possessing His Spirit. We
were more than happy to teach him this mystery.

## James the Lord's Brother
**after writing his letter**

If I say I am James, you may wonder
what James, for James is quite a common name.
As you know, two of the original
disciples were named James. And you may know
too that in my language James is really
Jacob. I am a Hebrew of Hebrews.

I am that very James who at the first
scoffed at the talk that Jesus was the Christ.
For a long time I was too near to him,
I think now, to see His divinity,
since it was then so well concealed beneath
the very ordinary things of life,
and since, some said, I was a brother of His.
Actually, I was His half-brother–
though for many years I ignorantly thought
that my father Joseph was His father too.

And if my father and mother (I judged)
are his father and mother then for sure
he is no more the Messiah to come
or Son of God than I myself could be.

He did some very remarkable things,
and, I confess, His words were very far
from ordinary, and sometimes shook me.
But I refused to believe that my own
brother who had worked as a carpenter
could be the one great hope of Israel.

And then occurred His swift unexpected death–
at least, it was unexpected to me–

and then the stories began that He lived.
This, I said to myself, I must explore.
And I did, going to Jerusalem,
and closely questioning His followers.
With one voice they told me He had risen
from the dead and had appeared to them all.

I thought I should believe them but wasn't sure
until one great day I saw Him with my
own eyes in His body raised from the dead,
and knew He was the very same Jesus
who had lived in our home and trod our streets.

Now I call Him not "brother," but the Lord,
our glorious Lord Jesus Christ, Savior,
and Israel's King. For Him I wait in hope,
so glad that the eyes of this stubborn man
were finally opened to who He is,
and full of joy to be His servant now.

Learn how truth concealed before our very eyes
may all of a sudden take us by surprise.

## Jude

If you have read my brief letter, you may
have noticed a fact that some do not seem
to grasp, thinking perhaps that I am a
contentious sort of person and like to
condemn those who are not of our belief.
I had a strong desire to write about
the wonderful salvation provided
by our Lord Jesus Christ. His gospel is
what grips my heart and mind as nothing else.
But when I sat down to write, my thoughts turned
to a need I both saw and deeply felt.
And I believe God's Spirit was at work
to produce those thoughts.
There are ungodly men,
raised up and sent out by Satan himself,
who worm their way into a church and there
attempt to corrupt the people of God,
both by what they do and by what they teach.
And could I remain silent at all this?
I resolved to speak out even if it
should cost me my life, as it well could do–
remember Stephen and James and others
who have been persecuted to their death.
(The world likes to accuse us of being
intolerant, but it is the people
of the world who oppress, torture and kill.)
But the truth of God is worth dying for
and a church at risk is worth fighting for.

This is why I wrote to believers in
general to earnestly contend for
the faith once for all given to the saints.
Nothing is so important as God's truth.

Without it we will remain in darkness
concerning all the really important
matters of time and of eternity.

These messengers of the devil, of whom
I speak, profess to know the Lord and to
be His servants, but they deny His true
deity and show by their lives that the
gospel has had no real effect on them.
They have their own agenda. They serve their
own lusts and their doctrine is hostile to
the Word of God. They teach that men can live
just as they please and deliberately
go on sinning as they wish, and then still
be covered by the grace and mercy of God.
From such teaching run for your very lives.

No more dangerous a thought has entered man's mind.
Its teachers are like brute beasts, spiritually blind.

## Antichrist
**(Revelation chapter 13)**

I have no equal on this whole broad earth.
I was born to command all other men.
Long have I waited; now My time has come.
My heart, review the plans now made and so
prepare to act to make the world one world
with one king over all, and I that king.

Energized by that great power none will
understand (there is One to whom I bow),
the entire globe will lie low at My feet,
where, as it will know, its true place should be.

Quickly it will learn what My rule will mean.
Democracy will be an unused word.
In every case there will be but one vote–
Mine. I will permit some few kings to reign
in their own lands in a limited way,
as long as they bow to My sovereignty,
which they and all their people will be keen
to do.
The method of the carrot and
the stick has worked so well throughout history,
that I am sure it will work again and
keep them all on their trembling knees to Me.

The only crime will be resisting Me.
All that a man has he will give to save
his skin. If they take My mark they will be
able to buy and sell and enjoy all
the wonderful benefits of My rule.

If they do not, the stick will crush their heads.

A full stomach (which is all most people
care about), and terror of punishment,
along with admiration of My might,
will be quite enough. None will want to fight
with Me.
                    But absolute control over
all the political, commercial, and
military powers of earth will not
satisfy Me. I crave more, and deserve more.
I will be God, and I will sit in the
temple of God and show I am God.
And the whole human race, every man,
woman, and child, will bow and worship Me.
If any draw back from the homage which
is My due, they will face the sword and the
the consuming fire. And no god in the
heavens or on the earth can change My plans,
or put a stop to them.
                    My heart, the times
cry out for action. So now boldly act!
Make all your mystic dreams bear solid flesh,
and clothe ambition with heroic deeds!

Strike now at the soft underbelly of
the body politic and bring it down.
Risen from the dead, the incarnation
of all that mankind has long yearned for, I will be
immortal. No "twilight of the gods" for Me.

## The False Prophet
**(Revelation chapter 13)**

I have long recognized that I am a
man of exceptional abilities,
and I have no desire to waste them in
this small land. I want, and have long wanted,
to be at the bright, hot core of power,
real power, power that aims to control
this globe from the far west to the far east.
Now I have the chance I've been looking for.

A remarkable individual
has appeared on the scene who views things as
I do. He is very charismatic,
very dynamic, and has great boldness
and intelligence. He is out to seize
power by the throat, and bring all finance,
politics, and religion under his
direct command, and reign, one supreme man
over one world.
I have thrown in my lot
with him, and will be his trusted helper
in all the working out of his great plan.

We are both totally persuaded that
this is the one way to save the earth and
make it what it should be–the abode of
prosperity and peace.
We all know the
severe problems and dangers which confront
us everywhere–the insane nuclear
race among even insignificant
countries, the constant struggle of nations,
big and small, to subdue one another,

the rebellions and wars that never cease,
the destruction of the environment,
the ups and downs of our economies
(with far too many downs), and the chaos
in the world of religion, with all its
inevitable rivalries and old
hatreds.
What we desperately need is
one government, one religion, one world,
one control over the world's finances,
and one army which none will dare oppose.

Yes, just as you, I have heard that power
corrupts and absolute power corrupts
absolutely. But this does not apply
if the person wielding the power is
totally incorruptible, does it?

The above mentioned individual
cares nothing for God, or gods, so he's safe
from corruption there.
And I don't think he
wants power for power's sake, but for the
good of man. His mind is brimming with grand
ideas, and plans of how to see them
carried out in the real world. And he has
that quite extraordinary vision,
that egocentricity (I use the
word in its best possible sense), and that
steely will which are found in only
the very greatest of leaders.
But some
may feel unease because he has no God.
I, for one, am sure this does not at all
disqualify him. Quite the opposite.
Is it not past time that man became his
own god, and spent his waking hours, his thoughts,
his strength, and his resources at the holy

shrine of man, rather than in temples made
for fictitious deities thought to be
hidden somewhere or other in the sky?

But if there is no God will not all things
be lawful (as others have suggested)?
Will not the whole of mankind fall into
violence, anarchy and lawlessness?
Far from it.
                    The man soon to be revealed
will actually put an end to that
sort of thing, once and for all. His will is
good and he will have full authority
to impose it. And not a man will lift
up a hand against his brother, except,
of course, those appointed by that supreme
authority to crush anyone who
resists it.
                    You may be assured that we
will deal very severely against such.
We can't have people opposing the state.
It would bring chaos to the world again.

Enough of words. It is time to act, for the grand
fulfillment of all my best dreams is now at hand.

## Satan

After all the slanderous, malicious
talk against Me, I think it proper to
say a word or two in My own defense.
If I had been satisfied with the way
God ran things, I would not have tried to take
his place. But who could have been satisfied?
With him on the throne, jealously guarding
his position, what hope was there for our
advancement to a more prominent place?
And what opportunity to express
everything that was in our minds and hearts?

I, for one, felt stifled and restricted.
Call Me proud if you wish, but always to
bow to the dominance of another,
especially to one so despotic
and arbitrary in his decisions,
was more than I could continue to bear.

I was not the only one who felt so.
A great host of others in high places
resolved to join Me in My resistance
to his arrogant abuse of power.
"Freedom!" was our glorious war cry then,
and it remains our one ultimatum now.

We have taken strong, heroic measures
to stop this hateful being from lording
it over us and this our universe.
That we have not yet fully succeeded
is not evidence that we never will.
Be sure that we will not give up the fight.

Question: If God has all power (as claimed)
how is it he has not destroyed us yet?
I think he has not because he cannot.
Certainly he must want to see us gone.
He knows that we create endless trouble
for him among those whom he considers
the crowning achievement of creation.
I mean the human race.
But use your head,
if this is really his great achievement,
what must we think of his wisdom and might?
Only that they are hugely defective.
In My time I've traveled to many worlds,
and have gone up and down throughout the earth.
Nowhere have I seen so pathetic a
creature as man. Not a one of them is
really attractive or forceful or wise
or faithful to what he says he believes.

I can make any of them crawl to Me
whenever I please. Just a little loss,
a little pain, and for relief they will
do anything I order them to do.
Tempt them even a little, and all their
fine resolutions instantly collapse.

Dangle a little money before them
and they will forsake honesty and truth
in order to seize it, and so will show
that all of their high-sounding principles
are as empty as their poor, barren hearts.
Offer them the pleasure of power–they
forget their immortal souls to get it.

In spite of God's many attempts to gain
their affection (he is always giving
them something), most of them still worship Me.
The rest care only for themselves, not God.

He offers men a high place in heaven;
they treat the offer with utter contempt,
because they want nothing to do with him.

If I could have even the least pity
for anyone, it would surely be for
this incredibly weak, stupid being
God seems to dote on so excessively.
But in My war against his unfair acts,
and his oppressive domineering rule,
I cannot and will not spare any
person or thing that he claims as his own.
My fixed purpose, My fierce opposition
will never slacken until I see all
human beings under My absolute control
and, at last, in hell where they all belong.

And never, never will My struggle cease
until I drive God from the throne, and he
suffers the same pains which have come to Me.
My humiliation! Can you even
imagine what it was like to lose face
and place as I did? I will humble him
if it is the last thing I ever do.

And hear this: I am also determined
to fully crush that precious son of his.
What right had he to invade this, My world?
He will find that the little victory
he seemed to win when he was in My realm
was just a brief, insignificant one.
He will not be able to overcome
the forces I will cause to be arrayed
against him in this age's final great days.

Since I will defeat him in the battle
to come down here, I believe I will be
well able to defeat him anywhere.

Do not believe that ancient fable that
says he will bruise My head. It is not true.
You will all do well to receive My words,
not his – even if you could find our what
his really are, a very doubtful thing.
At least believe My solemn word to you:
I do not hold existence dear to Me as
long as the adversary remains there
smugly in control of all worlds but this.

And I am utterly resolved that, soon or late,
I see staggering in defeat that one I hate.

## The Angel Michael
**(Daniel 12:1; Revelation 12:7-9)**

When Lucifer began his mad revolt
in heaven, I was in the forefront of
the opposition raised for his defeat.
So I could see how ambition and pride
devastate the heart, trample on good sense,
debase the will, and bring creatures God made
good to bitter ways and utter wickedness.
By them angels in the heights became fiends
attempting to dethrone our God Himself,
and fell to unimaginable depths.
And by them men, uniting with God's foes,
made paradise a wilderness of death.

Dissatisfaction with God's appointed
way is to place one's feet in ruin's path,
and rush toward folly and arrogance.
For who knows best what we should be and do–
we? or He who made us and knows us best?
I am well content to be ambitious
only to better serve the Most High God,
aspiring to remain in His good will,
and ministering good to those on earth
made lower than the angels for a time,
and fallen lower still in Satan's snare.
My heart must never give a place to pride,
or ever think that high position ought
to be engaged in more exalted tasks.

I know God has formed a surprising plan
for fallen mankind and will make a way
for them to rise to unexpected heights.
We angels try to peer into these things,

to understand the grace that is to be
unveiled to them in ages still to come.
It seems the eternal Father on His throne
now seeks companions for His eternal Son,
made up of those among the race of men
who hear His voice and put their trust in Him.

And now we find ourselves engaged in war
because of Satan's rash and evil acts.
Determined to destroy all that belongs
to God which he can contemplate and touch,
especially this world in which men live,
holding, as it does, the interest of
our almighty, all-wise King as no place
besides in the created universe,
the devil goes about to do his work.
And our fixed purpose is to keep him low,
and to give aid to lowly men who are
being freed now from his pernicious ways.

And because of this, we all rejoice and sing,
giving our unfeigned thanks to our heavenly King.

## Jesus

I am. In the beginning I was with
God, and was God. And in the beginning
I am the one who laid earth's foundations,
and the heavens are the work of my hands.
They shall all perish, but I will remain.
As a garment they will be folded up,
but I will go on, the same forever.

I did not think it robbery to be
equal with God, being in God's own form.
But for Him, and for you, I was willing
to lay aside the glory that was mine
which I had with the Father in heaven
before the worlds came into existence,
to make myself of no reputation,
and then to become a servant of men.

My own people did not recognize me.
They wanted pomp and military might,
and someone who would cater to their pride.
They did not wish to receive someone so
meek and lowly in heart. They did not know
the great hour of their visitation.
In blindness they gave me up to the cross,
on which I had already planned to die.
For I had come to obey all of God's
good and perfect and acceptable will.

The prophets told of my coming and death.
Beforehand they spoke of my agony.
My own disciples wrote of my spirit's
trembling and shrinking from that dreadful hour.
I was made sin, I who had known no sin.

Perfect holiness, complete sinfulness–
these two joined together on that one day,
when the divine redemption of mankind
was being worked out on the cross of shame.

Forsaken by God, alone and condemned
I paid the full price for you to be free,
free from your sin, from Satan's dominion,
from fear of death, and judgment after death.

The grave could never hold me. I came out
at my Father's appointed hour. And now
I stand before you, risen from the dead,
triumphant over all that could hurt you,
having loved you to the shedding of my blood.

Freely I offer to you forgiveness
of sins, peace with God, and eternal life,
looking down in love from the high and holy place.
Believe in me. Live. Enter God's kingdom of grace.

# Appendix – Poems

## HYMN TO CHRIST
**(after Milton)**

Great dweller in eternal light
Who filleth all the holy place
Thou radiant Image of God's face
High throned above all other height,
O Jesus, wouldst Thou dwell with me?
Canst Thou desire my company?

Pure unexampled Love Thou art,
And all my yearning soul demands.
Come Saviour, though all hell withstands
Since Thou wilt stoop to such a heart;
Since Thou wilt stoop to such a throne,
Take Thy great power and reign alone.

O Lamb of God, I groan for Thee
With sighs too deep for feeble speech
Come, grant the gift beyond the reach
Of words, or thoughts, or imagery.
Cleanse this Thy temple through Thy blood,
And make my heart Thy fixed abode.

Depart, ye thieves of unbelief!
The high and lofty One above
Will show the measure of His love,
Will early speed to my relief.
He, to this contrite heart, draws near
To make His habitation here.

By faith I seize the joyful prize.
My Lord, come to Thy house in peace.
My heart awaits Thy bright increase,
My Master, O my Master, cries.

And from the bliss Thy presence brings
Eternal adoration springs.

Across the threshold of my soul
He comes, a holy, heavenly Guest,
He enters now within this breast,
Destroys the sin and fills the whole.
By faith I claim Him as my own
And know that which cannot be known.

My prostrate spirit worships Thee.
My tears are seen, my prayer is heard.
I rest upon Thy promised Word
To live and work and walk in me.
What splendid things shall I not prove,
Filled with the fulness of Thy love?

## LINKS
**(Romans 5:12-21; 2 Corinthians 5:17)**

I am the one who ate
Of the forbidden fruit.
There was a fearful cost–
For death slunk through the gate,
Ruin leaped in pursuit,
And Paradise was lost.

*

And so men killed God's Son.
I too was there to use
The whip and nails and lance,
Doing all that was done,
And ready to excuse
Hatred and arrogance,

*

I in those ancestors
Adamically linked.
Denying this was vain;
The past had open doors
And nothing was extinct–
It all surged out again.

*

The roots of fallen trees
Sprouted in me, put leaf,
And reproduced their kind.
From ancient pedigrees
Darkness and unbelief
Spread through my nascent mind.

*

The themes heard on my lyre
Were written long ago,
Were like old tapes replayed.
Kilns baked in distant fire,

Stirred and fed from below,
Is where my bricks were made.

*

From torches long burned out
Flames blazed on to the full,
Shot deadly sparks in me.
Sailed ships aren't seen about,
But I still feel the pull
Of anchors drawn from the sea.

*

And is there no release
From those chains to the dead?
From what old actions mean?
Will bygones never cease
In me? Has all hope fled?
Must I be what I've been?

*

Ah, God's Son came to die.
I in Him also died;
Then was raised a new man.
In that real death of "I"
My past was crucified.
A future then began.

*

Flesh holds on, and begs, but
On that original day
God did what man can't do:
In Christ those links are cut.
Old things have passed away,
And now all things are new.

# THINKING

I think, therefore I am, he said.
I say, I am, therefore I think.
Thought is evidence of being,
but being is not always wed
to thought. Many there are who sink
below the state of beasts, fleeing

*

the demands of truth, senses quite
voraciously alive, but brain
dead, urging on their shattered keel
to deep waters, in pitch-black night,
with mutinous crew, and captain
now fallen lifeless at the wheel.

*

I would press on toward this goal:
To keep intelligence awake
in me, and to love Christ with all
my mind, and heart and strength and soul,
and, for myself and for His sake,
always to have ears for His call

*

to use the power of thought for Him,
who is the source of it (seeing
He is our Maker), and not yield
to those dark forces that would dim
clear thinking, and so give being
a partner on life's battlefield.

## BIRD IN THE EYE OF A HURRICANE

Water, leaping high, shattering to spray,
darkly surging against the trembling coast,
now made to stand by the convulsing air,
and racing on tall across the pale sand,
plunging over waiting streets and houses
and dreams.

Wind, aroused sky dervish on its strange mission,
sweeping sea and land, uprooting the rooted,
shaking all in its path which can be shaken,
raining howling blows on selected places,
numbing minds, breaking hearts, demolishing
foundations.

I, safe, soaring on wings,
at peace in the maelstrom,
in the embracing calm,
in the eye of the storm,
in the calm gaze of God.

## BUTTERFLY

**(See Isaiah 41:14; Philippians 3:21)**

From leaf to leaf devouring
I inch my bristly shape along,
and seem a most unlikely thing,

with all my days now spent among
fellow worms in this ragged tree.
And I am ignorant and young

and cannot guess all that will be,
but sense a move about to come
and feel a stir of change in me.

So I will make my changing room
suspended from a silver tie,
rest in God in that fragile tomb,

then lay my wormy body by
and giving a triumphant cry
rise on bright wings into the sky.

## AS A DEER PANTS FOR STREAMS OF WATER

**(Psalm 42:1)**

Alone now by the dry stream bed
its hot hooves beat across the caked
and splintered ground.

Its desperate head points beyond
the barren hills to the river,
its one, last hope.

It does not stop, or slow its pace,
or look behind. It does not dare
to turn aside.

Gasping sounds break from aching lungs,
but still it flies toward the goal.
Even so pants

my whole soul after you, O God.

## THE ARTIST
**(written in India to a friend in America)**

Here evening comes. Its palette fills.
Gold, reds and grays streak the pale blues.
But dawn stirs there. Its opaline hues
Touch umber fields, dark purple hills.

Ah, this our revolving home in space
Turns myriad faces to God's heart.
He shows the splendors of His art,
These clear, bright tokens of His grace.

His brush the rays of light up there,
His oils the prism of the air,
With constant hand He paints the skies.
God has no sunset, no sunrise.

## THE LIFEGIVER

**(Ephesians 2:1-5)**

Long my spirit lay wrapped in its shroud,
Sightless stared in the gloom.
Oh, proud was the wall that encircled,
Hard the stone on the tomb.

So who then could enter that darkness?
Or raise one dead in sin,
Creating new life in the lifeless?
Who could even begin?

God could. Taking my head in His arm,
Moving my lips apart,
He breathed in the Spirit of life, warm,
Mouth to mouth, heart to heart.

## THE SLAVE
**(Philippians 2:5-11)**

The One who made the stars
Stoops down to wash our feet.
With toil-worn hands He prepared a feast
And calls to us all to eat.

Descended from on high
To lower depths He went;
Was made a slave, and weighed down with us
His back (oh, his heart) was bent.

Obedient to death,
Three days He spent apart.
Then He drew near, still loving to serve,
Still meek and lowly in heart.

## THE REDEEMER

**(John 8:36; Ephesians 1:7)**

The thought would come: "Can there be hope?
Who can harm a king and be free
From the shackles, the cell, the rope?
A just and fearful penalty

Must wait for those who will not cease
To wrong the Majesty on high.
Who then, oh who can bring release
For criminals helpless as I?"

The King came down–men's cries were heard.
His heart was pierced, His blood was spilt.
He speaks the liberating word.
All go–fear and chains, doubt and guilt.

## THE ARCHITECT
**(Hebrews 11:10)**

It must take plans to make a world.
What should one use for its foundation?
What cornerstone? What collocation
Of its many parts? What space curled

Around its walls? Who will live there?
What kind of city on what kind of hill?
What hopes and promises to fulfill?
What glory to shine in its air?

I speak of that real world abroad,
Not this shadow world we now see,
But one made for endless occupancy
Whose Architect and Builder is God.

## The CROSS

**(Galatians 3:10-14; 2 Corinthians 5:21; 1 Peter 2:24)**

"Cursed is everyone who hangs on a tree."
He hung there, the Prince of heaven, Son of God,
and Son of man, through whom the worlds were made,

and hanging there He was made sin for me
and for us all, and so a curse. The rod
of God's wrath struck Him, and the flaming blade

of justice, which at Eden's gate once barred
Paradise's way, pierced His loving heart
and brought him down to death and rocky grave.

His beard plucked out, His pale countenance marred,
spit and blood streaking His face, there, apart,
alone, the holy and righteous One gave

all that He had to make eternity
blessed beyond our ability to chart
for all those who receive this grace displayed.

## RESURRECTION
**(Matthew 28:5,6)**

Death was there, crouching over the torn
body, its bared claws flaunting the stain
of the blood of God,

its brutal weight pressing on the thorn
wounds and pierced side, attesting its reign
over the whole broad

earth, coldly resolved to keep things so,
not knowing that its defeat was near.
The way for death to

die had come. The One brought down so low
lived again, could not be held, came clear
on out to bring new

life to dying men, to take away the worn
sad looks, and give hope in place of fear
where dark death had trod.

## THE VOICE

**(Psalm 19:1-4)**

Listen! A voice is sounding everywhere.
Even in this dark night its tones are heard.
From ancient portals an insistent word
Comes beating through the trembling atmosphere.

The fluent moon calls out, and there the glow
Of lucid wheeling constellations girds
The globe with speech, while animals and birds,
Hill, stream and field join in here below.

Lovers of beauty, are you not aware?
The message comes from every stone and tree.
Searchers of nature, is it not yet clear,
This universal voice that vibrates there?

Still are you deaf to earth and sky and sea?
He who has ears to hear, now let him hear.

## MAN AND THE SEA

**(Psalm 69:2; 18:16)**

I stood upon a lonely shore
That bordered an unfathomed sea.
Dashed inward by that giant's roar
Were ruined things and dead debris,
Lying there within my reach,
On that stretch of dimlit beach,
Confronting me.

But other things now out of sight
Had sunk beneath the ocean's wave
Had drifted down below the light
To groping weeds and oozy cave,
Fallen out beyond the reach
Of that strip of windswept beach,
Into their grave.

The wreckage gone, the ruin near
Were portents I could see full well,
Were copious causes for my fear.
But why I stood so near the swell
Of the ocean's greedy reach,
On that edge of sodden beach,
I could not tell.

I could not swim. I would not try
To breast the wave or ride the spray.
But just to feel the ocean I
Walked warily down to where it lay
Surging there within my reach
On that strange and tempting beach
Filling the bay.

I could not swim, but still to wade
Along the edge and feel the din
Of that unceasing cavalcade
Of white-plumed breakers charging in,
Keeping always within reach
Of the margin of the beach,
I did begin.

The sea inscrutable and wild
Rushed at my legs and hurled me down.
And I dismayed, still but a child,
Lost hold of land and in a swoon,
Drawn beyond the utmost reach
Of that frail and futile beach,
Began to drown.

The sea, its sullen exploit done,
Closed coldly on my dying shout.
I perished there, amazed, alone,
In mortal dread, in desperate doubt,
But Christ, the Heavenly Diver,
Plunged those depths to deliver,
And drew me out.

## A CURE FOR ATHEISM

**(Psalm 29:4; Revelation 3:20)**

The bombs fell and burst in the town.
Infants were twisted and maimed.
Bayonets stabbed where they were aimed
And helplessness was trampled down.

A little child lay burned and blind;
A wicked, and seeing, old man
Lived in health and peace his whole life span
With nothing but self on his mind.

A tornado ripped up one street;
A whole city was smashed in a quake.
I said, "What sense could all of this make?
Or what mad plan could this complete?"

I watched the night sky and thought,
"A cold thing with no heart at the source,
A field of dark impersonal force
In which, for no reason, we're caught.

"It is clear there can be no God.
What God would make a world like this?
Here is a truth no one can miss,
So belief in him is what's odd.

"Its inglorious flag unfurled
Indifference, not God, sits to reign
Over scenes of chaos and pain,
With blind chance the law of the world."

Not hearing one heartening word
I became so sad, so forlorn

I wished I had never been born
To suffer a world so absurd.

Then God, who I said could not be,
Whose Book I had left scorned and unread,
Refuting the wild things I said,
Suddenly drew near and spoke to me.

## DOORS OPEN TO SOMETHING ELSE

We all live in a door,
Bound now in its substance.
Its particles are stars,
Its atoms galaxies,
Its dimension is space,
The measureless expanse.

A door without a house?
We should not assume so.
We are on one small speck.

Being now of the door
We must not open it
To see what is inside
Or to see the outside.
And all we see is part,
A small part, of the door.

Is it wise, is it safe
To say there is nothing
On either side of it?

It is sure–all doors have two sides.
Dying, I will go through the door,
And I am not afraid to see
What splendors there are in the house,
What sublime shapes and sights and sounds,
And what Great One makes His home there.

## HOLE IN THE HEART

Cavities are instructive.
They tell us of infection.
They ache and want correction.
A decaying tooth can give

a blow to our sense of well
being. More so heart decay.
This can even make men lay
reason aside, and go sell

their future to ease the pain.
Their whole inner man will cry:
"Fill up the hole," and they try
anything, and try again,

and never once think clearly
that what they buy is rubbish,
can never fulfill the wish
to obtain a remedy.

There is one who will remove
the rot in the heart, will drill
to the root of things, then fill
all the emptiness, and prove

his perfect skill. And apart
from him more is always less,
will only increase distress.
Christ is the cure for the heart.

## EVERYTHING IS INEXPLICABLE

Everything is inexplicable.
Even the most giant intellect
cannot understand a worm. It's range

falls short of that. Life is a riddle
it cannot solve. So we must suspect
that the pride of scholars is most strange.

## LOOK IN THE MIRROR, AHAB

*Ahab said to Elijah,*
*"So you have found me, my enemy."*
(1 Kings 21:20)

Elijah was your friend
For he told you the facts,
Condemned your ways and acts
To encourage you to bend,

A messenger from God
To undo your doing
To bring about renewing
To save you from anger's rod.

Why not be like Rahab
Who changed foes into friends
Attempting to make amends?
Look in the mirror, Ahab.

Put men in their true class.
Look at yourself and see
The face of your enemy.
Look, Ahab, look in the glass.

## MONEY

Use all for self, and it will be
a tyrant using all your years
for useless ends, and making friends
with death and tears.

Give it to Christ, and you will see
it is a servant sowing seeds
in fertile earth, bringing to birth
most godly deeds,

and placing in eternity
a treasure far beyond men's power,
safe in God's care, stored for you there
until death's hour.

Love it, and it is a deity
demanding all that you have got–
your sweat, your soul, your heart, your whole
sad future lot.

## PARTIAL BIRTH ABORTION

Now it is December.
I sense a sudden difference.
For eight months twenty-five days
I have waited, sleeping, dreaming,
here in the peace, the safety.
What joys await me in the world?
What hopes of goodness and glory?
What growth in love for man and God?

The stirring has begun.
Caught up in powerful forces,
I move toward the bright future.
I feel the doctor's gentle hand-
But what? My head! The probing! The pain!
I have fallen into the hands of murderers!
Is this the meaning of Christmas?
Oh, the...

## TRANSMUTATION

*Jesus looked at him and loved him.*
*"Go, sell everything you have and give it to*
*the poor; and you will have treasure in heaven.*
*Then come, follow me."*
*At this the young man's face fell. He went away sad,*
*because he had great wealth.* **(Mark 10:21,22)**

In former days, or so I am told,
many a curious alchemist
tried to convert base metal to gold.
They learned an element will resist
the change they wanted to bring about,
that no apparatus could exist
which would take lead in and send gold out.

But there is a finer thing to try,
a method that works any day–
changing gold here into gold on high
by cheerfully giving it away.
This is the way for money to live.
And this the teaching we must obey:
we really keep only what we give.

And we will lose what we try to keep.
So being faced with the eternal
is not an ordeal to make us weep,
but opens the way to have it all.
This faith accords with reality.
All wise ones will respond to Christ's call
and employ this divine alchemy.

## THE REAL COLUMBUS?

**(an ironic answer to Mr Joaquin Miller's Columbus)**

Columbus was an eager man;
his heart was set on gold,
and India was in his plan,
and sure his plan was bold.

"I see the world as round, not flat.
And India can be found
by sailing west–no doubt of that.
I know this route is sound."

This our Columbus proudly said,
and sailed into the west.
And still sailed on till almost dead,
and still said this was best.

Over the wide sea's curving space
he made his ships go on,
hoping to see that country's trace
before all hope was gone.

One day from far he saw some spot,
and natives on its beach.
"Ah, India at last," he thought,
"And gold within my reach."

His ships dropped anchor in the bay,
his eyes explored the sand.
You can imagine his dismay
at what he saw on land.

Half naked savages stood near
and gazed at his three ships.
And when he saw their mindless fear,
these words fell from his lips:

"No region this of wealth and fame.
This gives me some surprise,
for here I hoped to gain a name
and find our journey's prize.

"This is a realm untamed and mean.
But still I will go near."
When he reached land, some gold was seen
on some poor woman's ear.

His hopes grew large when everywhere
he saw the yellow wealth
on necks and feet and hands and hair.
"Oho, by force or stealth,"

He mused, "These riches will be mine.
I've earned them in this case.
No man has ever sailed a line
so near death and disgrace

as I have done these awful days.
And now is my reward.
"Get all the gold, with no delays,
and store it safe on board,"

He told his men, and they complied,
and left none on that shore.
Then off they sailed with joy and pride,
greedy to find some more.

# EXPERIMENT WITH RATS

The rats went around their cage
And saw some levers in a row.
In time they learned to engage
The right lever, and doing so,

Grain came rolling down the chute.
"We see," they said, "what brings supplies.
At last we are at the root.
To postulate Man is not wise.

"Now we have done a great deed,
And we will not at all admit
(And surely there is no need)
That Man had any part in it.

"We grasp this truth with relief,
For our minds have never been free.
We abandon old belief
And march forward to liberty.

"Not giving up self-reliance
To believe in someone 'up there.'
We'll learn all truth through science
And lay every mystery bare.

"Some say Man made the lever,
The cage, and everything in sight.
But we will now endeavor
To show this can hardly be right.

"A 'big bang' began it all–
At least that's our present notion.
Slowly evolutional
Are our selves, cage, time and motion.

"We're moving to a new height.
That's proved by our words and our acts;
And anyone who is bright
Will agree that we have the facts.

"Some misfits will not hear it.
They say something about a Book.
They speak of soul or spirit.
We won't even give it a look.

"How can any adult rat
Believe those airy fairy tales?
We will keep ourselves from that–
Unless our power of reason fails.

"All this obsession with Man–
It is hard for us to be still.
We'd like to put a full ban
On talk about him and his skill.

"For faith in Man makes no sense.
Far better to trust what we see.
We'll use our intelligence
And shun irrationality.

"So this we can safely pledge–
And you'll find that we're hard to move:
We won't regard as knowledge
Anything we can't test and prove.

"Pondering on creation
We put thoughts of Man on the shelf.
This is our explanation:
Creation created itself.

"The maladjusted may clutch
At straws, as they always have done,
But we do not need a crutch
And will never try to find one.

"For us no 'pie in the sky.'
In this world we'll be quite content
To let the old fables die,
For we have found enlightenment.

From this day on we will never believe in Man,
Or that a cage was ever designed with a plan."

## THE UNCERTAINTY PRINCIPLE

*"They walk about in darkness"* **(Psalm 82:5)**
*"They hatch the eggs of vipers*
*and spin a spider's web"* **(Isaiah 59:5)**

"When we were young and naive,
Before our seminary days,
We felt that we could believe
In the old conservative ways.

"To us things were false or true,
Black or white. No questioning look
Was ever given–all we knew
Was blind acceptance of the Book.

"We were not sensible yet,
Not having arrived at our prime.
Of course, it's of some regret
That we wasted so much time.

"But now we're fully prepared
To distrust what some think is truth,
To say things we never dared
to let in our minds in our youth.

"Things that once were mysteries
Before we knew philosophy
Are now mere dubieties,
Not as real as they seemed to be.

"Now we've read Kant and Descartes
Darwin, Dewey, Freud and Hegel
Bultmann and Teilhard and Barth–
Anyone intellectual.

"Facing the mythical curtain
We have learned by conjecturing
To be sure we can't be certain
That we're certain of anything.

"God? We can begin with Him.
We now think we should not resist
The logic of the theorem
That He might not even exist.

"On the other hand, He might.
The Bible? A fine book; so far
Some parts still seem to be right.
If only we knew what they are!

"Jesus? We now have in mind
A very great person indeed.
We are still hoping to find
Just how He meets anyone's need.

"But as for a virgin birth
Or resurrection from the dead–
We're not sure that He lived on earth,
So how did He do what they said?

"His death? If He lived at all
The way of His dying was sad.
But we doubt that you should call
It a sacrifice for the bad.

"About being born anew–
Can we now think for a minute
That it was ever for you,
Or that there's anything in it?

"What about heaven and hell?
It's nice to be sure of one's facts,
But doubt will do just as well,
Since none of that bears on our acts.

"So we doubt the ancient creed.
But in all of our many bouts
With the faith, we've seen little need
To seriously doubt our doubts.

"For in all our theology–
Do we really have to explain?
Dogmatic uncertainty
Is what we've labored to attain.

"This is our message. You may
Or may not, approve of our stance.
But see that we've come a long way
From the days of our ignorance."

## WELCOME CHANGES

**(1 Corinthians 15:49; 1 John 3:2)**

Sand? To make a lovely pearl?
A worm? To make a butterfly?
Coal? To make a great blue diamond?
Me? To make a glorified child of God?

## CHRISTMAS LAMENT

Oh,
Santa–
the big belly,
the big laugh, and
the big false sleigh
and reindeers,
the false presents,
the false stories, the false beard,
the false heart, the big idol of big-bellied,
false-hearted America, and all its false dreams,
its false outlook on life, its big craze for big things,
its big demand for pleasure, its big love for fantasy,
its big greed for wealth, and its little heart
for Christ whose birthday
this
is.
Children, keep yourselves from idols.

## REFORMATTED
**(2 Corinthians 5:17)**

You know computers–that
no matter how much stuff
is on the large hard disk

one can still reformat
the whole thing with one rough
resolve to take the risk

and get rid of it all.
I hope that you can see
a truth worth all your gold–

since Adam's ancient fall
each of us needs to be
reformatted, the old

blotted out, gone, removed,
the disk receiving new
programs. This is no dim,

doubtful thing, but well proved,
a great work God will do
in those who turn to Him.

## THE POWER OF WORDS

**(Proverbs 18:21; Matthew 12:36,37; James 3:5-10)**

Words can be boxcars hauling heavy freight
Or fragile snowflakes bearing wisps of cloud
A gentle hand tapping at the gate
Or sledgehammer blows breaking down the proud

Hot black fevers that burn in our heads
Cool feather pillows for our weary beds
Thunderings down Sinai's mountainside
A still small voice that seeks us where we hide

Multiform seeds sprouting in the field
Celestial showers on the dying ground
Untamed floods where all good sense is drowned
Lethal storms where hatred is revealed

Polished cannon firing deadly lies
Eternal light prismed for our eyes
Bright clever comets flashing through our skies
Dismal swamplands where love sinks and dies

Ambitious Caesars seeking to control
Silken spiders webs to ensnare the soul
Treacherous currents rushing to a shoal
A hidden harbor safe from ocean roll

A conflagration breaking out from hell
A world of evil uncontrollable
Pitchers of pure water from God's own well
Deep mysteries that no man can tell

Our judge that will condemn us or acquit
An executioner eyeing his rope
A tree of life bringing breath and hope
Urgent envoys warning of the pit

Poisoned arrows sticking in men's hearts
Nectar spreading sweetness through all parts
Ready instrument for the wise or fool
God's inspired agent or the devil's tool

The skeptic's dungeon sending out a curse
Or faith's dwelling where God's praise is sung
Or the exhortation of this verse:
Watch, all you talkers, yes, watch your tongue!

## THE SCHOOL OF CHRIST

**(Luke 14:23-33)**

There is a school for humble folk,
For all those who will bear Christ's yoke
And go with Him apart.
The teachings come down from above,
The one abiding rule is love,
The fee is our whole heart.

Printed in the United States
19539LVS00001B/363